50v

RING AND DIE

RING AND DIE

Stella Whitelaw

Severn House Large Print
London & New York

This first large print edition published in Great Britain 2007 by
SEVERN HOUSE LARGE PRINT BOOKS LTD of
9-15 High Street, Sutton, Surrey, SM1 1DF.
First world regular print edition published 2005 by
Severn House Publishers, London and New York.
This first large print edition published in the USA 2007 by
SEVERN HOUSE PUBLISHERS INC., of
595 Madison Avenue, New York, NY 10022.

British Library Cataloguing in Publication Data

Whitelaw,   Stella
   Ring and die. - Large print ed. - (Jordan Lacey series ; 6)
   1. Lacey, Jordan (Fictitious character) - Fiction 2. Women
   private investigators - Fiction 3. Detective and mystery
   stories 4. Large type books
   I. Title
   823.9'14[F]

   ISBN-13: 9780727875754

Printed and bound in Great Britain by
MPG Books Ltd, Bodmin, Cornwall.

Acknowledgements

Again, many thanks to my good friend and Chief Superintendent Detective who goes through my manuscripts with a laser beam; the Fine Arts Society; Dr D C Thomas; dog breeder friends and fishing enthusiasts on the pier and beach.

Also thanks to both Oxted Library and Worthing Library staff, who are wonderful in finding endless information.

Lastly, to my new editor, Tom Jordan (no relation to Lacey), whose meticulous work has reduced any errors. If there are any, they are all mine.

To Edwin Buckhalter,
friend and publisher,
who had faith in Jordan Lacey

One

The wind was too strong for me to round the end of Latching pier, even head down and nose forward. My breath was snatched away in gulps. The forecasters had warned to expect a gale force six but I had not believed them. Gale force six is twenty-two or more knots per minute. Pretty blowy.

I believed them now. The sea was churning like cappuccino in torment, the froth a dirty cream slewing the top of each crashing wave. It was mesmerizing. Never underestimate the power of the sea. It could swallow the strongest swimmer, rapacious as a beast, suck down an Olympic champion as easily as removing an irritant fly.

I hung over the railings as the wind unravelled my thick plait with determined fingers. My hair flew across my face into my eyes, my mouth, bent on choking and strangling me, both at the same time. My asthma went into howling indignation.

''Ere, Jordan. Need a hand?'

An arm snaked under my elbow, fingers digging into soft flesh. For a moment I froze.

There were too many villains after my blood for my liking, even in Latching. But few of them used my first name.

'Friend or foe?' I gasped.

'Come off it, Jordan, you know me. Get inside. Or are you going to jump off the pier? Strewth, I'm in no shape to jump in after yer.'

True. Jack was in no shape to do more than chase a black coffee. His eyes were rimmed red. He had not shaved for days. His clothes smelt of stale tobacco and beer. And this was the millionaire owner of the amusement arcade on the pier. The man who raked in a sackful of coins every day, ran a flashy blue Jaguar, would have laid down his life for me in normal circumstances.

I let him guide me into his arcade, where the flashing lights and jingle tunes almost drowned the gale outside. It was warm and steamy, his security-coded booth a haven of awful instant coffee and serious money. All the usual people were feeding coins into his machines, determined to shake a wall of ten-pence pieces into the chute and into their greedy pockets. Except that the coins, fivers and watches clung to the moving shelves. I swore that Jack used Blu-Tack. The punters rarely won but they had fun.

'You look worse than I feel,' I said, plugging in the kettle. The jug had not been washed for years, grimed with fingerprints

8

and splashes. I hoped the water was fresher. If Jack got it from the public loo, then I was going to be sick. He read my mind.

'I use bottled water,' he said, wearily.

'Sunshine,' I said.

'What are you doing on the pier in this weather?'

Now, I have a thriving private-eye business called First Class Investigations. Thriving as in flourishing and fortunate, not necessarily prosperous. Not a lot of people know that. They think I run a junk shop called First Class Junk. The private-eye office is behind the shop, which is a perfect cover. I don't exactly make ends meet but I am working on it. I get the odd strange little case that does not warrant police investigation. Sometimes I get a murder. I don't like talking about the murders.

'Someone is stealing fishing rods off the pier,' I said.

I could anticipate the reaction but Jack was too hung-over to react to anything. He was trying to find unwashed mugs among the clobber on his desk. Crumpled crisp bags slithered on to the floor.

'So what? Is this a crime?' he said.

'It is to serious sea anglers,' I said. 'I have one irate fisherman who has lost several rods recently, and is ready to pay me coin of the realm to find out who is doing it.'

'Not in this weather.'

'Yes,' I said. 'One got thrown into the sea this very morning.'

'Blown over more likely.' Jack was not impressed.

I made two coffees, using caked instant milk. I had to bash it with a spoon. He made the worst coffee in Latching. This offering was one degree better than usual because I was making it. He lay back in his leather chair, eyes closed. I had never seen him look so bad.

'What's the matter?' I asked. 'Tell me.'

'You know the barn I took you to?' he mumbled. I remembered the midnight barn boot sale with mountains of dubious items on sale that had no ready invoice history. Jack had bought me a leather baker boy's cap that I wear often. 'Well, it got raided. The police rushed in, sirens blaring, lights flashing. Your boyfriend was there.'

'He's not my boyfriend.' DI James was in and out of my investigations but not in the role that would have made my life perfect. My craving for his company had to be held firmly under control. Pride has a way of helping when you are not loved back.

'I only got away because I was parked in a good spot. The best getaway. I always make sure I park there.'

'Here's your coffee,' I said. 'What happened?'

'I went the wrong way. It was sheer panic.

I found myself going towards Portsmouth, of all places, lost in the side roads, driving through torrential rain, couldn't see, didn't get any sleep, no grub, sick with nerves. You name it, Jordan. I got it.'

'Sounds like a bad conscience,' I said lightly, trying not to be judgemental. Jack was a good friend. He had helped me out several times, even saved my life.

'Don't get mixed up in this, Jordan. Don't ask me nothing and then you won't know nothing.'

'Then you've nothing to worry about.'

'Look, Jordan. Don't come in here for a bit. Stay away.'

'If you promise to shut up shop and go home,' I said. Maybe they had something on him. He was obviously worried. His amusement arcade was above board. Perhaps he had been innocently laundering money for some villain. 'The customers won't mind. They'll understand. Say the arcade is in danger of being blown over.'

He drank some coffee and switched on the tannoy system. 'In the interests of safety, this arcade is now being closed,' he said. Dribbles of coffee snaked through his stubble. 'Please leave in an orderly manner. Do not panic. The pier is safe but this building is not. It could get blown off.'

'Very reassuring announcement,' I said. There was a rush for the exits but some still

11

continued their games, determined to score the maximum points for a win. They crowded round the machines, feeding in money, hoping the force six would dislodge a mountain of cash into the shutes.

'In the interests of safety,' Jack began again.

'Start closing up,' I said.

'I can't leave all this money,' he said. 'I've got to empty the machines.'

The machine emptying ritual was an eye-opener. I knew that a lot of change transactions went through his booth, but I had never seen the machines emptied. Cascades of coins came out of the buckets, bronze and silver. Did he expect to count it all now?

A sudden huge wave hit the arcade and the whole place shuddered. Sea water surged through the open doors, wetting the floor space. Addicted old ladies in belted raincoats and plastic rainbonnets screamed and clutched their skirts.

'Time to go home,' I said, turning them in the direction of the landward exit doors. 'Off you go. Hold on to each other. The wind is getting stronger.'

There was no way I could escort each one of them back to the promenade on Latching front. My priority was Jack. He was heaving buckets of coins into his booth, sweat pouring off his skin. He looked like a near heart-attack victim. It was all that junk food he ate.

'For heaven's sake, leave it,' I said. 'It doesn't matter. Come back tomorrow and collect the money. No one is going to make a night raid in this weather. No one with any sense, that is.'

'Do you know how much money is here?'

'I don't care.'

'Several thousand. It could get blown into the sea.'

'So what? Are you going to stay here and count it?'

'Jordan, it's important. The punters lose their money, I collect it, I count it, pay the bills. Regular as clockwork, every night. It's routine.'

Jack was determined. He was stacking notes into a battered old leather briefcase. I helped, trying not to look impressed.

'I can carry that,' I said. 'If you trust me.'

'I'd trust you with my life,' he said without blinking.

At least he had another hand free for carrying the bags of coins. Once on land he could dump them into his blue E-type and count the money at his leisure. I was not inviting him back to my two adjacent bed-sits. He might be horrified at my basic living style and go out and buy me a villa.

The gale was thrashing the waves into powerful crescents of water that rolled on to the beach, pounding the shingle. I walked crabwise, crouched behind Jack's body to lessen the force. Spray was drenching the decking closest to the shore.

Jack did not seem to care if he got wet. He did not even seem to notice. He trudged on, weighed down by the money. I hoped he varied his route and routine. Some nasty mugger would relieve him of his earnings one evening if he was not careful.

'You need an armed guard,' I said.

'I am armed,' he said, gritting his teeth.

I did not ask. I didn't want to know. He probably didn't have a licence to own a gun. If he had bought it at one of the midnight barn boot sales, then it would have a dicey history.

He hurried against the wind, worried now about the state of his car. A door might be torn off its hinge by some almighty gust if he opened it for Jordan to get in. Yet he could not leave her in this weather. She looked as if she might be blown away.

I could read his thoughts. 'I'll walk from here,' I said. 'The wind's not so strong in the backstreets. It's not far to walk.'

I put the leather briefcase on the pavement beside the bags of coin. Jack was wrestling with the boot. I helped him steady it while he put all the money in and closed the lid.

'Thanks,' he said.

I was disappointed in him. It was the first time that Jack's chivalry had been found wanting. And for a car. It was illuminating. I

14

rated second, but then I had never given him any encouragement so perhaps it was not surprising.

'Thanks for the help,' he said, pausing and revising his thoughts. 'OK, you'd better get in.'

I shook my head. 'No, thanks. You might get your door blown off.'

Jack leaned against his car, catching his breath, rain dripping off his face. 'One of the punters was pretty upset yesterday. Her dog got nicked or something. I told her about you and how you floored that robber in my place. She gave me her address on a bit of card. I got it somewhere.'

He was searching his pockets.

A lost dog. My heart contracted. Not another pet. But I was good at finding lost pets. I had a string of successes, including Joey, the famously lost tortoise. I could have a scroll naming successfully found pets to hang in the office with some tasteful photos along the edges. I was going for the idea.

'Here it is,' said Jack. 'A bit crumpled.'

'Still readable,' I said, putting it deep into my back pocket. It seemed the safest place in a gale. 'Cheerio, Jack. See you sometime.'

The side roads were like wind tunnels. Crossing the road was a hazzard of some dimension, i.e. near impossible. I clung on to a lamp post, waiting for a lull when I might launch myself across the road. My nine stone was a mere straw in the wind. My feet were having trouble meeting the tarmac, or even finding it. There was no way I was going back to Jack for help. By now he would have driven away to wherever he lived. I didn't know. He might have a big house on Kingsdown Gorse for all I knew.

The two bedsits are side-by-side rooms over an empty estate agent's. I took on both, not because I wanted two keys, two kitchen sinks, and two bells, which was what I got, but because my preference is to sleep in a different room from where I daily live. I do not want my undies perpetually on view.

The front bedsit is neatly divided into areas. The kitchen area: sink, microwave (new purchase), calendar, string of garlic. Leisure area: moral chair (small, stiff-back sofa), black and white television, books. Work area: desk, typewriter from charity shop, books, radio. There were more books and plants everywhere. It was fast turning into a literary jungle.

The back bedsit was smaller and housed a sink, now styled closely to look like a feminine Vanitory unit, bed, cupboard, chest of drawers and yards more books. It looked on to someone else's garden, the back of the church and a nice apple tree. Sometimes a tortoiseshell cat sat on the old pebbled wall and gazed up at me. Seagulls sat on the roof and peered down at me. I was pretty much on view.

I was drenched by the time I got in so I shed my clothes and changed into a dry tracksuit. My clothes are simple. Jeans and weather-wise tops. Tracksuits. I have one posh black dress donated by Guilberts Store, when I worked there on a case, a year back.

A cup of my brewed coffee took away the taste of Jack's instant. I took out the crumpled card and phoned Mrs Daphne Gregson. I did not really want to start looking for another lost dog, but partly I felt sorry for the dog, and anyway I needed the money.

'Hello?' It was a blunt voice.

'Mrs Gregson?'

'Yes?'

She did not sound like a friendly dog owner but perhaps she was upset.

'This is Jordan Lacey, First Class Investigations. I understand that you have lost your dog.'

'Lost my dog? Indeed, I haven't lost them, young lady. More like stolen. Stolen from right under my nose. The nerve. These amateur breeders will stop at nothing. Thieves, that's who they are. My dogs have pedigrees. I've cups ceiling-high to prove it.'

I let Mrs Gregson rant on for a few moments. She sounded as if she had an ample chest to get things off. It sometimes helped.

'Would you like me to come round and we'll see if I can help?' I said in my best client-soothing voice. A stolen dog would tot up more work hours than a lost dog wandering the streets of Latching looking for its next meal.

'Yes, Miss Lacey. Please come this afternoon, say in half an hour? Number fourteen Walbrook Grove.'

'That's fine. What kind of dog did you say it was?'

'I didn't. I breed short-haired and long-haired chihuahuas. And it isn't a dog, it's dogs. They've stolen four of my pedigree dogs. It's an outrage.'

The cash bells tinkled nicely. Four pedigree dogs. I must remember to thank Jack when he had recovered from his low spirits. I'd buy him a pint at the Bear and Bait. That might cheer him up.

Latching library has a good selection of books on dog breeding. I found a chair and made some notes. Chihuahuas were small, diminutive. I gathered that. The short-haired ones looked all eyes, big worried eyes. The long-haired ones like bundles of wool. They were perfect for flat-owners, only needing short walks on their short legs.

Mrs Gregson lived in a large house surrounded by a high beech hedge. She was moated by hedge. No one could see what was going on behind that hedge. I wouldn't

18

fancy trimming it. Perhaps she had to hire the fire brigade and one of their ladder lifts.

I parked my ladybird (ancient Morris Minor with spots) outside and hurriedly opened the gate and rushed up the path to the porch. It was still raining heavily but I made it without getting too wet. The house was fake tudor, beams and timber and plaster and a heavy slate roof. The porch was cluttered with muddy boots and other walking gear. I could hear dogs barking somewhere, a small high-pitched barking. She seemed to have the kennels out the back. I pressed the bell.

Mrs Gregson came to the door. She was indeed a large lady wearing cord trousers and a big green jersey. Her straight brown hair looked as if it had been cut with the kitchen scissors. But her face was like a Native American carving, high beak nose and full lips, brown eyes as deep as some river ravine.

'Miss Lacey? Come in. I didn't expect any-one so young.'

'Getting older by the day,' I said. 'I'm working on it.'

'You want to put it on and I want to take it off. And neither of us can do a thing about it,' she said, shutting the door.

I followed her through to a kitchen. It was full of pots cooking on an Aga stove and the hot, greasy smell was disgusting.

'I can't stop,' she said. 'I'm cooking supper.'

Their supper, I hoped, not her supper. It smelt very carnivorous.

'Home-cooked,' I said, trying to look knowledgeable. 'Nothing out of tins.'

'Absolute rubbish,' she said. 'I only use tins of dog food in an emergency. Otherwise my dogs get the best. I go to a butcher in Findon. Buy half an animal at a time, all the bits.'

I shuddered. I could not see the merit in feeding one animal to another. Cheese was the nearest I got to eating an animal. Sometimes fish, but I was even going off farmed salmon after reading how they lived in recycled water.

'Tell me about your dogs,' I said, taking a seat nearest a window. It was half open, rattling like aliens trying to get in. Mrs Gregson was not into central heating, nor did she seem to feel the cold wind.

'Dog-nappers, that's what they are,' she said, stirring some vile concoction. 'They steal to order. My dogs are valuable pedigree animals and obviously they have been taken for breeding. Two were prize-winning males, both got seconds at Crufts, one was a bitch already mated, and the fourth was a darling baby, an absolute prize-winner, going to sweep Crufts.'

'How dreadful,' I murmured, making

notes.

'It's a black-market trade, a ring, a gang, you know,' she went on. 'They've got someone in mind before they steal. Not like the old days when kids would steal dogs and try to sell them off in pubs for drug money or alcohol. This is big money.'

'How much?'

'The boys are worth over six hundred pounds each. The mated bitch is worth more and the puppy, my little Angel, is priceless.'

'Nearly £3,000,' I said, my maths not being GCSE standard.

'Some rare breeds are worth £3,000 each...' said Mrs Gregson, starting to look really upset. 'I just hope they are treating them well. My Angel will be pining for me.'

'Poor little Angel,' I said. 'Have you got any photographs?'

The floodgates opened. Did Daphne Gregson have photographs...? If the cups were piled to the ceiling then the photographs were piled to the roof. Album after album came out on to the kitchen table. I went cross-eyed with photos of little dogs jumping up, little dogs jumping down, dogs on leads, dogs on cushions.

'And which are the ones that have been stolen?' I asked, bewildered. If this was an organized rustling gang, then Mrs Gregson's four dogs might be the tip of an iceberg. 'Have they got identity chips?'

'Of course,' said Mrs Gregson, miffed. 'Except Angel. She's too young. Here they are: Jodie, Mel, Jude and Angel.'

'All film stars' names.'

'Naturally. They are all stars in the dog world.'

I took some of the photographs. Angel was indeed a sweet bundle of fluff. 'Do you want me to contact FCI, the lost pet agency? I can't promise results but I can try. Are the local police involved?'

'I reported it to them but they don't have much time for valuable stolen dogs. They are too busy chasing motorists who drive at thirty-one miles an hour past Latching's cameras.'

I got out my contract form and explained the hourly and daily rates. She was very practical about it all.

'I'll pay the hourly fee,' she said. 'I doubt if you'll spend a whole day at a time looking for my dogs. You'll have other things to do.'

Like disappearing fishing rods, I thought. 'You'll get a proper invoice,' I said.

'I should expect it,' said Mrs Gregson, putting away the photographs. 'The very least.'

'May I see what security you have in place? Alarms etc,' I said. 'And show me how the thieves got in.'

'Of course. It's all high-tech. I don't know how they got in or out.'

It was still raining. I pulled up my anorak hood. The kennels were out the back, well-built wooden buildings in a yard. The yapping was a lot louder, as if supper time was imminent.

'I hope you like dogs,' said Mrs Gregson, a spring in her step, a gleam in her eye. 'They'll give you a wonderful welcome, my little darlings. They don't bite.'

It was not so much a welcome as a stampede of little feet. Thank goodness the dogs were only ankle-high. Mrs Gregson said they did not bite but they certainly enjoyed taking a few chunks out of my jeans.

Two

The sign on the door of my shop, First Class Junk, said CLOSED FOR LUNCH. It had been a long lunch hour, maybe one of those gourmet feasts that businessmen call power lunching. But I'd had nothing more than assorted coffees and nuts. Hardly a balanced meal.

My corner shop used to be an old-fashioned optician's. None of this two for the price of one and free sunglasses thrown in. It had small octangular windows on both sides, which suited me as I am not into window dressing.

The front window currently displays an array of cute china cats in silky stillness. There are also two sepia photographs of a little girl with golden hair, cuddling a lively kitten. The delight on the child's face is worth my six pound price ticket. Everything has a six pound price. It saves time.

The side window is into old comics this week. *The Eagle*, *Dandy*, *Boy's Own*. There were copies going back to WWII. Some grown-up boy will come along and buy the lot.

But there were no customers waiting for me to open. No mail, no calls on my answer-phone, no food, not even a wrinkled orange. It was time to call on Doris, my source of nourishment, at her shop two doors down.

'I'm just closing,' she said as I put my head round the door. She was painting her nails a hideous dried blood red. I'd seen enough of that red on roads in my WPC days.

'I'm starving,' I said, stepping inside. Doris sold everything, except exactly what you wanted. If you wanted mushroom soup, she'd only got tomato. If you wanted brown rolls, then she'd only got day-old bagels.

'You should have come in earlier,' she said. 'I've been open all day.'

Doris is a very good friend. She looks out for me, but it is part of her remit that she can tell me off as much as she likes. It's a kind of ritual.

'You can help yourself,' she went on. 'Put the money in the till. I daren't touch anything till this dries.'

'Going somewhere nice?'

'Mavis and I are going dancing at the Pavilion tonight,' she said. 'You don't need a partner. There's plenty of spare men. They may not be able to dance but they each have two legs.'

'I don't dance,' I said, roaming the shelves. I gathered lentil soup, Marmite, yogurts from the cooler, a bag of satsumas. I added up the total and put the money in the till. I tried not to notice that Doris had not done well that day. Her grocer's shop was too far off the beaten track and the big supermarket was taking all the trade.

'Some of the sea anglers go dancing,' said Doris. 'The ones that don't have a home to go to. You might be able to pick up something about the missing rods.'

'How do you know about the missing rods?'

'Mavis. Her latest fisherman told her. Bruno's got a big boat and he's a dishy man. The best of the bunch, I should say. Not too young, brown, muscular and very sexed-up. That's the phrase these days, isn't it? I'm not sexed-up, I'm sexed-down. You're not sexed in any direction.'

'Thank you, Doris, for those kind words. I'll retreat to my shop and see if I can find a well-thumbed sex manual that will help my morale.'

The words rankled. They touched a raw nerve. Every day I thought about DS Ben Evans and his death. If I had changed the train of events, maybe I could have prevented the accident.

Guilt is an odd thing. I was guilty of not loving him, but letting him think that I did. If I had gone on that holiday to Cyprus instead of accidentally missing the plane, maybe DI James would have felt primeval jealousy and had Ben posted. Then Ben might not have been killed in a car chase.

There were endless if and maybe permutations. I thought up a new one every day. Sometimes I lean over the pier railing and send thoughts into the night sky, recounting my failings, my weakness, my guilt and shame. I didn't believe he would suddenly appear at my side, wreathed in misty vapour. But I did hope thoughts locked on to his wavelength.

All I got were seagulls, screeching overhead, using me as target practice.

I had a rough list of the anglers who fished from the pier. Seven of them reported rods disappearing while they ate their sandwiches or went to buy a coffee. I had searched the second-hand shops. It was weird. Who would want to steal rods with all those grue-some bits of bait on hooks?

I made up my notes about Jodie, Mel, Jude and darling Angel and pinned up their photos. My notes were meticulous. A tiny detail that meant nothing can suddenly reveal exactly what you want to know. I ate yogurt and a satsuma. Fishing rods and diminutive dogs do not add up to a thriving investigative business. I needed some real work.

So some anglers went dancing. I rustled through my charity box to find something suitable for dancing. The girls going to the nightclubs wore tiny skirts and crop tops. I was young enough and slim enough but not stupid enough. It was freezing outside, mid-winter, and I had no mind to collect chil-blains on my rear.

I found the long flowered skirt I'd worn once as a social worker cover. It looked OK with a plain black top and sandals. I tied my hair back with ribbon and set out on my late-onset dancing career. Too tall, ever, to find a partner.

It was bitterly cold, a north-easterly attack-ing the shrouded palms along the front. I huddled into anorak and scarf and cursed the Hebridean draught blowing up the skirt.

The music sounded good, lots of stand-ards. I paid for a ticket and went into the pavilion ballroom. The warmth and sound hit me like a fuzzy blanket. It was canned music hosted by a DJ on the stage, not my big band jazz but foot-tapping tunes. The polished oval floor was crowded with couples dancing. Most of them knew what they were doing, fancy steps and holding each other in the proper ballroom stance. I went into the bar and bought orange juice. It was time to cruise the boards.

Spare men? I couldn't see any spare men. Doris must have double vision. She was dancing with a rotund partner who was light enough on his feet. Mavis was locked in the arms of her new fisherman, Bruno. They were barely moving.

The ballroom was a well-proportioned room, long velvet curtains at the pier windows, the stage proscenium arch decorated with garlands, cherubs and quotations from Shakespeare. The glass-domed ceiling was spectacular. It was covered at night but the curves gave the promise of endless sky above. I come here to listen to jazz, when famous names descend on Latching to play a one-nighter. My trumpter had played here with a big band. He gave me a free ticket.

'Like to dance, Jordan?'

It was the voice that would go with me to the grave. I did not have to turn but I did because I wanted to see his face. My own expression did not change. It paid not to let Detective Inspector James know how I felt about him. It was better to wear this year's mask.

'James. What a surprise. Do you come here often?'

'Not if I can help it. Dancing is not my scene.'

'Then this is work and you want me as a cover?'

'Something like that.'

'OK by me, but I might call in a favour myself some time.'

'I can do this quickstep.'

He lead me on to the floor. He had never held me in his arms socially. The hold was politically correct and the dancing lone-ranger stuff. He did his steps and I did mine. Basic movements. But he was close enough for me to smell his skin, to see how finely his dark hair was crew-cut to his head, to notice the lashes that flickered over those hard granite-blue eyes.

'Am I allowed to ask why you are here?' I said.

'You can ask but I may not answer.'

'I'll tell you why I am here.'

'I'm riveted,' he said without feeling. 'I thought maybe this was time off in lieu of good behaviour or Mavis had fixed you up with a blind date.'

'This is work. I'm hoping to talk to some anglers. I know it's small fry – joke, James – compared to your cases, but I have to earn a living somehow.'

The music ended and people clapped. Who were they clapping? The taped music, themselves or the cleaner who polished the floor? James relaxed his hold but did not move away. Were we going to dance a second time? The heavens had decided to shower me with joy. James was wearing his usual black shirt and black belted jeans. I guessed the black jacket was on the back of some chair.

'The stolen fishing rods? Yes, they came into the station but we don't have the resources to follow it up.'

'Too busy chasing motorists?'

'Not fair, Jordan. I don't make the rules.'

'So why are you here?'

'To dance with the prettiest girl on the floor.' His voice was emotionless. He was looking everywhere except at me. Something had happened to his family a long time ago and it had made him remote and bitter.

'Bollocks,' I said. 'I'm not the prettiest girl.' I'd never be pretty. My hair is tawny red and my five foot eight means I need a man who is taller. My face is normal, no spots or acne. And this was a black mascara night.

'I didn't say it was you.'

I would have walked off and left him standing, but the next tune was 'Someone to Watch Over Me' by Gershwin. I love Gershwin. James did not change his hold. No cheek to cheek, no folded hand against his beating chest, as I had often dreamed. Bruno was eating Mavis's ear. Doris was sitting this one out, making her drink last.

When my jazz trumpeter played this number, it had soul. But this version was terminal, chemical. I knew the words. Perhaps if I sang them, James would melt. But I couldn't find my voice. It was stuck halfway down my throat.

'So who, among these assorted dancers, are you watching?' I rambled on. 'Is the gorgeous Bruno smuggling drugs across the Channel in cod stomachs? Does the DJ run a ring of phone-girls from his mobile caravan? I know, it's Mavis. She has contravened some ruling from Brussels and the Fat Squad are threatening to close Maeve's Cafe.'

'Do you always talk such nonsense? Yes, you do. Please be quiet and let me concentrate on my dancing.'

'If this is concentrated dancing then I'd hate to be around when you're relaxed.'

His mouth twitched. It was the nearest he got to a smile that evening. He was still searching the floor.

'Doris said that some of the anglers come here to dance. A few beers and they might talk to me.'

'They are part of a brotherhood. A brotherhood of messy bait, extreme cold, stiffness, cramp and patience.'

'Perhaps I ought to sniff around.'

'They wash and use deodorants. Super-drug give them a discount for quantity.'

The music ended and I drew away from James. I lost his warmth. I could have danced all night.

'Thank you,' I said. 'But I have work to do.'

He nodded and walked away. I stood, marooned among the dancers, wondering where I had parked my orange juice. My feelings had been under control for weeks. Now the longing and craving were back, coupled with the dread that he might be posted to some outpost in the north. He'd been in sunny Latching longer than most. He was due a grunge posting.

I found my juice. If not mine, then I was drinking someone else's germs. The movable theatre seats were grouped around the edge of the floor and I found a good view. Doris was dancing with a very tall partner who was obviously treading on her feet. Mavis was wrapped round Bruno. I envied her addiction to fishermen. Not an age spot in sight.

'Miss Lacey?'

It was a man in a green fleece sweater and brown slacks, not normal dancing gear. He had a ruddy face and hair that disobeyed every rule in the comb book.

'Hello,' I said. 'Do I know you?'

'I'm Dick Mann. I fish off the pier, all

weathers. Mad about fishing. My mate, Arnie, has spoken to you about the rods being whipped. Can I have a word with you?'

'Of course, Mr Mann. Sit down.'

'You may have seen me,' said Dick Mann, putting his glass of beer on the table, slopping the froth. 'I always fish in the same spot, second stretch, east side, facing the skyscrapers of Brighton and the Seven Sisters.'

'Ah, yes, I know the spot. I walk the pier in all weathers.'

'We know. We've noticed you. Nothing much to look at when you're fishing, a lot of sea and a lot of sky. You tend to get to know the regular walkers.'

'But anglers tend to look the same,' I said. 'Huddled in waterproofs and hoods. You must get very cold.'

'Enough to freeze the ... off you, begging your pardon, miss.' He took a quick gulp of beer and coughed on it. Dodgy chest too. 'Arnie says you're looking into this rod business and we're all chipping in to pay for you. So it's up to us to give you as much information, right?'

'Right? What do you know?'

'Well, I was fishing just the other morning. I work shifts at the hospital and I'd done a night shift. I had two rods out and the fish were running well. I'd a couple of flounders and a nice bass. The bass was going to be my supper with a bit of bread and butter.'

'What happened?'

'I was crouched down, cleaning the bass, out of the wind, when suddenly my rod was jerked off the pier. It went up in the air like a whiplash and fell into the sea. I rushed to look over the rail and it had disappeared. I couldn't believe it. Vanished in seconds. Rods float, they don't sink. Something had pulled it down like a whale or a shark.'

'Or a small boy? We don't get whales or sharks lurking off the Sussex coast,' I said.

'That's what's so odd. I'm only telling you what I saw. We all thought it was a gang of boys thieving for a lark but I reckon it's summat more sinister.'

'Sinister? You mean like a Latching monster or south-coast jaws? We might make national headlines.'

'Rods are expensive. There's little insurance to cover fishing equipment.'

'Perhaps I'll come fishing with you, Mr Mann, catch a sighting of this monster. When would be a good time?'

Fish surveillance. It might be better than sitting in a car for hours, watching an empty house. But it would be cold. Both thermal vests on, Jordan.

'How about tomorrow afternoon? It's my half day. Wrap up warm. I'll bring a thermos and some sandwiches.'

'OK,' I said, resigning myself to a cold, wet

afternoon. There was no shelter on the open deck. 'I'll see you on the pier, east side.'

Dick Mann finished his beer and stood up. 'Want another?' He nodded towards my orange juice.

'No, thank you. I need to circulate.'

He ambled off towards the bar, to the men who were there to drink and not to dance. I didn't want to talk to any more anglers. I wanted to talk to Bruno.

Bruno was a hunk, even more gorgeous than Miguel, the owner of the Mexican restaurant near my shop. His teeth flashed against a weather-beaten skin. He had dancing eyes and masses of dark curly hair streaked with silver. His sexual attraction was dominant. He was clearly taken with Mavis, touching her, pulling her close. There was nothing detached or distant about those two.

Mavis was another long-time friend. She owned the best fish and chip cafe on the south coast and we were especially close since the time she was beaten up. She had never forgotten my help, little as it was. Mavis was one of those ageless women. She could be thirty, she could be fifty. And she was addicted to fishermen.

'Mavis,' I said, making no attempt to conceal my admiration of her escort. 'Please introduce me to Bruno.'

'He doesn't like detectives,' she said.

'Then you're safe from any competition,' I said. 'I only want to ask a few questions.' I turned to Bruno, trying to look less like a detective. This was stretching my acting ability and needed a plain face. 'Hi, are you having a good time? It's great music for dancing to.'

'Jordan?' He inclined his head towards me. 'I've heard a lot about you. Mavis told me.'

'Don't believe everything that Mavis tells you. She thinks I'm a heroine.'

'You are occasionally very brave, often foolish and always a nosey-parker,' he said.

His statement took my breath away. I gasped. It was pretty accurate but I did not want to hear it. The dancing had gone out of his eyes and had been replaced by a coolness and hint of hostility. I had never crossed swords with any of Mavis's beach lovers and I did not want to start now. Even Mavis looked disconcerted.

'Hey, Bruno,' she said, stroking his arm. 'Jordan is a very good friend.'

'That doesn't mean she has to be mine, too,' he said curtly.

'It's OK,' I said, retreating. 'Mavis means more to me than asking a few questions that you might or might not be inclined to answer. Keep checking those cod stomachs.'

He blinked, puzzled. Mavis flashed me a look. It said sorry, I'll explain later, come and see me soon.

I headed straight across the floor, oblivious to the couples swirling round me. The skirt was flapping and annoying my ankles and I was tired of it. The DJ announced The Last Waltz to a buzz of disappointment from the dancers. I looked around the ballroom for DI James. He owed that much to me.

But he had gone, disappeared without a word. I found myself dancing with a green fleece sweater and listening to tall fishy tails about bass, bream, huss, Dover sole ... I wondered if I would ever eat fish again.

Three

Nobody walked me home. I was left to cope with the muggers and drunks and flashers. Happily there were none about and the windy walk back to my bedsits in the dim yellowed lamplight was incident free, although I clutched the cut-in-half credit card in my hand, ready to thrust it up against any nose. Guaranteed to draw blood.

The encounter with Bruno was disturbing. Why did he dislike me? The detective label had been like a red rag. But why? I had never met him before. I did not have an international reputation. That wasn't in dispute.

I needed my sleep. I curled up under the rose-patterned duvet and thought of dancing with James. My guardian angel had been watching out for me for once. Then thoughts of fishing rods and little dogs invaded my dreams and James vanished, pushed away by other problems. I had vulnerable four-legged creatures to find. Pass me a pair of binoculars.

My shop opened to a flurry of activity. I sold three glass cats in half an hour. I ought to join the Cats Protection League. The window display looked empty. I added a couple of frogs. It was not a bad move since one went before coffee time.

'Those comics,' said a customer who had been browsing the book shelves. 'How much for the lot? I can pay cash.'

There were a lot of comics in the window. The man was thin, balding, wiry and intense. He smoked continuously, his scrawny fingers stained with nicotine. I did not like to point out the No Smoking sign. Stock had to be kept moving even to an unpleasant customer. I couldn't choose who came into my shop.

'Thirty pounds the lot,' I said, picking a number out of the air.

'Done.'

I'd obviously underpriced them. He counted out new notes at speed in case I changed my mind.

'Does that include the annuals?' he said, confident that he was dealing with a dimwit.

'No way,' I said. 'You asked about the comics. There was no mention of the annuals. They are priced separately.'

'How much?'

'Six pounds ... each. They are collector's items.'

He shook his head and watched me take the piles of comics out of the window. I wrapped them carefully. They were old but in good condition. One careful owner. A schoolboy who had treasured them, read them and reread them until time had plucked him to university and adulthood. I could not clearly remember how I had acquired the collection. Some job lot at a house clearance.

'Thanks,' he said. 'I might come back for the annuals.' Now he had got the comics, he seemed to be itching to get away.

'Annuals are for the reader who has put away the comic books but is not yet ready for the editorials,' I said, slightly altering the quote.

'Oh yeah? Who said that?' He'd opened the door.

'A critic called Gloria Steinem. She was reviewing the book *Valley of the Dolls*, I think.'

'She wasn't referring to annuals,' he said from the step, already half out.

'No, she wasn't,' I said. 'I was rearranging

her words.'

'You can't do that,' he persisted.

'Probably not. But I'm sure Miss Steinem would be pleased that I remember half of her one-liner. Hope you enjoy the comics. Do come back anytime and browse.' But I hoped he wouldn't.

He and his cigarette left. I opened the door wider, waving it on its hinges to dispel the smoke. A cold draught blew in looking for somewhere warm to hide out. It had been a good morning's work. I could begin orchestrating my hunt for four little dogs. Start with the local dealers.

I thumbed through the Yellow Pages, marking Dog Breeders, Dog Trainers and Dog Grooming from all over the county. It took the rest of the morning phoning the owners and managers, assuming the role of keen dog owner wanting to buy several chihuahua puppies.

'Have you got a long-haired female?' I said. 'I'd really like a long-haired female. They are so pretty.'

I was offered puppies of all ages and varied pedigrees. Detailed notes filled several pages. None of the puppies exactly matched Mrs Gregson's lost puppies but then they would not have the correct documentation. Prices were mixed.

'Oh lovely, a long-haired female. How old? Are you sure? When can I come and look at her? Tomorrow, fine. Ten o'clock. And you'll have all the documentation ready?'

Mrs Gregson had warned me that an unscrupulous breeder would produce false pedigree papers. How would I know whether they were false or not? I doubt if they had a watermark or official seal.

'Rowland Kennels, Potters Lane. Yes, I'll be able to find it. Tomorrow morning. Look forward to seeing you.'

Puppies and fish. I was fast becoming caught up in a web of veterinary cases. Not that I was knocking the seriousness of the crimes. The puppies were valuable and Mrs Gregson was upset at losing her babies. The rods were also valuable and their disappearance was theft.

Before I left the shop I had the side window to dress. It looked forlorn without the garish piles of comics. I combed through my boxes out the back, looking for a theme, any theme.

'Pub jugs,' I said triumphantly. There were six pub jugs, a bit chipped and stained but still interesting pieces of brewer's advertising: Bell's Whisky, Grant's, Buchanan's and a really battered one picturing Kenco Old Blended, which apparently sold for two and six per bottle in those days and in your dreams. I had a feeling that I ought to sell that last one on to a special dealer but the effort required was beyond my resources.

The pier felt as if it was wobbling. Gusts shook its sturdy iron girders. The anglers were out in force, clustered in companionable groups with their canvas seats, thermoses, and boxes of unmentionable bits of squirmy bait. I was unrecognizable in layers of sweaters, scarves and knitted hat. But still the wind found its way up untucked layers and into neck gaps.

'Hi there, Jordan,' they called, banging gloved hands and stamping feet. Their assorted hats were pulled down low over eyebrows, scarves hoisted ear-high, as they patrolled the row of rods, lines streaming out to sea.

'Caught anything?' Stock phrase. I was invited to inspect a motley selection of fish, some still gasping. It was not pleasant watching the last thrashes even of a creature as unattractive as a wet-eyed fish.

'Isn't that one a bit small?' I said.

'She wants you to throw it back,' someone sniggered.

'Anything to oblige a lady,' said Dick Mann, tossing it back into the waves. I hoped it was in time and leaned over the rail to watch its descent. But the fish had disappeared beneath the churning water in a second.

'I've brought some sandwiches,' he went on. 'Hope you like cheese and pickle.'

42

'My favourite,' I said. I was glad he hadn't brought fish.

He looked pleased and continued baiting the hook. I stepped out of the way of his cast. It looked as practised as a golfer's swing.

'Any action?' I asked Arnie. He was easy to find, being a big lad. Arnie Rudge was the original complainant, who had come to me seeking help. He seemed to think it was dead easy and I would solve the mystery in a couple of hours.

'You wait around and watch. You'll catch them, I know that. Piece of cake for someone like you used to catching criminals,' he'd said, signing my contract for the hourly rate. 'We'll stand you a pint in the pub after-wards.'

'I'll deserve it,' I said.

I deserved it already and I had only been on the pier ten minutes. The fish were quite clever. The bait was repeatedly yanked off the hooks and had to be replaced. The anglers discussed types of bait, merits and demerits. I didn't want to know about lug-worms and sliced mackerel.

'Have you tried bread?'

'Falls off. Too soggy.'

'I think I'll take a wander round,' I said, tired of the inactivity. 'Maybe keep an eye on anything happening under the pier.'

'Good thinking.'

I would never make an angler. It required

hours of patience. Yet I've spent hours on surveillance, up a tree, in a car, pacing a pavement. It was possible that I was not looking at this case in a positive way. Another kind of surveillance, plus fish. It was the smell that was difficult to accept. Surveillance up a tree was an essay in leaf and mould, bark and essence of sap.

It amazed me that Mavis was never put off by the smell of fish. Perhaps they spent a lot of time in the bath.

The tide was nearly on the turn. It was a very high tide, 6.4, helped by the ferocious wind. The wind was good for my asthma, blew through the sticky pipes in my lungs. A few people were out strolling the pier and the seafront, the ones who enjoyed battling with the elements. It helped if you had an arm to cling on to. An extra ten stone alongside promoted stability.

The white cliffs of the Seven Sisters were lost in a distant mist. Even Brighton's monstrous architectural skyline was mercifully blotted out. Rain was on its way. Dark pewter clouds were scurrying across the Channel from France hung with a touch of garlic.

It was not easy trudging over the wet shingle. I slid and slipped, pebbles rolling away from under my feet. I took up a position with my back propped against a wooden groyne, where I could watch the anglers on the pier. I counted the rods, six in all. Shopping list: better binoculars, waterproof hat. Rain was dripping down my neck and I was starting to feel sick. Had I eaten or was it the prevailing smell of fish?

My current state of cases did not cheer me. I suppose that depression had set in with the death of DS Ben Evans and it was not something one could shake off. I am not registered with a doctor. My frequent visits to Latching Hospital and other Sussex hospitals have been due to my own foolishness in getting injured, one way or another.

I did not know all the names of the anglers but Dick Mann was positioned furthest from the shore and the bulky Arnie was the nearest. I just kept counting the row of rods, nodding off ... Six ... six ... five.

Five! Nothing had happened. No giant Jaws thrashing the water or slithering twenty-foot black thing emerging from the depths out at sea. I told myself to calm down. One of the anglers had packed up and gone home to watch *Emmerdale*.

I tracked back to the seafront. The rain clouds were gathering darkly over Latching, biting into the wind. Surveillance in a car was a lot drier. Latching's permanent bag lady, Gracie, was huddled into one of the beach shelters, surrounded by her laden shopping trollies like a Wild West corral. She was in for a miserable night.

'Hi, Gracie!' I shouted.

She never answered.

I hurried on, skirting the palatial Pavilion, home of last night's dance, amateur musicals, touring comedians, pop groups, jazz bands, antique fairs, bridal shows, computer exhibitions. The curtains were drawn against the sea-facing windows as staff put the theatre seats back in rows for tonight's performance of *Songs from Sinatra*.

Arnie was crouched down, trying to light a cigarette in a pocket of calm. Judging by the oily papers around him, he'd finished off a big portion of fish and chips and a take-away coffee and was now on his last course. He'd caught some fish for his supper. Huss by the look of it, a long shark-like fish with a centre bone but firm white flesh when cooked.

'A bit wet now, isn't it?' I asked, rain dripping off my face. I wanted to go home, dry out.

'No way,' he said. 'Only a bit of drizzle. Fish are running. We're doing well.'

'Well, someone has gone home. A rod has gone.'

He stood up and groaned. 'Hell's bells. Not another one. Jordan says a rod has gone.' He rushed up to other crouching figures and there was a general melee as they counted rods. The new decking had darkened with the rain.

'Mine is here.'

'And mine.'

'Who's gone?'

'It's Dick's.'

The furthest from the shore had gone and that had been Dick Mann's. It had gone from right under my nose. I had not seen a thing. It was uncanny. No small boys larking about under the pier, although the tide was going out now and the first girder legs were straddling pools of whipped water.

I strode the length of the pier and round the double-tiered jetty end where occasionally paddle steamers tied up. The wind at the far end was almost impossible to breach. Head down, I battled round, gulping for breath.

No sign of Dick Mann.

'He's gone home,' I said, surprised at his departure. 'He's not on the pier. He's not anywhere.'

'He hasn't gone home,' said Arnie, agitated. 'He's left all his gear.'

It was neatly piled on one of the bench seats. A sodden newspaper, waterproofs, bait boxes, a pint thermos and an Iceland carrier bag. I peered into the plastic bag. Wrapped cheese and pickle sandwiches. They had not been opened. Untouched. He'd brought one for me and now he had gone.

'He's gone to the Gents loo,' I said, inspired.

They looked at me and each other,

unconvinced. No angler would reel in his rod for a call of nature. But one of them went off to check just the same.

'No, he's not there.'

I went into Jack's amusement arcade to see if Dick Mann was also addicted to the machines. But a quick reconnaissance drew a blank. Jack was busy changing money from inside his booth, bagging up coins. He looked up and saw me, shook his head vigorously. Not the usual welcome and no sign of Dick Mann in the arcade. He slid open a window.

'Get out, Jordan,' he shouted. 'It's not safe.'

I was starting to panic, unusual for me. I do not panic even in dire circumstances. Ask DI James. I ran back to the anglers. They were peering over the rails as if expecting to see Dick dangling from the iron girders. What was not safe? The pier? Or was Jack warning me about something else?

'Has he done this before, gone off without a word?'

'Never.'

'When did you last see him?'

'Don't know. Wasn't looking, really.'

'No idea.'

'We were standing about talking. I thought Dick was with us as usual. We don't take much notice of anything when we're fishing,' said Arnie.

'Well, he's gone,' I said. 'And so has the rod. But he has left his gear.'

The group went silent. Dick Mann had vanished. Like the rods. Not a sign. Not a clue, not a trace. He had vanished off the pier in broad daylight. Perhaps the police would take some notice now.

'I'll report the circumstances,' I said, anxious to set foot on dry fish-less land, except it was wet and puddled land.

'Let's wait and see if he turns up,' said Arnie. 'It might be something personal. Perhap's he won the lottery, lads, and has gone off to collect his winnings.'

'Bet he's in the pub, right now, opening the champers,' someone laughed.

I was not so sure. No true fisherman would leave his bait.

Four

The new police station at Latching was clean, open and airy, with automatic doors and as yet without any character. They had closed the old building, dismantled the offices and cells, moved everything and everyone to a custom-built grey-bricked structure in the centre of town.

In order to clear a site for the new police station, some old shops were bulldozed. They were not Georgian or historically worth preserving but they were part of old Latching.

Sergeant Rawlings was no longer accessible behind a big desk with a mug of tea. He came forward to a glass-screened counter and nodded to me.

'Hello, Jordan. Come to watch feeding time?'

He looked unhappy. The office behind him was spacious and newly painted, well equipped with desktop computers and telephones. Several rows of desks, tops bare, were unoccupied. The area was well heated and there were seats in the foyer for the public.

'Where is everyone?'

'We don't need so many now to man the front,' he said. 'The shifts have been cut.'

'It's very ... clean,' I said. 'Do you like it?'

'No. I liked the old place. It had character. OK, it was ramshackle and draughty and in need of a make-over, a few licks of paint. But it felt homely.'

'I've never heard of a police station being called homely before. It does seem strange, all this glass.'

'Don't get too near. We've got terrorist shutters too,' said the sergeant, eyes alert. 'I've only got to press a button and, watch out, your fingers are off.'

'Sign of the times,' I said.

'CID offices are upstairs,' he said, telling me what I wanted to know. 'But you can't get there without going through several coded doors. You have to know the code, Jordan. And it gets changed regularly. No more slipping past me and using our data system.'

'As if I would. Slip past you? Never.'

'How can I help you?'

'It's about a man being reported missing. A man called Dick Mann. Does it ring a bell?'

'Is he local?'

'Yes, but I'm not sure where he lives, somewhere north of Latching. I don't have many details.'

'Recently missing?'

'Yes, since yesterday afternoon. He went missing off the pier.'

Sergeant Rawlings is used to hearing odd things from me. This was nothing unusual. He did not blink but retreated to a bank of computers at the far end of the room. I couldn't see what he was doing but I guessed. He was accessing the Police National Computer. All the latest software. I wanted to know if anyone had reported Dick Mann as missing. It was possible that he had taken off of his own accord, but it seemed strange, leaving all his belongings behind on the pier. No one had seen him go.

The other anglers had not known much

about Dick's private life. No one knew if there was any family around. He turned up regularly with his rods and his thermos and no one asked any questions.

Yesterday we had all searched the pier, inch by inch, looking for torn anoraks, any clue. We found nothing. His expensive fishing rod had gone, so had Dick Mann.

'Jordan, I don't know what to make of this,' Arnie had said, perplexed. 'He'd never just go off like that. It's not like him. We all go for a pint together after fishing. Never misses it. Dick likes his pint. We're all mates.'

Sergeant Rawlings came back with a printout. 'Nothing, no one,' he said. 'Sorry, Jordan. What about this Mann person? Did he jump off the pier?'

'No, he disappeared off the pier. Quite suddenly. One moment he was fishing with his friends, and the next he had gone. Completely disappeared. No one saw him go.'

'Lost his bait?'

'Left his bait box behind, full of horrible squirming things. Revolting.'

'And is this one of your cases?'

'Not really. I'm investigating the disappearance of fishing rods. Now, don't laugh, Sarge, please. It's serious. Some of them have very expensive equipment. You can pay thousands of pounds for state-of-the-art gear.'

'I remember them coming in here,' said

Sergeant Rawlings, leaning on the shelf, then finding the sheet of glass was in the way and having to stand up. He looked weary. 'We couldn't do much to help.'

'Too busy spending your resources on a brand new police station. How much did this building cost?' I asked.

The automatic door opened, allowing a chilly draught to blow in. A man hurried in and stood beside me, fairly cold and distant.

'That tongue of yours will get you into trouble one of these days, Jordan,' said DI James, flicking through his notebook.

'Going to put me in a cell?' I said.

'We haven't got any cells here. We'd have to drive you to Durrington. It's called centralization.'

'What a shame,' I said. 'I've always counted on getting an overnight bunk here if I ever lose my house keys.'

DI James looked tired. His face was drawn. Maybe he had been working all night and the last person he wanted to see was me. I know I annoy him. It was unfortunate, especially when I felt so differently about him. Ben's death had sobered me somewhat, but my passion for James was now laced with fear. I could lose him as well. It could happen so easily. I did not want to think about it.

He shook my sleeve with a rare familiarity. Maybe he had seen that fleeting fear in my eyes. 'Come and have a guided tour, Jordan, while I'm in a good mood. Everywhere is still tidy, but not for long.'

'When did you move in?'

'Over the weekend. It was diabolical. We're still living out of boxes. It's all high-tech.'

He patched in some numbers on the door code, too fast for me to remember them, two, three, something, something.

'We change the code every month,' he said as the door swung open. 'No point in you trying to remember them.'

'I'd soon work it out. Try me.'

'Come upstairs to the CID suite. All mod cons. Even a shower and walk-in locker room. Percolated coffee in the kitchen. Same old instant drinks machines in the corridor.'

'To make you feel at home,' I murmured.

'You haven't been to visit me recently,' he said, striding down the well-lit corridor to a door at the end.

'You haven't asked me.'

'You don't need an invitation, Jordan. Come any time to Marchmont Tower. I can't guarantee that I'll be there.'

'No point in making the journey then,' I said briskly.

It was open-plan upstairs, but so different from the old building. Far more space and walking room between the desks. They had been overcrowded in the old police station, barely room to close a filing cabinet. I recognized several officers. They were unpacking boxes in a fairly disorganized way.

'Why don't you employ civilians to do that?' I asked. 'It's a waste of manpower.'

'Classified files.'

'I could help,' I heard myself offering.

'Thank you, but no. You'd be reading everything and making notes. Besides, everyone knows that you used to work here. An ex-WPC might be bearing a grudge.'

'Only against the rodent who got me suspended,' I said. 'And he's not here any more. Waving his brand of justice for rapists somewhere up north, I understand.'

James ignored my remark. I knew he had looked into the case and thought I had been unfairly treated. It was mud under the gangplank now but it still hurt. I'd always wanted to be in the police force, a girlhood ambition. But my life now was one surprise after another. First Class Junk paid the bills. First Class Investigations paid for the jam and the cream, or, in my case, the yogurt and the brie.

'These are much better working conditions,' I said, trying to sound judicious and encouraging. 'Pretty good.'

'We never complained.'

'It's called progress.'

'They are going to put up flats on the site of the old police station. A block of eighteen round a central courtyard.'

'Sounds like a developer's dream. I shall campaign for a tree, a single tree in the courtyard, to encourage the birds.'

'Excellent idea, Jordan,' said James, taking off his black leather parka and hanging it behind a desk. 'Invite me to the ceremonial planting. I'll hold the shovel for you.'

'Do you know anyone called Dick Mann?' I asked. 'He's an angler who fishes off the pier.'

'No, sorry. Should I?'

'He seems to have gone missing.'

'Probably nipped across the Channel to buy some fresh lobsters. Quicker than hanging off the end of the pier for hours.'

'Anglers take their fishing very seriously,' I said, defending my clients. 'And his disappearance is a mystery.'

'Ah, the dreaded Latching Munching Monster emerges from the depths of the sea again,' said a uniformed joker from the other side of the room. 'Nothing it likes better than a juicy angler.'

'This move has obviously unhinged some of your team,' I said. 'They forgot to pack their brains. Perhaps you ought to go back to the other station and rummage around the rubbish.'

'What have we got on the Burns case? Coffee anyone?' said DI James, already forgetting I was there. I turned away, hiding the ache. One day it might heal.

Fortunately the way out did not require the door code procedure. I waved to Sergeant Rawlings and thanked him for his help.

'Take care,' he said, looking more miserable than ever.

Sunny Latching was in hiding behind a dark roller-coaster cloud. It was going to rain again. I shivered and double-tied my scarf round my neck, dug my hands in my pockets. My gloves ought to be strung through my sleeves, like a toddler. I was always leaving them around. This time on the coffee counter in the CID suite.

Dogs, four, small. It was time to visit the Rowland Kennels armed with photographs of Jodie, Jude, Mel and Angel. Shopping list: disposable camera, doggie snacks, disinfectant. This last item was purely in case of doggie accident.

The ladybird had not been out for days. She started up first time like the grand old lady she was. I'd planned my route and arranged appointments, filling up the tank at the first petrol station on the way. I'd learned my lesson about leaving it till the last drop.

This was a moment I savoured and enjoyed to the full, driving out of Latching in my classy Morris Minor. Those early months of cycling everywhere had been healthy but damp. Nor did my arrival, soaked and out of breath, make a good impression. But my ladybird was the tops. She broke the ice. Her black spots on red were a sure-fire talking point with young and old.

'My goodness, that's some car you've got there. She's pretty old, isn't she? What year?'

'J-registration. Classic. I call her my lady-bird.'

'Not difficult to see why, Miss Lacey!'

Rowland Kennels were full of yapping animals. I should have brought earplugs. The little creatures were prancing around, all hopeful of a doting owner. I produced my photos and spun a yarn.

'These were the puppies of a very dear friend of mine and I want to buy some exactly the same,' I said.

'You want to buy four puppies?' I was asked. The owners were seeing megabucks changing hands.

'If I can find identical puppies. You said you had a long-haired.'

'These puppies have passed on?' They nodded sympathetically.

'You could say that.'

I was shown yards full of gambolling puppies. They all seemed to be well looked after and the puppies were bright and intelligent-eyed. At first they all looked the same. Then I began to notice the differences in coat and face, a dark patch here, a more pointed ear there. It was pretty exhausting. I made notes of near misses. All the owners confirmed the value of these little creatures. We were talking a lot of money.

'About the long-haired female,' I said. 'Could I see her?'

'I think we've sold her. Yes, late yesterday. An impulse buy by a couple moving into a seafront flat in Brighton.'

I wondered if they would give me the address. Probably not.

'There's a great demand for chihuahuas,' they went on. 'In these days of flats and apartments, people want a small dog. Much easier to look after.'

'Shorter walks,' I added.

'You've said it.'

'I'm sorry,' I said, with a big theatrical sigh. 'But none of your lovely puppies are quite right in size or colouring. It's a shame. I really like this place and feel that puppies from such a good home would have been delightful.'

This was my parting speech at each of the kennels I visited. It went down well. I felt that none of these people had crept in at dawn and stolen Mrs Daphne Gregson's valuable foursome. I did not see any creature resembling the ball of fluff that she called Angel.

I drove back to Latching, deep in thought. I did not know where to go with this one. Perhaps I needed to dig around the underworld, ask about a bit. I sniffed at my sleeve.

It smelt decidedly doggy.

Pub crawls are not normally my scene. A glass of a good red in pleasant company is a welcome relaxation, but this was going to be different. A drink in every pub that I passed on my way back to Latching. It would need stamina.

The first pub en route was obviously popular because the car park was full. I hung around, then grabbed a space when someone backed out pretty fast. A blue Mondeo missed me by inches.

'Hey buster!' I yelled, perfecting my road rage. 'What's wrong with your eyesight?'

The bar was full. I had to inch my way between burly shoulders to get served. I will never understand why men have to drink leaning on the bar when there are ample seats and benches around. Perhaps the bar represents some solid maternal support which is now missing from their life.

'A St Clement's please,' I said at last.

The barmaid went blank. 'We don't stock it,' she said.

'Yes, you do.' I went on to explain. 'It's orange juice and a bitter lemon. The nursery rhyme ... oranges and lemons, say the bells of St Clement's.'

She was still blank. 'Oh, you want an orange juice.'

'And a bitter lemon.'

She still had not got the hang of it and

served the bottle of bitter lemon separately. Maybe I was going to have this trouble everywhere, I thought, as I mixed the drink myself.

It's not easy to start chatting to strange men in pubs. They are always in close groups, turning their backs on any stranger who intrudes. And chatting is difficult even in the best of circumstances. It's always an act. The perfect opportunity came when the door flew open and in burst a tubby man being pulled by a black labrador on a lead. The dog went straight to the bar and sat down, grinning.

'On time, Bert!'

'That dog knows your habits better'n you do.'

'Lovely dog,' I said while the barmaid was letting his brimming Guinness settle. 'What a beautiful head. And such intelligent eyes.'

'My Maggie,' said Bert. 'She's the best. Wouldn't change her for the world. I'd give up the missus before I'd give up Maggie.'

So I knew where I stood with Bert. We talked dogs for ten minutes. At least, I listened to dog talk for ten minutes. Bert did all the talking.

'I'm looking for a small dog,' I said when I could get a word in. I was part of the group by now. 'One of those tiny dogs that people have in flats. What are they called? I've only got two rooms.'

Time to look petite and vulnerable and helpless about choosing a dog.

'King Charles spaniel?'

'Jack Russell?'

'No, much smaller.'

'What about one of them pedigree chihuahuas?'

'That's it. A chihuahua. Anyone know where I could get one? I'm not interested in pedigrees or papers. Just a nice little dog. I'd pay, of course, but not the top price.'

'Now you're asking.'

'Loopy's the man you want. Whatever you want, he'll get you. Dog, microwave, swimming pool. He can get anything.'

'We don't know his real name but he's loopy about dogs. So we call him Loopy.'

'When can I meet this Loopy?' I asked, finishing my St Clement's. I'd made it last.

'You just missed him, miss. He just left. He drives a blue Mondeo.'

It was time to move on. Perhaps I'd come back, check on Loopy. I gave Maggie a farewell stroke. She had sat there with more patience than a human and her head was like velvet.

'Goodbye nice dog,' I said.

That evening I went for a meal at Miguel's, the expensive Mexican restaurant in the same row as my shop. Miguel is a brilliant cook. He looks like Omar Sharif and acts a bit like him too.

'Jordan. I have missed you.' He came straight over, took my hand, kissed my fingers. I was wearing the poncho he'd given me.

In moments he had found me a table and was pouring out a large glass of his best red wine. He had beautiful glasses, more like crystal goblets. He never measured a drink, poured by instinct.

'So, you eat with me tonight?'

'Yes, but I am paying for it. I insist.'

He had brown eyes, deeply flecked with gold, all glowing with admiration. He liked me. If DI James had not been around, I would probably have given him some encouragement.

'So, shall I choose a meal for you, Jordan, something special? Shall I sit with you when the customers have gone? It is too long since we talked.'

'That would be nice, Miguel. You decide, something light. I'm sure it will be superb. I've not eaten all day, so not too much. And one more thing...'

'Yes, anything for you. You know that.' Those eyes were smiling.

Miguel was so charming, I don't know how I can resist him. He would pamper me, take care of me, feed me, take me to South America.

'Please don't talk about dogs.'

'No dogs,' he agreed, nodding, not asking why. He was like that.

Five

Mrs Gregson was impressed by my report. It typed up far better than I had thought. She read the list of kennels visited.

'Excellent, excellent,' she murmured. 'You see, I couldn't have done this. They all know me. They'd get suspicious, wonder what I was doing. But you … ideal. You say that you didn't see any puppies that resembled my babies?'

'None, although I didn't search inside the kennels. Your puppies could have been kept out of sight but I doubt it. The owners seemed very open and genuine and I had a good wander round.'

'It was a gang of thieves, I'm sure,' said Mrs Gregson. 'There's a black market trade in pedigree breeds. My babies are probably halfway to Amsterdam by now.' She was near to tears. I passed her a tissue. Amsterdam seemed an odd destination.

'Have you found out how the thieves got in? I presume the police brushed for prints and things like that. Tell me again.'

'There was nothing exceptional. No one had broken in as such. They had used a key to unlock the padlock on the gate into the kennel yard. It's a five-foot-high gate.'

'What about your alarm system?'

'Yes, of course, it's a very good system but it didn't go off. Not a single bell. It must have been tampered with or turned off. Whatever happened, I slept right through it. I didn't discover the loss until I went to feed my lot. For a start, a couple of puppies were playing in the yard and the door to the kennel was swinging open. I knew at once that someone had got in. It was my worst fear.'

She looked so stricken by the loss of her puppies that I was shocked into vigilance. I assured her that the puppies were being well treated. They were a valuable commodity, to be sold on for top money. No one would harm them.

But Mrs Gregson was suffering. She got up and filled a kettle with water, a little unsteadily. I was pleased that tea was on its way. I was still afloat with St Clement's, having called in at several country pubs on my way back to Latching, hoping to see a blue Mondeo. I could be getting a reputation.

As I was leaving, I gave Mrs Gregson a glimmer of hope. 'I do have a lead,' I said. 'That's not a joke. I've been told of someone who sells dogs in pubs. Maybe he steals them in the first place, steals to order, I don't know.'

Mrs Gregson looked even more upset. 'Please be careful, Miss Lacey. In pubs, of all places. He doesn't sound a very nice person.'

'Don't worry. I can take care of myself.' They were bold words and I didn't believe them. I'd got into enough trouble in my time. Sometimes DI James came and rescued me, sometimes I got out of the situation myself. Some of the events were big, some small. I was a victim of my own circumstances.

I walked back to the shop. It was a dry, bright day but bitterly cold. The northeasterly wind attacked my teeth. I had to suck in my mouth to dull the ache. The farmers liked a hard winter but it was the devil to live through. One of the shops had a thermometer in the window. The needle was in the blue zone. It was below freezing.

Someone had left a bulging carrier bag on my doorstep. Did they think I was a charity shop? It didn't look like a bomb but did any of us know what a bomb would look like? I imagined wires sticking out and a ticking clock.

Still, I was careful. I skirted the bag and let myself into the shop. Shreds of yesterday's heat clung to the inside. The red light flickered on my answerphone. I pressed replay. It was DI James.

'Watch out, Jordan, when you're driving your ladybird,' said the message. 'Latching is being hit by staged car crashes. It's an insurance fraud.'

The machine clicked off. I almost played it again so that I could listen to his voice, deep, masculine, that faint accent. It was stupid, idiotic. I was trying to get over him. Wasn't I?

He had thrown my thoughts off kilter. I could barely remember why I was in the back of the shop. Ah, a broom.

My attention went back to the carrier bag on my doorstep. This time I took a broom with me and poked the outside gently. It seemed to give a little but was packed stiff with the size of the contents. The tied knot was straining and I caught a glimpse of pale material. Do they wrap bombs? I gave up being careful.

The bag was large and bulky. It weighed more than I expected. I untied the knot and the bag fell open with relief and spilled out a tumescence of gossamer-white material, yellowed with age on the folds. There were yards of the stuff. I held it up. It was a high-waisted chemise-dress, so old it almost fell apart. The breast-high girdle was of plaited primrose silk. The neckline was trimmed with lace and the train was decorated with a hem of artificial spring flowers. It was delicate, ethereal, unbelievable.

'Wow!' I said, putting it on a hanger.

I did not know what to do with it. My six-pound price label would be ludicrous. Anyway, I did not want to sell the dress. My own taste ran to jeans and T-shirts, but I could appreciate perfection in feminine apparel when I saw it. Leroy Anderson would like it. She would look a million dollars, wearing that gown.

The dress needed a date. I locked up the shop and cycled to the library, padlocking my bike on to the railings. People stole bikes these days. Once inside, I combed through an encyclopedia of fashion, looking for this dress. I found something very similar, printed in *Journal des Dames* 1799. It was French made and over two hundred years old. The model had her hair done à la coiffure hollandaise, whatever that was. I thought it was a sauce.

Why put such a dress on my doorstep? Was it some sort of message? People had done stranger things.

And I was still worried about Dick Mann. I was only employed to find out about missing fishing rods, not missing anglers. It was none of my business. No one was paying me. But it wouldn't hurt to ask at the hospital where he worked.

Latching Hospital is now a vast place, built on and built on again in different architectural styles. I skipped reception and went

straight to personnel. I used to have a friendly contact who worked there but she had
moved on. I was stuck with trying to find
rapport with new people.

'I'm enquiring about Dick Mann,' I said.
'He's a friend of mine.' I tried to imply more
than a friend but it was difficult remembering the ruddy face and green fleece. 'Is he
here? Did he come in to work today?'

A superior sort of supervisor came round
to see me. She was strait-laced and
imposing. They did still employ dragons.

'Why do you want to know?' she asked.

I did a sort of wobbly, as if I was intimidat-
ed. This woman was straight from a school
of witches.

'Er ... we had arranged to meet yesterday
and he didn't turn up. I'd like to talk to him.'

'His private life is none of our business,'
she said, clearing her throat. 'So he didn't
turn up? That's between you and him and
nothing to do with us. Please leave and don't
come back.'

'I only want to know if he came to work.'

'We're far too busy for this sort of enquiry.
If you don't go, I shall be forced to call
security.'

I wished I had a police badge to flash at
her. I also stretched my mind for a scathing
retort, but nothing surfaced. 'OK, I'm
going,' I said.

I made a note of the name on the shiny

badge fixed to her lapel. NINA DEODAR. I'd remember that name. Nein Deodorant. Not a nice lady. No sweetness and light. An NHS monster.

But as I left the personnel office, a normal-type person passed me in the outer corridor. She was carrying a stack of patient files and had a pleasant round face.

'Dick Mann left last week,' she said in a low voice. 'He gave in his notice. Such a shame. Everyone liked him.'

'Why did he leave?' I asked swiftly. 'Do you know why?'

'I think someone made his life a misery.'

I was left to guess who. It would be easy to put the blame on to the formidable Ms Deodar but there was no real evidence.

'Have you any idea where he lives?'

'An old cottage off North Mill Lane. He's doing it up.'

'Thanks,' I said, but the woman had already gone back to the lion's den. I hope she didn't get eaten.

Maeve's Cafe was almost empty. I had a choice of tables but took my favourite by the window, facing the sea. The water was grey, rising in angry surges, pounding the shingle into submission. It didn't like a north-easterly any more than we did.

'How did you enjoy the dance, Jordan?' said Mavis, coming over with a mug of tea for me, weak, with honey. 'Didn't see you on the floor much.'

'Shortage of partners,' I said. 'You and Doris had first pickings.'

'Don't try to hoodwink me. I saw you dancing with our dishy DI James. Don't tell me you didn't plan that one in advance. I love a man in a black shirt.'

'It was not planned,' I said through gritted teeth. 'I didn't know he would be there. Don't put me through another third degree, Mavis. Your boyfriend wasn't very polite to me.'

Mavis drew up a chair. I hoped she didn't have something frying out back that was going to set off the smoke alarm.

'I'm sorry about that, Jordan. He doesn't like you or anyone who sniffs of the police or authority. I'm not sure why. He hasn't told me. Perhaps it's to do with fish quotas. I've never seen him like that before. He's a real teddy bear, most of the time.' Her face softened as she thought of the times. Her hair was a strawberry blonde this winter.

'Bears can be savage and vicious. Never trust a teddy bear.'

'He'll be all right once he gets used to you,' Mavis promised. 'You must come round one evening. I'll get him to bring a friend for you.'

I went hot and cold with the implications that flooded my mind. It did not bear think-

71

ing about. There, Mavis had got me thinking about bears now.

'So why doesn't he like authority?'

'All the fishermen are uptight about the fishing quotas, the foreign trawlers, inspectors turning up and counting the catch. It's not fair. They are only trying to earn a living. They can't measure every little fish that is stupid enough to get caught in a net.'

'Do I look like a ministry inspector?' I said, sipping the hot tea. 'Fish coming out of my ears?'

'How does he know who you are working for? You could be spying for the Fisheries Board or whatever they are called.'

'I don't fancy sitting on the beach in this weather, waiting for his boat to come in, to count the catch. You can tell Bruno that I admire him going out in all weathers. They are a tough bunch.'

'He is tough,' said Mavis with a broad wink. 'In a certain department.'

I didn't ask. It was always best to pretend to understand. Mavis had a colourful love life and I preferred to spectate from the sidelines.

'I've some lovely skate,' she went on. 'Would you like a nice piece for your lunch? Grilled, battered or breadcrumbs?'

'Grilled, please, Mavis. Thank you.'

'Can't have you so skinny. You've lost weight.'

'I forget to eat.'

'That's your excuse.'

Mavis went back to cook the skate, leaving me to contemplate the wind tossing the sea, the palm trees swaying and the stray walkers battling against the force, overcoats flapping.

There were several old labourers' cottages along North Mill Lane but I knew no one who lived in them. Door-knocking time. Unless I spotted Dick Mann's fishing gear, tidily stored in some outhouse. But would I spot the owner? Would he be there at all?

I tried to put such thoughts out of my mind as the skate arrived with that delicious smell of perfectly fresh fish. I did not ask if Bruno had caught it. My fork went into the succulent thick flesh of the fish and hooked out a mouthful. It was perfect. I nodded my thanks to Mavis who was watching my re-action. She was well pleased and went back to serving some other customers who had taken refuge from the bitter wind.

It was a long time since I had eaten. I never kept to normal mealtimes but grazed as required. It suited my lifestyle. I could hardly break off a surveillance to go and have my tea.

DI James did not come in. We often met in Maeve's Cafe, shared a table, argued over a few points. But today he was elsewhere. He'd said something about car crashes. Perhaps there had been another one on the road to Brighton.

My two cases seemed insoluble. How could I find four little dogs, halfway to Amsterdam? And who had been nicking the fishing rods? There was nothing to get my teeth into, except this gourmet fish from the Channel. Poor skate. It had once been flapping about so happily at the bottom of the sea.

I paid for my lunch, promised to pop in again, went back to the shop to pick up the ladybird, which I always parked in the back yard. North Mill Lane was some distance north. Not exactly after-lunch walking.

The wintery sky was grey with scudding clouds, every wisp of grey taking on the shape of a witch. An NHS witch? It was pretty unnerving. I moved on to the main road, wished I had a car radio, wanting to listen to some soul jazz.

There was a lot of traffic about. I often wondered where everyone was going, wasting all this fuel, polluting the atmosphere. Why didn't they stay at home?

I am a careful driver. I spend a lot of time looking in the wing mirror and the overhead mirror. After a few minutes it occured to me that I was being followed. As I slowed down to a crawl, as if looking for a road name, the car behind me also slowed down. It was a green Vauxhall driven by a man wearing a woolly hat. A woman passenger sat beside him. My brain recited the registration number. It was an old habit. I slowed down to make a left turn off the roundabout towards the back of Latching. North Mill Lane was somewhere near the ancient windmill.

As I turned, the Vauxhall accelerated and overtook me. Then, for absolutely no reason, the Vauxhall braked and I went straight into the back of him with a shattering crunch. I was flung against my seat belt as I jammed on my brakes.

'Hells bells!' I groaned against the steering wheel. My breath was ruptured, banged out of me. All thought was for my beloved lady-bird. She was too old for much in the way of repairs.

I got out and staggered round to the front. The Vauxhall was hard against the bumper of the ladybird. Both the driver and passenger looked stunned.

'What the hell were you doing, accelerating when you could see I was slowing down to make a left turn!' I shouted at the window.

He let the window down. 'You were going too fast, you stupid woman.'

'You braked suddenly, right in front of me,' I fumed.

'No way, I never braked.'

I inspected the damage to my car. It was only the bumper. I could live with a dented bumper. Some mechanic must owe me a favour somewhere. It could be straightened out.

The Vauxhall must have been made of softer metal. There was much more damage and broken rear lights. The woman passenger was groaning. I went round to the side door and opened it.

'Don't move,' I said. 'I'll call for an ambulance. You may have hurt yourself.'

'I want to go home,' she moaned.

'I think a doctor ought to see you,' I said. 'Take some deep breaths and try to relax. Where does it hurt?'

'My neck, my neck...' she sobbed.

The man had got out and was writing down my registration number on a piece of paper. 'What's your name and address and the name of your insurance company? It was your fault. You crashed right into me.'

Alarm bells rang. I made sure my hair was tucked away under a hat.

'No, I did not, it was not my fault,' I said firmly. 'But your passenger is injured. First things first. How about calling for an ambulance?'

Other cars slowed down to view the accident. It really annoyed me. This was not a side show. 'Want any help?' someone called out.

'You could be a witness,' the man called back.

76

'Didn't see anything, mate,' said the other driver, moving on with fast acceleration.

I went to fetch my mobile phone from the front seat. The irate driver followed me. I noticed he was limping. 'You're not getting away,' he shouted. 'What's your name?'

'I'm phoning for an ambulance for your passenger. She's hurt. Keep your hair on, I'm not going anywhere. And by the way, your brake lights were not working.'

I made two calls. The first to 999 for an ambulance. The second call went straight through to James's mobile. He answered abruptly.

'I've had a crash in very odd circumstances,' I said in a low voice. 'By the roundabout that leads to North Mill Lane. I've phoned for an ambulance. Are you interested?'

'Be with you right away, Jordan. Try to keep them talking.'

'I wonder if he's interested in fishing.'

Six

He said his name was Derek Brook but he did not seem sure. It was as if he was trying to remember who he was. It had happened to me many times when I was on surveillance, being someone else, then forgetting who I was. But maybe it was the shock of the crash.

The woman was leaning back against the headrest, still moaning. Perhaps she had hurt her neck. It was difficult to judge without a medical examination. Maybe this was not one of those suspicious insurance scams. If it was a genuine accident, then I was going to lose my no-claims bonus.

An ambulance arrived, lights flashing, and the paramedics jumped out. They had a neck brace on the woman passenger in minutes. The car driver was sitting on the side of the road, saying he had a pain in his chest. Both paramedics knelt at his side. The light was fading and the scene turned grey.

'What's your name? Where does it hurt?'

'Brook, Derek Brook. Here, my chest. Ouch.'

I was confused. It looked like a real accident with genuine casualties. It had the hallmarks of a staged car crash, but now they were convincing me that they had been injured. I wished DI James would arrive. He would sort them out.

They were both being helped into the ambulance. The woman wanted her handbag from the car and I fetched it for her. It was the least I could do.

'How about you, miss?' one of the paramedics asked me.

'Oh, I'm all right,' I said. 'I wasn't going fast. They braked for some reason. Just a few bruises, I expect.' My chest was beginning to feel tender. I hoped it wasn't a cracked rib. They could hurt for weeks, as I well knew.

'Perhaps you ought to come along and be checked out,' he suggested.

'No, thank you. I'll go along to my own doctor,' I said. I nodded towards the ambulance. 'I don't want to travel with them. Not my favourite people.'

'OK. Go and have a strong cup of tea, plenty of sugar. By the looks of you, you need it.'

'Thanks.'

They closed the back doors of the ambulance, got into their seats and drove off, leaving me by the side of the road, feeling isolated and miserable. I patted the ladybird in a vague way, not quite sure if she needed consoling. I echoed the woman's words in my head: 'I want to go home.'

DI James had parked his car away from the roundabout and was striding towards me, parka jacket fastened to the neck. If he was concerned for my well-being, he was keeping it under cover. His blue eyes were glinting, taking in the details.

'You've just missed them,' I fumed.

'Delayed. I had to go to court. You know what it's like.'

'No, I don't know what it's like. I make every effort to arrive on time. Those villains have gone off in an ambulance. You could catch them at Latching hospital.'

'Gone off in an ambulance? So what's this vehicle coming along the road now? Or did you ring twice?'

An ambulance was slowing down round the roundabout, lights flashing. They drew up just ahead of the Vauxhall and the doors opened. Two paramedics in green got out, bags in hand, took in the two cars, bumper to bumper.

'Hello,' they said with professional efficiency. 'Are you all right, miss? What's your name?'

I swallowed. 'Idiot, I think.'

But that was not the end of the indignity. I had to be breathalysed. DI James insisted.

'It's for your own good,' he said. 'And it's routine these days for any accident.'

'I might have an asthma attack, breathing into that bag.' I was still glaring.

'OK. The paramedics are here. They'll deal with any problem. But you won't have an asthma attack because you haven't been drinking, have you, Jordan?'

'No, I haven't. Not for ages.'

'So why the sour grapes?'

DI James wanted a full statement. He drove me back to the new police station, to his new office, and I sat down on a new chair. He gave me a cup of tea because I had started to shake. It was strong and laced with sugar. Not my favourite brew but this was no time to be choosy.

'His brake lights were not on,' I said.

'I know. They were broken.'

'I didn't break them.'

'I know. There was no broken glass on the roadway.'

'Who's a clever detective then?'

'I am.' DI James was not smiling.

It is no fun being made a fool of. James said it had the marks of a scam, right down to the first, fake, ambulance. They did not want an official ambulance making on-the-spot clever observations. Their injuries, if any, would emerge later when they had seen their own doctor, and a lengthy medical report went to the insurers. And the fake ambulance would never be traced.

'So what happens next?'

'They make an insurance claim.'

'What about my claim?'

'You'll probably find that they are not insured. Sorry, Jordan. I know someone who can straighten that bumper.'

'Thank you,' I said in a humble voice. 'That's very kind.' I wanted to get back to my ladybird now. I didn't like the idea of her being left by a roundabout, people swearing at her. They could swear at the Vauxhall. That was their business.

'I'll need a statement.'

'That's OK. You'll get one.'

His phone rang. DI James was called away to the hinterland of West Sussex. No wonder he was so lean and tense. He did not have a minute to himself. A WPC came in and took my statement. She looked about eighteen, was stick thin, and could not spell. She did not know the difference between their and there. But we managed a statement between us and I signed it. I would have signed the pledge. I wanted to get away.

I knew I looked a mess when I left the police station. No time to tidy up or wash. I stopped and took a deep breath of fresh air. A flash blue Jaguar cruised by but I hoped the driver had not seen me. Jack thought I was sophisticated and beautiful, not the current wreck. I did not want him to see me.

But it was too late. He reversed with a

screech of gears.

He opened the passenger door. 'What'ya doing, Jordan? Get in,' he said. 'I'm your knight on a white charger.'

'It's blue,' I said.

Jack always looks unwashed, unshaven and a sartorial disaster. Today was no exception. But I was easily his equal. I wanted a shower and clean clothes and some decent coffee. I also needed some sleep. Sleep is the best antidote for shock.

'What'sa matter, Jordan?' he asked as he lent over to fasten the seat belt. It was the nearest he ever got to touching me. 'You look as done in as a pig's dinner.'

'I've been in an accident near the North Mill Lane roundabout. My car is still there. I've got to get her back. I can't leave her there all night. She'll get stolen.'

'Is your car still roadworthy or written off?'

'No, no.' I almost didn't have the strength to answer. 'She's got a bent bumper, that's all.'

I found myself telling Jack about the insurance scam. He kept nodding his head, all the time driving towards North Mill Lane. He was right on my wavelength. Funny how we had this mental affinity and yet no way did I fancy him, not in the way he fancied me.

'I'll get it fixed,' he said, getting on his mobile. 'Bert? Jack here. Look, we got a Morris Minor, classic, on the North Mill

Lane roundabout. Do me a favour. Get there, needs a bumper facelift. Ten minutes? OK.'

'You're not supposed to use your mobile while driving,' I said. 'It's an offence. You could get fined.'

'Worth it. I'd do anything for you.'

He would, too. I thanked him by briefly putting my hand on his sharp knee. Not a lot of thanks but it seemed to be enough.

The ladybird was still slewed halfway off the roundabout. The Vauxhall had already been removed. Quick work but then they were organized professionals. Pity. I wanted to know if the Vauxhall was a write-off or if they had driven it away. We waited for Bert. Jack produced a flask of vodka from a pocket in the door and insisted I took a swig. I'm not used to vodka. It tasted of nothing but lifted my wavering spirits to some degree.

'Are you feeling better, Jack? You seem more like your old self.'

'Yerse. It's all blown over. I thought I was in trouble.'

'So where are you going to now?' I asked him.

'A nice meal first, somewhere classy,' he said. 'I don't cook, ever. I eat out all the time and I fancy a decent steak. Then to the midnight barn boot. It's started up again. That raid was all bluff. Remember, you came with me once? They've got some good stuff tonight, so I hear.'

'Dogs,' I said. 'Fishing rods? Do they sell them at the barn? I'm trying to find some stolen dogs and some disappearing fishing rods.'

'Dogs, no. Fishing rods, maybe. They can cost from hundreds to thousands, y'know. Hardy's is the best make. I heard about the stuff disappearing off the pier. You involved in that? Hopeless, Jordan. You won't find out anything.'

'Why not?'

'Because it don't make no sense. How can a rod disappear off a pier with everybody watching like hawks for the slightest twitch from a flounder? What are they paying you? I'll give you double to give it up.'

'Jack, you know I don't work like that so stop offering me silly money. The anglers are concerned and it's a viable case.'

'That's Bert, in the van with a trailer. Soon get your ladybird sorted. He likes old cars.'

Bert was short, bearded, tubby, in a yellow sweater that had seen better days. It needed washing, mending and still putting in the bin. But he had twinkly eyes under bushy eyebrows and I took to him. He looked like a teddy bear I once had. And then I recognized him.

'Cor,' he said, walking round the ladybird with a bit of a swagger. 'What do you want for her?'

'She's not for sale,' I said.

'Classy. They don't make them like this anymore.'

'That's why I'm keeping her.'

'Let me know if you change your mind.' Bert was inspecting the damage. 'Couple of hours' work should fix this. I'll have it done by tomorrer morning.'

'Bill me,' said Jack.

I was past arguing. I'd repay him somehow but not in the way he wanted. A meal, perhaps. He grinned at me, reading my thoughts. I often thought Jack was probably a millionaire with a six-bedroomed house on Kingsdown Gorse. I didn't want to know.

'Thanks,' I said. 'Have you got a dog called Maggie?'

'Strewth, girl,' he grinned. 'You've got second sight.' He hadn't identified me as the woman in the pub.

'Relax,' Jack said as Bert took my ladybird away on his trailer. 'I'm going to buy you a decent meal and then take you on to the barn boot. You need lightening up. Fishing and dogs? You want a proper case, a bit of murder or arson. There's some right criminals at the barn boot. You'd better be careful.'

The decent meal was at a roadhouse called The Lantern which I had never been to before. The long, red-bricked restaurant looked horrendously expensive but then Jack never ceased to surprise me. He parked his car alongside a line of Rolls and Bentleys and BMWs. The Jaguar did not look a smudge out of place.

It was like something out of a dream. Jack escorted me into The Lantern looking like a tramp, but arranged for me to have a shower somewhere upstairs before the meal. It was an everyday type of thing.

'Please look after this young lady,' he said to a female member of staff. 'Shower gel, shampoo, hairdryer, wash and dry her T-shirt. Then we'll order. I'll wait for you in the bar, Jordan.'

'You're a sweetheart,' I said.

'I know I am,' he said with a wink.

Half an hour later and I felt better, looked better, was very clean, hair shiningly tawny, T-shirt surprisingly washed and pressed. I was ready for a good meal. Jack was drinking a shandy. He looked relaxed and happy. He had me all to himself for several hours. Apparently that was enough to make his day.

'Come on, Jordan, I'm starving and I bet you are too.'

'Wonderful,' I said as we were ushered into a long, low dining room. It was seductively lit with red lamps on every table, sparkling glass and silver, white linen. Even the spray carnations in slender vases were real. I felt their moist petals. 'Nice place.'

A waiter put a huge parchment menu in front of me. It was almost too dark to read and the italic print rather small. I don't need laminated orange-tinged photographs of dishes but it does help to be able to read the words.

'Home-made soup,' I said. Good bet that soup was on the menu somewhere. 'Then pasta with tuna, mushrooms and cheese.'

'Perfect,' said Jack, waving over a waiter. 'And I'll have a prawn cocktail followed by steak, rare, peas and chips.'

It was a good meal. The food delicious and well presented. I was hungry and every mouthful hit the spot. Jack was expanding with another shandy. I don't remember what we talked about, stayed with orange juice. The conversation was good, almost funny.

'This is a lovely meal, Jack,' I said. 'I appreciate the shower and the clean shirt. But why take me to the barn boot? I think I ought to go home and sleep off the shock.'

'Do me a favour. It does my image good to be seen with dishy arm candy. It keeps the piranhas at bay. You've no idea what some women will do to line their handbags. I work hard for my dosh and I'm not intending to freeload some dame with a shoe addiction. There's only one person in this world that I would spend my money on and you know who that is.'

It was nearly a blush. Jack knew how to

embarrass me. And he was grinning again. He waved over the waiter.

'Two cappuccinos,' he said. 'And the bill.'

It was nearly midnight when we strolled out of The Lantern and Jack drove the Jaguar into the heart of the tangled Sussex lanes where tonight's barn boot was being held. I had been there once before, working on a case. It had been an eye-opener.

'Take a sleep, baby,' he said as we drove through the lanes. 'A nap will perk you up.'

I tried not to sleep on his shoulder, but the bucket seats in the front of the Jaguar were close. I was past caring or arguing. I needed the sleep and I did drift off, lulled by the hum of the powerful engine and the scent of the night air.

I guessed we had arrived when the sound of the engine stopped. Jack parked in his favourite place, ready for a quick getaway. He let me surface from dreams and come back to the world.

'We're here, baby. No police cars. It's going to be a good night.'

It was like clawing through cotton wool. 'We won't stay too late, will we? I'm so tired.'

'Home soon, I promise.' But Jack was already halfway through the barn doors with me on his arm. I had no idea why I was there or what I was supposed to be doing. The old barn was crowded as it had been before, the walls lit with spotlights. Stalls were pitched around the sides with a centre lane piled with goods. Jack stopped to talk to a mate and looked set for a long conversation. I might as well look for fishing rods. I put on my tinted glasses. No point in being recognized.

'Any fishing rods?' I asked as I strolled round various stalls. 'No particular make.'

'No, miss. Want a nice leather jacket?'

'I've got a leather jacket.'

'What kind of fishing rod do you want?' asked another stallholder, lighting a cigarette, ignoring the No Smoking signs in the wooden barn, the smoke curling from his light.

'MasterRod? SuperCatch?' I said, producing names out of the air. 'Any make really. I'd like to buy one for my boyfriend.'

'I'll ask my mates.' He was a fishy looking character, eyes too close together, puckered mouth. I looked around for Jack but he had disappeared.

Then Jack wandered back through the crowd, hands in his pockets. He looked pleased. 'I've bought two new games. Kill the Giant Claw-Toothed Tiger and Space Man's Nightmare. Should be great. Got to keep giving them something new. The kids, these days, they get too good at the games. They win too many prizes.'

'Can we go now, then?'

'Just another little bit of business, darlin',

then I promise, home.'

I began a trawl of the side stalls. I was not into shopping for anything, but the goods were tempting. Stuff going for half shop price and I did need some new trainers.

Trainers, leather goods, batteries, mobiles, umbrellas, jeans all shapes and sizes, denim jackets, window frames, mirrors, garden furniture and gnomes. Was there a market in dodgy gnomes? I began to wake up, my sleepiness slewing off me like an old coat. DI James would have been proud of me, but then DI James never took me to The Lantern.

Then I saw them.

They were standing close together, haggling over the price of a new car battery. No sign of a neck brace. In fact they both looked amazingly lively and composed for a couple who had been in an accident earlier in the day.

It was Derek Brook and his woman passenger. She was wearing different clothes, make-up and hair immaculate. No sign of shock. I edged closer.

'Come on, you can do better than that,' Derek was saying. 'I'm a good customer. I ought to get a whacking discount. And what about our little deals? I've got a nice Vauxhall coming your way. Been in a slight accident. A few extra touches and they'll write it off. Then you can do what you like with it.'

Seven

My disposable camera was sitting on my desk at home, somewhat out of reach. But I was not deterred. I backed off, crabwise, without drawing attention to myself. I'd seen a couple of cameras for sale on a mobile-phone stall.

'Do they work?' I asked.

'Of course, miss.'

'Have they got a film in?'

'No.'

'How much?'

'Ten pounds and I'll throw in a film.'

'Eight.'

'Nine and I'll give you two films.'

'Has it got a flash?'

'Hold on, miss, what do you think you're up to? Bleeding Movietone News? Gonna be film stars, are we? You'd better be careful. We don't like people snooping around here and taking our pictures.'

'Me, snooping? Heavens, no,' I smiled, going all winsome and fluttery. 'I just want to take a few snaps of my mates tomorrow. We're going on a girly picnic to Patcham

Hill. All those lovely views of the South Downs.'

'A picnic in this weather? I should coco. You're a right one. Wear your thermals.'

It was lucky I had nine pounds on me. I slipped behind a group of rails hanging with sheepskin coats and denim jackets and put a film in a camera. I still remembered how to do it. Disposable cameras make sloths of us all.

No flash. But a flash might have alerted more than the couple I intended to photograph. I didn't want to be bundled out or get Jack into trouble. It was a dark and daunting barn, big and gloomy, so the definition would be poor. A high percentage of the traders present were illegal on a small scale, dodgy transactions and dubious goods. I had to tread carefully.

I wrapped my scarf round the camera, leaving the lens clear, and held it to my chest as if clutching a purse close for safety. Derek Brook and partner might not be in focus and I might take a lot of dud pictures but if I got one good shot of the couple, it would be worth it.

My finger was on the button, click, click, click, very David Bailey. I kept my distance, eyes down, circling the group. I did not want them to notice my manoeuvres. My hair, freshly washed, was loose and falling over my face in a curtain. A lot different to the old woolly hat I'd been wearing for warmth at the time of the accident.

The woman actually glanced at me for a second but without a flicker of recognition. She was smiling to herself. They had obviously won a bargain and were well pleased. The couple linked arms and were walking away. It was a very good shot. Click, click. No sign of pain or neck injury, no limping. I needed to date the photo.

'Ready to go, Jordan?'

'Yes, please, Jack. But first, could you hold that newspaper up so I can see the front page?'

'You want to take a photograph of a newspaper?' He was incredulous.

'It's cool.'

'I always knew you were barmy.'

'Thanks...' The two figures were in the background and the front page dominated. The photo could be dated.

'Finished? Come along, then. Bought anything?'

'Odds and ends.'

'I knew you'd enjoy yourself.'

The next morning I finished up the film on the seagulls. They were reluctant to sit on the rail that ran along the pier. They squabbled among themselves, complaining that I hadn't brought any food, so why should they pose for pictures?

The sea was calm and silky. Not a breath of wind stirred the surface. But it was still bitingly cold, the kind of cold that took a hachet to your breath. My fingers were numb, my eyes watering from the cold and the brilliance of the winter sun. It was a day of contradictions.

In January 1907 the temperature had plummeted to something unregistered in Latching and the sea foam froze along the wooden groynes on the beach, forming sculptures of incredible beauty. There were dim photographs of crystal droplets petrified into cascades of ice, and Edwardian fishermen breaking off chunks of frozen sea to prove it had happened.

I tried to put a briskness into walking, so that my blood circulated a bit faster. It was reluctant to move into any area that had less than three layers of clothing.

Boots photography counter was warm enough for me to unwrap marginally and hand over the camera. I ordered the fast service even though I could hardly charge it to any client's account.

Then I put an advertisement in the local free newspaper.

> WANTED: Chihuahua puppy,
> must have excellent pedigree.

I added my phone number and the woman

at the counter said it would be in tomorrow's newspaper. She asked for my name and address.

'We have to ask these days, purely for our own records,' she explained. 'We get such a lot of crackpot adverts. You never know.'

'This is not a crackpot advertisement,' I said.

'How am I to know it's genuine? Chihuahua might be a code for something else. Y'know, drugs or porno.'

'It's a very small dog.'

'That's what you say, miss.'

My investigations had more or less ground to a halt without wheels. I was too mean to hire a car and too cold to get out on my racing bike. Since both clients were paying me by the hour, I could with a clear conscience spend the rest of the morning in my shop, keeping busy, warm, and refuelling my brain.

I switched on both heaters, which was sheer extravagance, and the coffee percolator, in that order. As I sipped a strong black, I wrote up my notes. It was easy to forget details if they were not written down. I included the insurance-scam incident. I was my own client in this case. And if I didn't get myself some justice, I would be disappointed.

Customers drifted in and out, handling things, asking questions, buying, not buying.

Even shoplifting. Someone lifted a china frog out of the window display when my back was turned. And I had no idea who it was because I didn't notice the empty spot till some time later.

'Someone has lifted a frog,' I told Doris, indignantly. I was buying more soup. I was living on tinned soup. It was a sign of appetite deprivation.

'Looking for a prince,' she nodded.

'What?'

'You know ... kiss a frog.'

'It was a china frog.'

'Maybe they want a china prince.'

I gave up on this conversation. Doris looked pleased, as if she had won on points. She dug out a carton of cuppa soups and pushed it over the counter.

'It's a new soup, broccoli and Stilton. They give you an extra packet free, special offer. Do you want to try it?'

Not really. I did not fancy reconstituted broccoli and Stilton. I did not see how they could manufacture such a combination. It was a soup I often made with fresh ingredients, sometimes for James, in the days when he had sat on the floor of my front bedsit with a huge china bowl of home-made soup and crusty bread. Those days seemed to have gone, along with all the dirty water under bridges.

Love is a kind of illness, I suppose. An

obsession with a love object, alternating with manic happiness and depression. And the falling in love was a fall from normality. I was in the melancholy love state. After Ben's death I was much less interested in the manifestations of romantic love and was wary of loving James too much. I had become frightened of being in love. It held the seeds of pain and hurt.

'Are you listening to me, Jordan? Your eyes have gone off somewhere.'

'Sorry, Doris. What were you saying?'

'I was saying I had a boy in here just now wanting to buy puppy food. Didn't seem to know what he wanted. Of course, I don't sell cat or dog food. No shelf space. Thought you might be interested, seeing that you're after some stolen puppies.'

I woke up. 'This boy, where is he? What did he look like?'

'I've no idea where he is, because he has gone. And he looked like any ordinary boy does these days. Skinny, baggy clothes, baseball cap on backwards. About fifteen or so.'

'Earrings?'

'What?'

'Any earring or stud? Boys wear them too.'

Doris shook her head. 'I'm sorry, Jordan. If you want me to give you accurate descriptions of my customers, you'll have to send me on a course or put CCTV in the shop.'

I was on my way out. He might still be in the road. I'd take a chance on not locking up my shop. There was no time if I was going to catch him.

'Sorry, I'll be back for the soup.'

'He had the letters H-A-T-E tatooed on his fingers,' Doris called out as I left.

One day I would buy Doris a really big present. I flashed her a thank-you grin and ran out on to the pavement. It was not busy, the cold having thinned out the normal crowd of shoppers. Fifteen? He should be in school, or was it half term? Was he truanting? Buying puppy food. It was such a slender chance. Hardly worth bothering about but I was desperate.

The boy was sauntering along, hands lost in baggy pockets, chewing gum. He stamped on a mineral-water bottle and the plastic exploded with a satisfactory bang. Then he kicked it into the gutter. No wonder Latching Council go bananas spending a fortune on street cleaning.

'Hi,' I said cheerfully, as if I knew him. 'I hear you've got a puppy for sale.'

'How d'yer know?' he said, glaring at me suspiciously.

I tapped my nose. 'Grapevine, or should I say dog-vine?'

He was oblivious to any form of wit, however pathetic. He had foxy eyes. They swivelled.

'How much?' he asked.

'How much what?'

'How much you gonna pay?'

I stalled for time. 'For what? I haven't seen your puppy yet. I don't know what it's like or what breed. I've got to see the puppy, haven't I? Is it a pedigree?'

'Pedi-what?'

'History, parents, etc.'

'It ain't got no parents. It's an orphan.'

This was a losing battle and I was nearly lost. Yet I hung on, hoping for some glimmer of information that would justify this conversation. I glimpsed the letters H-A-T-E on his fingers as he scratched his head.

'I'm looking for a very small puppy. They are called chihuahuas. Flat-owners like them because they don't grow very much, never more than about five inches high at the shoulder, and they are Mexican.'

His young face brightened a fraction. It was an extraordinary sight as the blankness lifted like a veil. 'Look like rats, do they? Large pointed ears and big eyes? No fur, all skinned like a rabbit?'

'Well, not quite ... you can get long-haired ones as well.'

'There's a bloke down our street got puppies like that. Wot you said. Chi-hahas? He wanted to sell me one for forty quid. I said, you're bonkers. I like proper dogs. My puppy is a bull mastiff. Right macho.'

I could not stop a shudder. I had once been locked in a room with a raging bull mastiff dripping saliva over my ankles.

'Chihuahuas may be small but they are not short on courage,' I found myself saying. 'They have brave hearts.'

This went past him. He was getting restless, moving the chewing gum in his mouth, feet shuffling.

'Well, if you don't want a bull, I'm off.'

'Where do you live?'

'Springfield Close.'

'And what's your name?' He was already moving away. A conversation of longer than two minutes was brain-draining.

'Norman.'

Bet he liked that.

I went back to my shop, collecting the soup on the way. Nothing else had been lifted. Springfield Close. I found it on the street map and plotted a route. Not one of my usual haunts. I could cycle there and start logging time for FCI. At this rate of earning, I was going to be very, very poor. If only the winter would end, then spring might bring a few lucrative cases. Cases where people would pay, up front, not counting the pennies, like the vandalized garden on Updown Hill. I'd made a profit on that one.

DI James was waiting on the pavement, his car parked close to the kerb. He was in a patrol car so there was no warden hot on his heels.

'Can I come in?' he asked.

Could he come in? Anytime. Anywhere. Didn't he know? I was drinking the free cuppa soup. It tasted like free chopped cardboard.

'This fishing case that you have ... any news of the missing angler, Dick Mann?' he asked.

'No,' I said. 'I don't have a case on Dick Mann, only the missing rods.' I didn't say I'd been on the way to his home when the Vauxhall staged the accident scam. Nor did I mention the barn boot photos in case they were a failure. Failure is my middle name.

'We've a report of a body, no identification.'

My insides did their usual plunge. I'd never forgotten the shock of finding the nun on a meat hook at Trencher's Hotel. It would stay with me for life. I would never forget her feet slowly turning in the air above me.

'And there are no missing persons from that particular neck of the woods?'

'We've no missing persons fitting the description. And no one has reported Dick Mann as missing, except you. And that's not on record, as you reported him as a disappeared person. Disappearing people are not necessarily missing people.'

'Perhaps Dick Mann doesn't have any wife or partner,' I said. 'No one to notice that he was not around any more. He hasn't turned up for work at the hospital, but then that's to be expected, since he gave in his notice last week.'

DI James was sitting on the edge of my desk, long legs crossed at the ankle. I had not invited him to sit there. He had his usual gaunt, no sleep, no food look. I could offer him both but the odds on being turned down were high.

'Would you like some cardboard soup?' I asked.

'No, thank you, Jordan. But a mug of your high-octane Brazilian bean coffee would be acceptable.'

'Too much coffee is not good for you.'

'Let me decide that.'

I switched on the percolator, added freshly ground beans and water, praying it was not a day for scummed water. Shopping list: one of those filter jugs for water. Latching had not yet got its water supply right. Local factories poured effluent into the sea. I dreaded to think where it came from or what the scum consisted of. Sometimes my tea was swimming with oily blobs.

He drank the coffee without comment. I took the slight relaxation in his body language as a degree of appreciation. It could have been sheer fatigue.

'Tell me what Dick Mann looks like.'

I got out my notes. It looked efficient even

if the description of Dick Mann was sparse. I could barely remember his face. His clothes were more memorable.

'Aged about forty, maybe a few years younger, I don't know. Height about five ten.' I tried to think what it had been like, dancing with him. Zero recall. 'Ruddy complexion. Round face. Straight nose, I think. Eyes ... no idea of colour, except there were two. Light-brown hair cut in a short, spiky style with gel. Oh dear, that's not much to go on, is it?'

'Not much for a detective. You are a detective, aren't you?'

'OK, I challenge you to get a better description of someone done up to the neck in waterproofs and every device known to man for keeping out the cold. There was nothing showing. He was walking waterproofs.'

'Do you remember any other clothes he wore?'

'Brown slacks and a fleece jersey. Green. Dark green like Sherwood Forest.'

'Very medieval, Jordan. Anything more?'

'I'm sorry, James. I really didn't take much notice of his clothes. How was I to know that he was going to disappear?'

James put down his mug and half smiled at me. Half smiles were all that I usually got and they were disturbing enough. It was a haunting sort of smile. I wondered about his past life and all the traumas that he had barely hinted at. What had happened that put him off women, even me, for the duration?

'So where has this unidentified body been found?' I asked. 'Are you going to tell me? You've asked enough questions.'

'In the bell tower at St Luke the Divine, the church on the road to Patcham. The bell-ringers found him when they arrived for practice yesterday evening. Not a pretty sight. They were very shocked.'

'Had he hung himself?'

'Not exactly. More the opposite. He was suspended by his right ankle, upside down, some thirty feet above ground. He'd been there some time. Apparently he'd died from dehydration and drowning.'

'Drowning?'

'That's what happens, I'm told. If you are left hanging upside down for any length of time, water drains into the lungs and you drown.'

'Not suicide then?'

'It looked more like some sort of punishment ritual in a house of correction, you understand? If we find who strung him up, it'll be murder.'

'And you don't know who he is ... he was?'

DI James slipped off the desk and stood up. He was cradling the mug, keeping the last vestige of heat against the palm of his hand. His face gave nothing away.

'He was wearing a dark-green fleece, the green of Sherwood Forest, and the only item in his pocket was a copy of the tide timetable for Latching.'

A tide timetable. A hollow feeling of quiet despair spread through my limbs.

Eight

Was it Dick Mann? Who else but an angler would carry around a tide timetable? I told James about his cottage in North Mill Lane. He made some phone calls on his mobile, rinsed out the mug in the sink and made to leave.

'You'd better come with me,' he said. 'I have an unidentified body and you have a missing person. It's crucial that I get the earliest identification in a murder investigation.'

'Yes, I understand,' I said, my heart sinking. I hated the chilly, vaporous atmosphere of the morgue. 'When?'

'Now.'

I pulled on an anorak, mentally reminding myself to update my clothes with a trendy fleece. I followed him out to his car. Even a drive à deux with James did not lift my spirits. We did not talk much. I can't even remember what we talked about.

I followed him everywhere like a tame dog, down corridors, through swing doors, into the hospital morgue. We had to put on protective clothing. By this time I did not care how I looked.

I hate those refrigerated shelves. I hate the clanging doors. The sliding body trays made a rasping sound. I'd probably hear that nerve-twanging sound even if I was dead.

James turned back the cover from over the face. The hair still had gel on it.

'That's him,' I said. 'Dick Mann.'

'Thank you, Jordan. That's saved us a lot of time.'

Outside the hospital, he was on his mobile, making tracks to leave me stranded. 'Where are you going?' I asked, almost on his wavelength.

'To Dick Mann's cottage in North Mill Lane.'

'Can I come with you?' I asked. 'The mechanic hasn't brought my car back yet. I'm cycling everywhere.'

He narrowed his eyes. 'This is a police investigation,' he said. 'We don't take civilians along.'

'But I've been very helpful and saved you hours of fruitless enquiries. The missing rods are my case. There might be a clue in Dick Mann's home. You owe me.'

He paused. 'All right. But no weird stuff, Jordan.'

'No weird stuff,' I promised.

'And don't touch anything.'

'As if I would.'

He took me via the shop. I put up the CLOSED FOR REDECORATION notice and locked the door. DI James said nothing. Maybe he thought I did have the decorators in. The shop was beginning to look shabby. Shopping: tin of paint, apricot white; brush; a magic product for mopping up drops.

I sat beside James in a flashy yellow and blue patrol car, trying not to look as if I was being taken in for shoplifting. At least he had turned off the sirens. The radio link was on, crackling with messages that were difficult to understand.

'I don't know how you can make out what anyone is saying,' I said. 'It sounds like a foreign language.'

'It is a foreign language,' he said. 'Who's fixing your car?'

'A teddy bear,' I said. 'A teddy bear who is into old cars.'

'You mean Bert? That's the mechanic I was going to recommend. He's good with cars and reliable. Knows what he's doing and doesn't overcharge. It'll be interesting to see the claim from Derek Brook, how much they go for.'

I said nothing about the barn boot. 'Yes, it

will. I suppose they'll add on injury time.'

'That's the point of these staged accidents,' said James, negotiating the roundabout that led to North Mill Lane. I tried not to look at the crash site. 'The damage to the car is the least of their worries. They probably bought it for next to nothing and they'll write it off. They'll claim for loss of earnings, legal costs, compensation for injuries. There have been payouts of more than a hundred thousand.'

'I don't have to pay that, do I?' I said, going cold.

'No, your insurance company pays out. Norwich Union, Royal and Sun Alliance, whoever they are. But they don't like it. If we could nail someone, it would be a big plus.'

I began to feel a glimmer of hope. Perhaps I could be the big plus PI who nailed these fraudsters. Another career opening. Investigator to car insurance companies. It sounded dull and boring but if being bored meant a regular pay cheque, then I'd sit at a desk and investigate car claims all day.

James was turning into North Mill Lane. It was an ancient parish road, narrow and twisting, laced with overhanging trees. I could imagine horses and farm carts making their way up the lane to the mill. It was meant for horses, not cars. But the muddy track had been tarmacked and the cottages had lost some of their front gardens to accommodate the rise of four-wheel-drive ownership. The cottages were scattered along the lane, built higgledy-piggledy over the years with different angles of frontage, before the days of planning permission and urbanization.

North Mill Lane had a rustic charm, totally cut off from anything resembling a supermarket or a library. It did not even have token street lighting. I wondered if the cottages had gas or electricity or whether Dick Mann read the tide timetables by candlelight.

'So which cottage is it?' James asked.

'I don't know. I was only told North Mill Lane.'

He shot me a look of total disbelief. 'You start this side and I'll take the other side of the lane.'

'Yes, sir,' I said meekly, as if he was my superior officer. We got out of the patrol car and started the trawl.

It did not take long. Tan Cottage was very small, built of Sussex flint cobbles with a slate roof, but the shed door was open and propped inside there were enough rods to catch the entire fish population of the English Channel. I got a horrible feeling. Surely no one angler would own so many rods? If so, why the collection? It did not make sense.

DI James knocked on the front door. It was tiny, probably two rooms up and two down. That is, twice the size of my two bedsits. The

Sussex flint cobbles were laid diagonally by a right-handed labourer, the windows like tiny eyes, the roof a slope of mossy slate. I liked it immensely, but out here, miles from anywhere? No one in their right senses would chose to live in such an isolated place.

Unless you had something to hide.

It came into my head unbidden. I let the winging thoughts creep in. They sometimes know better than I do. What would Dick Mann have to hide?

No one was answering the knock and the front door was secure. We wandered round the side of the cottage. Dick Mann was no gardener. It was a wilderness of weeds and overgrown shrubs. The back door was also locked but the wood had warped. It gave way on pressure. It creaked open like in a horror film.

'Hello?' DI James called out. 'Is anyone there?'

He went into the kitchen and I followed. It was a tiny kitchen but everything was neat. Not exactly IKEA but late forties style. A metal kitchen cabinet. A plain wooden table with a chair tucked under it. On it was a half-drunk mug of tea and a sliced loaf of bread. An old-fashioned gas stove at the wrong eye level. Some wall cupboards of different styles. On the windowsill was a pot of chives. It needed watering.

'I don't think there is a Mrs Mann,' I said.

111

'Unless it's his mother, someone who occasionally visits.'

'Hello, Mrs Mann?' called DI James again as he moved through the kitchen and into a front sitting room. No answer. The cottage sounded empty. 'Anyone at home? Hello?'

Again it was a room lost in time. It had an upright vintage wireless and an old television set in a cabinet, two sunken chairs bracketing a green-tiled fireplace. Rag rugs on the floor. A row of faded Reader's Digest condensed books on a wall shelf. No flowers, no plants, no cushions. No comforts.

'No Mrs Mann,' I said.

'Are you sure?'

'No woman lives here. There's not a single sign. Except the chives on the windowsill, but even that's not certain.'

We made a tour of the empty house. The upstairs rooms only had the bare necessities for sleeping, washing and storing clothes, a bed, a cupboard and a washbasin. There was nothing that was any clue to Dick Mann's existence. No photos, no letters, no phone numbers, no personal belongings. It was as if he did not exist. Only the rods in the shed were any clue to the man.

'We could be in the wrong house,' said James finally. 'The rods might belong to someone else. I'll try next door.'

The woman in the next cottage came to the door surrounded by several small child-

112

ren and barking dogs. She looked harassed, pushing back frizzled hair, trying to prevent toddlers following the dogs out into the garden. I caught one determined youngster by his denim dungarees and hauled him back from the front gate.

'I'd tie that one down if it didn't mean the Social would be after me. He'd be off down the pier and fishing with his dad if he had half a chance.'

'Fishing?' I said weakly.

'His dad fishes every hour he can get off. Does it to get away from the kids. He can't stand them.'

'Arnie?'

'Yes, Arnie.'

DI James showed his badge and introduced himself.

'We're looking for Dick Mann's cottage,' he said. 'Do you know where he lives? Is it the one next door?'

'Right next door,' said the woman, hanging on to two wriggling toddlers with both hands. 'Dick and my Arnie go fishing together. Arnie Rudge is my husband and the breeder of this unruly brood. Arnie keeps his rods in Dick's shed. Handy for him. We ain't got no room for them here, what with the kids and the dogs. And we've got hens out the back. I said I'm not having those smelly things in the house. So Dick said Arnie could use his shed.'

'Very useful,' I said.

'Do you know anything about Mr Mann?' said James. 'Do you know if he has any relations, a brother or a mother perhaps?'

'I don't know anything about him. Keeps himself to himself. Nothing much more than a polite good morning or good evening. Sometimes he gives me a bit of fish if Arnie's had a bad day. I once said to him, for a laugh like, you could be one of them great train robbers hiding out here in North Mill Lane and no one would ever know.' Her wiry blonde curls bounced with laughter.

'I bet he thought that was funny.'

'Oh yes, he thought that was funny, he did.'

'Do you know when you last saw Mr Mann?' said James, trying to get Arnie's wife back on track.

'No idea,' she said with a vigorous shake of her head. 'I hardly know the time of day with this lot.' She hauled back the small monster in dungarees again. 'This one's going to be an explorer or the first man on Mars. No one'll stop him once he gets out there.'

'Please try and think,' James persisted. 'Was it yesterday or the day before?'

'I don't have a clue,' she said. 'Arnie might know, though they weren't great mates or anything. Only for the fishing and a pint afterwards. They both like their pint. I'm lucky if I see a vodka and lime at Christmas.'

'Well, thank you very much,' said James,

retreating from various sticky fingers pulling at his trousers. 'You've been very helpful.'

'Nice to have somebody to talk to,' she grinned. 'Here, do either of you want some eggs? Cheaper than the shops and fresher.'

We both left with a dozen eggs packed in cartons. They were fresher. They were so fresh they had bits of straw sticking to them.

She saw us off, trying unsuccessfully to get the kids to wave. 'What do you want him for, anyway?' she called out as an afterthought.

'Great train robbery,' I waved back.

'Thought so.'

I trudged after James. 'That's a woman who has her hands full. All those kids. One a year by the look of it,' I said as we walked away. 'I counted five.'

'I think that vodka at Christmas is her downfall,' said James with a rare glint of humour. 'She should stick to orange juice.'

'And what about Arnie? What should he stick to? It takes two, you know.'

'Fishing. I'm going back to the station now. Where would you like to be dropped? I've got a hunch about Dick Mann and I want to run a few checks on the PNC.'

'I've got a hunch, too,' I said.

'What is it?'

'Oh no, I'm not telling you my hunch unless you tell me yours.'

James got into the patrol car and push-ed the passenger door open. 'This is too juvenile for words. I haven't time for games.'

I tore off a page of paper from my note-book and wrote some capital letters on it. 'There it is, my hunch in writing. I shall fold it four ways, fasten it with this paperclip and give it to you, showing my complete faith in your integrity not to open it till you have checked your hunch.'

'Ridiculous. I said no games, please, Jordan.'

'This isn't a game. I'm deadly serious.'

'All right.' He took the folded paper and put it in his pocket. 'My integrity is at stake. If I succumb to the temptation to read your priceless information, I'll make you a supper with my cheaper and fresher eggs.'

'Omelette or scrambled?'

'I was thinking boiled.'

He dropped me at my shop before re-turning to his brand new station and their brand new computers. He was waiting for the pathologist's report before confirming formal identification. The incident room had already been set up at the station and witness statements taken from the bell-ringers. The exhibits were being collated and forensic evidence sent to the experts. I knew how vital and how busy those first few days of a murder investigation would be. If it was murder.

'Thanks.'

'Watch your back, Jordan.' He shot me a

brief, sweet smile which rocked my solidity. For a second he looked as if he really cared. It was a heady moment that brought a surge of emotion, fracturing the shell that I had carefully built around me. Butterflies were fluttering in waves, luminous and glitzy, carried by my breath in the cold, sharp air.

'I will.'

He drove away, accelerating, leaving me to reassemble myself on the pavement. It had been a useful visit to Dick Mann's cottage. One is not supposed to remove evidence, if you could call it evidence. It was something small and insignificant. James had not thought it of any interest and had passed it over. It was a brooch, the letter 'A' surrounded by a circle of gilt leaves. It had been tucked behind a curtain in his bedroom.

The next day there were three messages on my answerphone, each offering me a choice of chihuahua puppies. They had seen my advertisement. Two were genuine. I recognized the names of kennels that I had visited earlier. The third was interesting.

'I got a nice little puppy,' said a man's voice. 'Just what you want. If you're interested meet me at the Sow's Head tonight at eight o'clock.'

No name, no carrying a copy of the *Dog Breeder's Annual*. The Sow's Head, a fair distance away, was not one of my watering places, because the name was unacceptable. How would I know him? How would he know me? Do chihuahua people have a certain look about them? Small, big-eared?

I'd put my acquisition from Tan Cottage in a plastic specimen bag and added it to the fishing file. There was not much else in it. The fishing investigation was not going well. Perhaps I ought to fit in a surveillance.

Then a brilliant idea struck me. Ideas are around all the time, waiting to be recognized. I should be under the pier, watching. But how would I get there? I could hardly climb over from the decking or climb up from the wet sand. Then I remembered the work going on for the new decking on the pier, section by section, length by length. I could climb over the barrier and work my way along the girders under the pier till I found a good surveillance spot, somewhere to perch. Sandwiches, mobile phone, water ... it would be a doddle.

Late winter was still surfing through Latching, with minus temperatures, bitter cold and winds that froze my breath. Then suddenly a morning of sun would bathe the promenade with sharp radiance and people hurried down on to the beach, half believing that spring was on its way. It must be coming soon. It had been a long, long winter. Sunsets were glorious, a rosy flush tinging the clouds with the splendour of a painter on a high. Sometimes I stood and gloried in the sky, unable to leave the changing scene as the sun slid, huge and orangey, into the sea.

The Sow's Head. Did I go as Jordan Lacey or did this require a new persona? Persona is the aspect of personality corresponding to the attitude of the moment. Exactly. I needed a new personality of the moment. Bert had brought back the ladybird, straightened out. I had wheels. Her spots weren't known in that part of the country.

Even Doris would not have recognized me. It was *Stars in your Eyes*, Latching version. Jordan Lacey ... you are now Dusty Springfield. The beehive hair-do was right, the pink clothes were right and so was the dark eye make-up. *Call me Irresponsible* or whatever she used to sing. It was amazing. Except for the shoes. I couldn't walk in her stilettoes.

The bar was full. The Sow's Head was obviously a popular place. It was hard to order a drink as the men were two deep at the counter and not moving. But Dusty shed her usual magic and the men parted like biblical water, eyeing the hair, the clothes, the make-up, sniffing the perfume.

'Thank you, thank you,' I said. The barman brought me a large glass of Australian Shiraz without my saying a word. It was a big glass, practically a third of a bottle.

'How did you know?' I said, passing a five

119

pound note over the bar and not expecting any change.

He slid a few pathetic coins in my direction. 'I always know a Shiraz woman when I see one.'

There was no answer to that.

I took my drink over to a corner table where I could watch people coming in, first wiping the top with a tissue. I didn't know who I was looking for. It could be anyone.

The large glass of wine lasted a long time. At about twenty past eight a man came over to my table. He was thin and rangy, narrow-eyed, wearing a faded red T-shirt, jeans and a grey anorak. He needed a shave. There were nick marks on his chin.

'All on your own?' he asked.

'No,' I said. 'I'm waiting for a friend.'

'They all say that,' he smirked.

'And in this case it's true.'

'Mind if I sit down for a minute?' He was carrying a brimming pint of Guinness, dark and frothy. 'You look just like Dusty Springfield,' he added.

'So?'

'Do you mind?'

'Yes, I do mind.' I was tired of this game already. I wanted to be alone and to appear to be sitting alone. The man with a puppy for sale might appear at any moment. The pub was filling up, the noise level rising, wafts of cigarette smoke clouding the air, irritating my sticky airways. I ought to charge danger money.

'I'll go when your friend arrives,' he said, pulling out a chair. 'Don't mind me. It's nice to talk sometimes. I haven't seen you before. Have you many friends?'

This was getting difficult to handle. I did not want to antagonize the man but I didn't like his face. He was one unpleasant specimen. Not exactly shifty, but his eyes were unfocused, roaming the room. And his breath smelt of stale nicotine.

'Yes, masses of friends,' I said. 'I'm waiting for one now. He's a fireman. He should be here very soon.'

'Do you live around here?'

'Yes,' I said. It was a spur of the moment thing. 'I live in this road, right opposite, number eighty-seven. With my brother-in-law and his family. They are all mad on rugby. You should see the mountains of muddy shirts I wash.'

It didn't work. The man took a sip of his Guinness and leaned forward. A pulse was throbbing in his scrawny neck.

'I don't believe you,' he said. 'There isn't a number eighty-seven. Get up quietly now and take my arm. Walk out of the pub as if we are leaving together, like old friends.'

'You're joking, mate,' I snapped. 'I'm not going anywhere with you.'

'Oh yes you are.'

He leaned across the table and opened his hand. In the palm lay a nasty-looking knife. 'I'm rather good at face-cutting. What would you like? Criss-cross? Or a daisy pattern?'

Nine

James. DI James, where art thou? I sent out a silent cry for help. There was no answer, not a tremor in the air. I had enough sense to know that I was going nowhere with this thug. My skin cringed. I did not want to end up in a ditch of nettles. Nor did I want him to practise his face-cutting on me.

'I need to go to the ladies' room,' I said. Age-old excuse. Works every time, but not this time.

'I'll come with you,' he said.

'I think not. Doubt if the bar staff would approve. They could object, with reason. Public decency and all that.'

'I'll tell them that you are sick, female time of the month stuff, need a friend to keep an eye on you.' His face was twitching, so was the knife. 'Get up, Dusty. Come round the table slowly. Smile, baby, smile. You won't get hurt if you do what I say.'

The pub was crowded, pulsing with

people, yet no one seemed to have noticed the drama that was going on at this table. The fruit machine lights were flashing. I searched the room for someone that I knew but it was not my local. I'd never been here before. No one would even notice my departure. They were too busy discussing soccer, Six Nations rugby, horses. And my wits had deserted me. I was on an island of my own making, feeling sick. Come on, Jordan, think up something. Be positive.

I broke out into a sweat. The varnished table was marked with overlapping beer rings, wet and white, like a game that has gone wrong, a game without rules. My focus was fuzzy, blurred with fear.

It was an impulse. I swept my hand over the table, fast as an ace service, and the glass of Guinness shot straight up into his face. He swore and cursed as the brown liquid drenched him. His hand flew up. It gave me enough time. I ran like the wind. Gone with the wind. Through the bar, shouldering people aside and out into the damp street.

The cold air hit my face like a wet flannel. I ran to my car, fingers already searching for the right keys. This time they were there, in my pocket, and I found the ones I needed. I only had seconds. There were footsteps pounding after me. My fingers were trembling as I unlocked the door, slid in, slammed it shut, found the ignition. There was thumping on the rear of the car. He was alongside, wrenching at the handle, but I had locked the door. I threw the car into gear and the ladybird responded instantly. She was halfway to heaven. There was no one to run over except him. I had a clear getaway ahead along an empty road. Thank you, St Peter, I did not want to precipitate a new arrival.

At first I drove anywhere, taking right turns, left turns, losing myself, making distance. I was not being followed. Then I realized I was on the road towards Marchmont Tower on some kind of homing instinct. It felt like coming home. I recognized the overhanging trees, whispering with rain. I began to slow down, feeling calmer, fastening the seat belt, my hands loosening their manic grip on the wheel, the moon sliding behind a cloud, out of sight. I had got away.

Marchmont Tower loomed ahead, straight-stoned, shadowed and medieval, flat crenellated roof etched against the sky. DI James might not be at home. DS Ben Evans would never be home again, with his warm arms and even warmer kisses, welcoming me with fondness and ardour. The grief came back, musty and dry.

I drove round to the back of the tower, to the parking space. Lights were on in the tower. I did not know if this was a good sign. Maybe James always left them on for security. I parked, ran to the back door, rang the bell and hung on to it.

It was like waiting a million years. I crouched back, in suspense, dying by inches, expecting the knife man to appear at my side, blade glinting. But it was James who opened the door, light streaking behind him.

'Jordan?' he said, peering out. It was like seeing him for the first time. Tall, grey-tinged crew cut, eyes deep as the ocean. He was in casual slacks, black polo-necked jersey.

I fell apart. He was still unsure, looking surprised. My Dusty Springfield outfit was only a lash short of a full make-over. I pulled off the wig, crumpled it in my hands, my own hair springing out. 'It's me, Jordan. Can't I come in?'

'Of course it's you. I know it's you.' He pulled me inside. The big kitchen was familiar, still untidy, still a bachelor's den. He had not washed up for days. It smelled of ancient bangers and beans. 'You look awful.'

'So would you if you'd been threatened by a man with a knife. It was not funny. I had to run and run. I don't know how I managed to drive here.'

I was still shaking. I pushed my hair back, feeling a dampness on my skin. Something warm smeared my cheek. James took my hand and turned it over. There was a cut across the fleshy part of my palm. The knife man had caught me.

125

'Not funny at all,' he said, leading me to the sink. He turned on the hot-water tap, first letting it splash over the plates and mugs. 'He cut you.'

It was not a deep cut, just a slight slice. I remembered his hand flying up. The blade must have nicked me. I didn't want to have it stitched. I was sick of hospitals.

'I'm not going to hospital,' I said firmly.

'No need,' said James. 'I think we can cope with this. It doesn't need stitching. Hold your hand here, under the water. Wash out the germs thoroughly. Don't worry about the blood. Let me make a phone call first. Which pub was it?'

'I didn't say it was a pub. The Sow's Head.'

'It's always a pub. I'll make you a drink in a minute. You're still shaking.'

I allowed him to cosset me. It was an unknown pleasure to watch him administering TLC. He phoned the station, giving the bare details, then made some tea, remembering the honey. He put stinging antiseptic on the cut and a whacking great plaster that looked like a pink tarpaulin.

'You'll live,' he said.

'Yes, but for how long?' I was beginning to wonder.

'Perhaps you had better tell me what has been going on and why. Start at the beginning.'

He guided me up the narrow stairs to the

first-floor sitting room. It was as untidy as the kitchen, but chock-full of his personality. Newspapers and cuttings, magazines, tapes and videos, unopened mail. I longed to be his secretary, his housekeeper, his anything. Pass me a notebook and a magnetic duster.

He sat me down on the long sofa, as if I was incapable of sitting down by myself. There was more tea on a classy wooden tray, and a tin of digestive biscuits for dunking. From a hidden wall cabinet he brought out a bottle of Bell's whisky. He'd thought of everything. He tipped a small dram into my tea.

'Feeling better yet?' he asked.

I nodded. Normal words had disappeared. I hoped I was not going to say something I would regret. My feelings had been bottled up for so long, like the genie in the bottle. If they all came whooshing out in a purple mist of passion, DI James might run for cover. He would hide in some primeval cave on the South Downs, the Cissbury Ring Iron Age Fort probably, where I would never find him again. He might fall down the shaft of a flint mine.

'Very kind,' was all I managed to say. I was starting to feel warmer. I shed my shoes and tucked my feet up on the sofa.

'Do you mind?'

'No. Feel at home.'

He sat on the other sofa, loafing, at ease. It

was a big, octangular-shaped tower room. He returned to a glass of pale gold liquid which he had been drinking when my arrival interrupted a quiet evening of rest and recuperation.

'Feel like telling me about it now, Jordan? Take your time. I want to know what happened. I'm listening.'

It took quite a time, like gathering a dream that was in shreds. I had forgotten what James knew and what he did not know. We were talking both fishing and puppies. I told him about my newspaper advertisement for a puppy and the call-backs, going to the Sow's Head, and the man who sat at my table, who suddenly turned nasty with a knife hidden in the palm of his hand.

'Nothing to do with fishing? It might not be connected.'

'No, not fishing, I'm nearly sure. But I'm confused. Does anyone kill, maim, cut, threaten, for the sake of stolen puppies? James, I ask you. Is this some sort of international crime? What have I gotten into? Are you keeping something from me?'

I was starting to shake again. The whisky-laced tea had been comforting but the effect was not lasting. It was a combination of lack of sleep, lack of food, total down-the-drain feeling. James fetched a fleecy blanket, daddy syndrome. All I wanted was to sleep in his arms but he did not know that. James, please, come alive and recognize this long-ing that stems from within me. But he had his own problems and I couldn't solve them.

'I've sent a patrol car out there but I think we ought to report this more fully, Jordan. He's still out there with a knife.'

James noted down my description of the man. A guess at height, age ... it wasn't a lot. I couldn't really remember much about him. It was more a feeling, an impression of his malevolence. His words were imprinted on my brain.

'Can't you remember anything else?' said James, tapping his pen with irritation. 'The colour of his eyes...'

'I didn't look at his eyes. I didn't have time. Eyes are small in a face. You don't really see the colour of them unless they are very bright or very dark. Or special in some other way.'

Special like deep ocean-blue. James had these amazing ocean-blue eyes. And deep velvety brown. Miguel had the velvety eyes. I could remember them but I had no idea of the colour of Doris's eyes or Mavis's eyes, and yet I see both of my friends on most days. And I'm a detective. Pathetic.

We went over the facts time and again, getting nowhere. He was being paid a regu-lar salary. I was not. I fell asleep on the sofa while he went to phone again. Someone tucked the blanket round me. I could only guess that it was James.

Marchmont Tower was dark and empty but for me ... James had gone. I could feel the emptiness. He had left a note on the table. I wanted to keep the note, put it under my pillow like a love-sick teenager.

'Called out to Shoreham. Someone tried to steal a plane. Make yourself at home.'

It was nearly morning. I hurried round Marchmont Tower, locking every door with a déjà vu feeling. I had done this once before. He wasn't getting in, that man, who-ever he was. I was slightly, ever so slightly nervous. This was not like me. Perhaps I was sickening for something. Flu, shingles, bubonic plague. I took a quick look for spots or blisters.

There was no more sleep for me. I did the washing-up to take my mind off the silence. I switched on the radio and found the Jazz FM band. The building was high enough to get the frequency. I went into housework mode and put all the cereal packets and pickle jars away, cleaned the surfaces, scrub-bed the table, polished the taps. James would not be able to find anything for weeks. So much for breakfast, if I was still here.

There was no way I could sleep if James was not somewhere in the tower. I did two-thirds of the crossword in yesterday's paper.

I started writing up my notes, including now the man with the knife, in case he was connected. I didn't know. And yet, why me? Was he stealing puppies to order? Maybe he was into fishing rods. Nothing seemed right. He'd been on the lookout for a woman on her own and I fitted the bill.

The tower was four rooms, each one on top of the other, with a spiral staircase going up an inner wall. It was a folly built by a nineteenth-century landowner wanting to spoil his neighbour's view. James paid the rent and DS Ben Evans had been his lodger. I had slept in Ben's bedroom, once, but he had not been there at the time. I did not even peep into the other bedroom though my curiosity longed to see where James slept.

Meanwhile I was getting older, crabbier, starved of love in every sense. I could feel my juices drying up. Ben had been so right for me, as second best. Miguel would be happy to accommodate my other needs, anytime, but I couldn't use him as a sex toy. He was too nice, cooked like an angel, always gave me the best wine.

Miguel. I had my spare mobile. Not lost today. It still worked. I phoned his Mexican restaurant, a few doors down from my shop. Even though it was early, he was already there, probably working on last night's accounts.

'Miguel? It's Jordan.'

'Ah, bellissimo. La belle Jordan.' His voice was as deep and velvety as his eyes. He launched straight to the point. 'You eat with me tonight, yes? I cook something very special. It is quiet. The bookings are down. I shall sit with you and listen to all your troubles. Maybe I shall solve them for you.'

'I'm not sure you'll want to hear them,' I said.

'I would listen, as they say, to your talking down the phone book,' he said with a deep chuckle.

'Reciting the phone directory.'

Life lifted itself a few notches with incurable optimism. Miguel always had this ability to lift my spirits. It was something to do with his one hundred per cent admiration of my talent, my non-existent looks, my femininity. It never failed.

'I should like that,' I said cautiously. 'But I shall also want to ask about where you get your fish. And some other fishy questions.'

'Anything. I am an open book. I keep no secrets from you. All I ask is to sit with your beautiful face and your sparkling eyes.'

This was too much for me at this time of the morning. My hair was looking a wreck and my eyes were bagged and shadowed. I needed quite a bit of restoration. Cold tea-bags and a friendly herbal shampoo.

'This evening then? Eight o'clock?' he

suggested.

'Nine o'clock. I am an owl.'

How was I going to last till then? I needed a quick fix. There was no sign of James returning but I could not stay cooped up in Marchmont Tower like a chicken. I roamed restlessly, plumping up cushions that did not need plumping, reading old newspapers. It was capitulation time. I showered in the downstairs bathroom, put on yesterday's unwashed, unclean clothes and went out, closing the door carefully, the latch down. No getting in again. I looked like a tramp who had slept in a shed.

The ladybird would not start. She whined and moaned and shuddered to nothing. She was stone cold. It was either because water had got in, the battery was flat or she was out of petrol. Perhaps the getaway had been too traumatic for her.

This time I did not go to the windmill. I'd had enough of being locked in a windmill, especially when the steel shoe catches fire. I set off for the downhill trot to Latching. Why James lived so far out, I didn't know. The isolation suited him. He isolated himself from everything except work. I remembered then that I had not left a reciprocal note. Not even a thank you. Ah, well, etiquette was not high on my CV.

It was an unexpected morning with a hint of spring. The waysides had the thin spiky leaves of daffodils thrusting through the grass. Birds were fluttering about, gathering fluff and moss for their IKEA home-built nests. Spring in Latching is wondrous. Some enterprising counsellor a long time ago, now under some cold slab, sanctioned the planting of the bulbs everywhere. The dual carriageways were transformed with carpets of yellow. The lanes were banked with golden glory. The Beach House gardens were glorious until the late-night drunks staggered by, crushing the blooms, breaking slender stems of tulips. It was enough to make you weep. Yellow heads strewn everywhere like soggy cornflakes.

I alternated walking and jogging, eating up the miles. The distance narrowed and I could smell the sea. It sparkled far away, a sheet of shimmering silver, mirroring the sun. Another half an hour on the road and I should be home. They say the average walker covers two point three miles an hour and I was faster than average.

No one was paying for running time. I couldn't charge for thinking. But my cases were still unsolved. I was no nearer to finding the puppies or who stole them, nor to solving the mysterious disappearance of the fishing rods. Dick Mann was dead and no one seemed to be concerned about the rods anymore. No one had reported him missing or come forward to identify him.

My calves were aching by the time I let myself into my bedsits. I shed my clothes, wrapped myself in the duvet and rolled into bed. I was asleep in moments. I slept for some hours, being woken by my phone.

It was DI James. His voice was controlled. 'You got home all right?'

'Yes.'

'I told you to stay where you were.'

'I couldn't stay. Sorry, I had to get out. I needed air.'

'Open a window.'

'I don't wish to be lectured,' I said. 'I'm home and I'm safe. It doesn't mean that I am not grateful for you allowing me to stay at Marchmont Tower last night. But it was only temporary. Sorry about my car. It wouldn't start.'

'Will it help if I tell you that we were both right about Dick Mann?'

I did not understand what I was hearing. I shook off the blur of sleep, hoping my brain would start to function.

'Right about what?'

'You wrote it on a piece of paper. Remember? Some initials, WPP.'

'Oh, that. It was a hundred years ago.'

'Well, it was spot on.'

'Does this chalk up favours for the future?' I asked. 'This was definitely assisting the police in their enquiries.'

'It was my line of enquiry, too.'

135

'So?'

'We were both right. Dick Mann came to live in Latching under the Witness Protection Programme with a new identity. And, as yet, no one will tell me who he once was. It's true. No one will give me a name.'

'Perhaps they will when you tell them he's in a morgue.'

'But why is he there? Is it murder ... or suicide?'

Ten

Witness Protection Programme. They provided a new face, new home, new occupation but maybe not a new hobby. He could not give up his fishing. Whoever Dick Mann had once been in another life, he couldn't give up his fishing.

'Would you tell me who he was if you knew who he was?' I asked but I already knew the answer.

'No.'

'Then I don't believe you. Why should they keep his identity from you? No way, Inspector James. You know, but you aren't going to tell me, and why not?'

'We're not joined at the hip.'

'Thank goodness. How very inconvenient and most uncomfortable. That suits me down to the ground. Don't ask me any favours.'

I put the phone down. I was on my own again. Detective Inspector James had gone officious. It was not the first time. I never knew where I was when it came to James. He had crept into my heart and was destined to stay there. Sometimes it hurt and the pain was like a window in my head. When we were working together, as occasionally happened, then I could live with the rejection.

Rejection? I was not sure that it was a rejection. Sometimes he did not even notice me. It seemed that his marriage and his wife's actions had damaged him forever. Maybe one day he would tell me what had happened.

But what if he died on duty, like DS Ben Evans? I would churn in a sea of sorrow. I could not imagine ever getting over it. Work would be my solace ... if there was any work around. At my present rate of success, I would be stacking shelves.

The phone rang again.

'Hello?'

'Suddenly I've found this funny attachment to my hip. Sort of Jordan-shaped.'

I was stunned into silence. I tried to imagine where he was, sitting at his new desk with his new computer. Piles of files and papers. A black coffee within reach, already cold.

'Jordan? Are you still there?'

I nodded into space. 'What do you want?' I said.

'Derek Brook came into the station today to make a statement about the accident in which you were involved.'

'You sound like a policeman.'

'Flippancy will get you nowhere.'

'OK. Tell me something about the statement that I don't already know.'

'There was a passenger in the back seat. And the passenger was also injured.'

I gasped on a short intake of breath. 'No, that's not true, James. Totally wrong. There was just the two of them. I ought to know. I was there. I looked.'

'They claim that their fourteen-year-old daughter, Miranda, was a passenger in the back seat, lying down, asleep. She was apparently hurt and had to have medical attention.'

'No way, there was only the driver and the front-seat passenger. The back of the car was empty. Oh, maybe a few carrier bags on the seat full of shopping.'

'Are you sure you're not making a mistake? Memory lapse due to trauma?' James asked cautiously.

'A girl doesn't look like carrier bags full of shopping. There was no one in the back, I swear it. This is an extension of their scam. More injuries and more claims. It's disgusting. And now involving a child. I don't know how people can do it.'

'I agree that it's pretty low. But they swear that their daughter, Miranda, was with them. And there is evidence that she has recently been seen by a doctor. A painful injury to her neck and arm.'

'Poppycock,' I said firmly. 'It's an old injury. She probably hurt herself at school in the playground. It happens all the time. I'll prove it.'

'Taking on another case, Jordan?' James's voice assumed a more serious tone. 'You be careful. These people might not be above faking a second and more lethal accident.'

'They wouldn't dare.'

'You stay with puppies and fishing rods.'

'And look what's happened to Dick Mann. He's dead. And he died in a horrid way. What was he doing in the church? Was he learning to do a grandsire or a plain bob?'

'Pardon?'

'Patterns. They are bell-ringing terms. Want a lesson? I do private tuition for several large glasses of Shiraz. Oh, it's starting to rain, James. I have to go.'

'Left the washing out?'

'No, I don't do washing. Just throw everything away and buy new.'

'That's my Jordan.'

139

'Not your Jordan, sorry.'

But I wished I was his Jordan. I put the phone down. It wasn't raining in my patch of Latching but he would not know. I had to sort out my brains and see if they were still working. Photographs: they needed picking up. I'd paid for the fast service. Where had the time gone? I put on a clean tracksuit, trainers, anorak, and went to pick up the photographs. It was paying for fifty per cent blank paper, a couple of vaguely dim groups, one recognizable close-up of Derek Brook and partner laughing, good shot of front page of newspaper, and three excellent David-Bailey-class snaps of supercilious seagulls perched on pier rails. Maybe they'd make next year's calendar. Calendar Gulls.

Perhaps I should consider a career move. Would they pay expenses?

Arnie. I had to talk to Arnie Rudge. He was on the pier, wrapped up in waterproofs, munching a burger, a line of rods leaning across the rail. I wondered how he got so much time off work. He probably never went home until the kids had gone to bed. He looked at me, remembering my involvement.

'I heard about Dick Mann,' he said.

'How do you know? It hasn't been announced.'

'It was all the talk in the pub. I haven't seen him around. It must be Dick Mann. Poor sod.'

A flash of silver disturbed my vision. It was odd. It had happened before. Was it a reflection?

'What did you hear?' I asked.

'That a body had been found in a church. Hung himself, I heard. Don't ask me why. He didn't seem depressed, enjoyed himself most of the time. A bit of work, fishing, dancing, the pub. Like the rest of us, made the best of it. We aren't all millionaires. Have to do what we can.'

'How long had he been your neighbour?'

'A couple of years.'

'Did he tell you anything about where he lived before he came to Latching?'

'Can't say he did. Wasn't much for saying anything. Bit on the quiet side. Nice enough chap. Could mend things. Did a few repairs for the missus and me. Wouldn't take anything for it. Said I would buy him a beer, which I did, of course.'

'Of course.' I wasn't getting anywhere.

'Hang on, something's happening.' Arnie went over to a rod that was trembling. He began to reel in the line, his impassive face not showing any excitement. The hook appeared, dripping green weed. 'The b— got the bait. They do that all the time.'

'Clever, for a fish.'

'They bite it off, like something on a cocktail stick. It's amazing. You've got to hand it to them.'

Arnie was fingering around in his bait box. I didn't look. The contents were too revolting for words. No wonder there were few women anglers. Royal anglers probably have a bait boy, someone to do the messy part for them.

'Can you remember anything about Dick Mann's life? Did he have any other friends? Did he have a woman friend, for instance, at the dances?'

'Dunno. Dunno anything really about Dick. He kept himself to himself. Only saw him here on the pier or in the pub. Didn't know he was into bell-ringing. They ring the bells on Sundays, don't they? Well, he was here every Sunday, with the tide. Never missed. So he wasn't ringing bells. The only bell he ever rang was Bell's Whisky.'

Arnie nearly doubled up with laughter at his own joke. It was the first time I'd seen him laugh and it was explosive. The rod shook in his hands.

'Thanks, Arnie,' I said. 'Do you want me to continue with the disappearing rods enquiry?'

'Couple more days should see it out,' he choked. 'None have gone missing recently. Funny that.'

A thought slithered by before I could catch it. I scrambled my brain trying to bring the thread back but it had gone.

'Don't forget to give me an invoice,' said

Arnie. 'Me and the boys have got some money in the kitty.'

'OK.'

I went to Springfield Close. It was a dead end. The man with puppies for sale was selling King Charles spaniels. I suppose they had big eyes.

'Nice little chaps,' he said. 'Make good pets.'

'No, thank you. Sorry to have troubled you.'

There were no more answers to my puppy advertisement. I put in a second, altering the wording. I had no idea what else I could do about the stolen puppies. Mrs Gregson was not going to be pleased.

I spent the afternoon phoning local schools to find out where Miranda Brook was a pupil. No one had heard of her. Private schools next. The Brooks could afford a private school if their scams were paying off. My phone bill was rising and this was not a case I could charge to anyone. I could hardly charge myself.

The 1799 chemise dress was hung on an old dressmaker's model that had come my way and stood in a corner, the train pinned to the floor. It looked beautiful, so delicate that I was afraid a sudden gust from the door would blow it away. Many of my customers commented on the dress. Several wanted to buy it.

'It's not for sale,' I said.

'They don't make clothes like that these days,' a woman said. 'A skill long gone.'

'They do, if you have the money for hand-stitching. But not in that style. It's all glitz and glitter at todays fashion shows. Weird-cut outfits on skinny models that no one would think of wearing.'

There was something about the dress. It made customers linger and eventually buy something, as if in token payment of being in the presence of an exquisite garment from another era. I still had no idea who had left it on my doorstep.

It was a magnet. I could not count the number of small purchases that had been made while the dress graced a corner of my shop. My personal talisman. I had the feeling that I would never let it go, even to a woman on her bended knees, dripping twenties like confetti.

Miguel was expecting me for a meal this evening. It seemed aeons ago that it had been arranged. I almost thought I'd missed a few days out and that the date was long gone. I wrote up my notes and planned what to wear. I only had one dress, the black one from my days as a shop assistant at the town's department store, Guilberts. It would have to have another outing.

It was an action replay, although I hoped

not in every aspect. The last time I had eaten, or not eaten, at Miguel's restaurant had been the evening that DI James came through the door, ashen-faced, with news of the road accident. I did not want that kind of replay.

Francis Guilbert had given me some expensive Floris bath gels and foams and lotions for Christmas. I poured half a bottle into the bath. It frothed and foamed like Niagara Falls. I sank in up to my chin and wondered what I was doing wrong in my life.

Francis was a handsome and charming man, but, at sixty, a little over the hill for me. Miguel was a darling, but too ardent. I had got rid of the two spongers, the malicious one and the hungry Joshua. That left my jazz trumpeter whom I rarely see, whose music I adore and who is happily married. There was James. And Ben, who had died.

It was quite a list. And I wasn't even thirty yet. Men were largely reponsible for things that happened to women, and I was a cold flame in their lives. I felt stretched out by their manipulations.

I made up my face carefully. That meant both eye shadow and mascara. As I stared back into the mirror, wand in hand, I glimpsed my mother's face and that was unnerving. I was nothing like my mother. She and my father had been besotted with each other. I was merely an afterthought. They died together, which was alright for them.

I did my hair in a long plait in case any loose ends fell into my food. Hair dipped in spicy Mexican sauce was not worldly enough for tonight's image. The black dress looked good and I dusted off the low-heeled pumps that completed the outfit. The silk scarf would be a perfect touch, but it had been sent to me by a murderer. It had never been worn since I discovered that unsavoury fact. Either I accepted it for what it was, a beautiful piece of material, or I put it in a charity shop.

A pair of long earrings won the day, or evening. I went early, tempted by a glass of Miguel's best wine while sitting at a corner table, watching him work. He was a brilliant cook, moving at speed between tables and kitchen, with a word for everyone. His restaurant was besieged by Latching's divorced women and widows, all hoping for personal service.

'Jordan, querido. Bueno to see you. Elegancia ... as my eyes pleasure,' said Miguel, beaming, his words in a twist as usual. He was seeing me to the corner table, a single rose in a vase, the red wine ready to pour into a mega-sized goblet.

'Tonight I will eat with you. Last time was not good, no. Tonight you will be happy. I will make it happen. I am cooking the prawn for you, with asparagus and rice. The sauce is secreto.'

Wow, a whole prawn to myself. I smiled at him, wondering if I could manage a whole prawn. 'Lovely,' I murmured.

He brought a dish of nibbles to keep me going. I nibbled at ease, relaxing into the atmosphere of good food and wine, the sparkling glassware, good linen, real flowers. Miguel ran a classy joint. He wouldn't wait for me forever. One of these well-dressed, immaculate, flaxen-haired women, flashing their diamonds over the rim of a wine glass, would snare him. It was my own fault.

But it was a lovely meal, cooked to perfection. Miguel was a charming host. He told me about his family in South America. He had children but he did not mention a wife. He described his home, his hacienda.

'You will come with me, one day, yes? For a holiday. You would like, Jordan. No more rain. No more the wild winds. Always such sunshine. And I would look after you, bring back the sparkle into your eyes. It's not good, this work you do. Always particular danger.'

'There's not much danger about stolen puppies and missing fishing rods,' I said. I didn't tell him about the Sow's Head. 'Very tame.'

'Not if you find these thieves. They could become mucho apretado, dangerous.'

Miguel's velvety brown eyes were full of

concern. He really seemed to care what happened to me. I couldn't understand why, because I have never given him any encouragement. I openly sponge on him when I need a civilized meal with civilized company. Once I had served in the restaurant over the Christmas period. It was hardly a seduction technique.

'You're so kind,' I said. 'My favourite neighbour.'

'After the Doris?'

I laughed. 'Doris, too, but she's in a different category. Her packets of cuppa soup are hardly gourmet food.'

'Doris worry about you. She tells me to look after you. She says you will be in bad trouble one day.'

Miguel's English actually improves the more he talks to me. The Spanish disappears and he thinks in English. It would be so easy to go along with whatever he suggested and let him look after me. A hacienda sounded fun. Rolling space and eternal sunshine. He hadn't mentioned any ponies.

'Bad trouble, never,' I said. 'Maybe some small trouble now and again but nothing to worry about.'

I took another sip of my wine, enjoying the fruity flavour. His gaze was so fervent that I had to unlock our eyes. Instead I shifted direction and looked over his shoulder. The wine almost froze in my mouth.

Sitting together at a small table on the far side of the restaurant were two people that I knew. But I did not know that they knew each other or were on expensive dining terms.

It was Derek Brook, he of jump, bump and claim fame. The woman sitting opposite him was Nina Deodar, the less than helpful, witch-like personnel officer at Latching Hospital. They were engrossed in animated conversation, ignoring the menu, the candle-light illuminating their faces.

Real wife, lover, mistress, girlfriend, accomplice? The permutations ran through my mind.

I rose carefully, shielding my face with the edge of a linen napkin. 'Excuse me, Miguel. I need the ladies' room. Be back soon.'

Eleven

I stayed in the ladies' room as long as I dared, washing my hands like a compulsive, listening to the busy clatter of the kitchen. Miguel's kitchen was out of bounds to me of my own making. I did not want to catch him opening a packet of frozen beans. But I had to find another way out or stay in the ladies' until Brook and Deodar had finished their meal and left.

I came out and leaned flat against the door, holding in my stomach. Miguel passed, opening a bottle of wine. He took a quick look at my face and it all registered.

'This is some little bad trouble?' he asked.

'Sorry, I have to go. It was a lovely, lovely evening but I can't stay any longer.'

'You wish the back door?' he guessed.

'You can read my mind.' I reached up and kissed his cheek. He smelled so nice. Some sexy Latin aftershave and a whiff of a good wine. If only I went for older men.

He showed me to a door that led into a yard, similar to the one behind my shop. He opened it and cool night air blew in with a touch of salt and sea.

'We could have walked along the beach,' I said. 'It would have been perfect.'

'I only wish we could,' he said sadly.

I might have said: 'One day, perhaps...' but it didn't seem fair to him when I didn't know if I meant it. I legged it round to the new police station at the fastest trot these pumps would allow me. It was so cold. The automatic doors wafted open at first sign of my human warmth and presence. I wondered if they opened for dogs.

A smart young WPC was at the desk, behind the protective glass shield. She smiled a lot of lip gloss. 'Can I help you?' she

150

asked nicely. She'd been on one of those customer service courses.

'Is Detective Inspector James still here?' I asked, hugging my arms for warmth.

'I'll find out for you.'

She went into button-pressing mode and eventually found a human voice to speak to. 'Who shall I say it is?'

'Jordan Lacey. With information on a certain case.'

It was some minutes before I heard his footsteps coming down the concrete stairs. He never used the lift. He was shrugging into a dark coat. He took a longer than usual look at the black dress and earrings but did not comment.

'Aren't you cold?'

'I left my wrap behind. No time, it was a quick getaway. It was urgent.'

He took my arm and moved me out of the station into the crisp dark air. The temperature hit me again. 'Have you eaten? I haven't. Food first, information later.'

'Let's eat then,' I said. Anywhere to keep warm.

'Chinese or Indian?'

On top of Mexican? My stomach cringed at the thought of more food. Maybe I could pick. A prawn here, a grain of rice there. Perhaps they'd give me a doggy bag.

'Chinese.'

He frog-marched me round to a popular

Chinese restuarant near the gardens. They stayed open to all hours, till the last diner had gone home. I applauded their fortitude, let James order a set menu, only sipped the indifferent pinkish wine, alcohol content of about four. Straight out of a box. James ordered a Chinese beer for himself, which he drank from the bottle. That showed a degree of desperation. One of my social skills is chopsticks. I was glad to see that he knew how to handle them.

'So what's this information?' he said, stuffing a spring roll into his mouth. I don't think he had eaten a normal meal for weeks. I have no control over his life.

'I've discovered that Derek Brook has a friend at Latching Hospital. Nina Deodar, who works in personnel. A very hard, pushy sort of woman. It could be an interesting link. They were there tonight, eating at Miguel's at a table for two. It's an expensive restaurant. I saw them together. A funny sort of coincidence, don't you think, after the accident?'

'How very cosy,' said James with a mouthful of green seaweed bits. This selection was the starter course.

'I've checked all the schools around here. Miranda Brook doesn't seem to be a pupil anywhere. Unless it's a private school right out of the area. Could be, of course.'

'Out of the area,' said James, tackling a

spare rib.

I picked at a shred of seaweed. It glistened with sugar and fat and calories, melting like honeycomb in my mouth. 'I've acquired a photograph, not a very good one, I admit. But they are both in it, Derek Brook and his passenger or partner, whoever she is, the woman in the accident – having a good time, laughing, no sign of a neck brace, the same evening as the accident. And he wasn't limping anymore.'

'Is there any way of authenticating the time and date this photograph was taken? Was it at a scheduled event, something I can check on?' His teeth were white against the bone of the spare rib.

No way, I thought, and I wasn't going to say where I took it. It had been an illegal barn boot, nothing James could check on. He'd be more likely to close the place down, sending a posse of police cars, sirens screaming. Another friendship up the spout. Jack would be hurt and suspicious.

'It's rather more difficult than that,' I hesitated. 'I'm not sure I should tell you where it was. Sort of top secret.'

'Some coke cave?'

There had been a lot of talk and newspaper stories about illicit drug taking in Latching recently. I didn't like it. Not in my half-asleep seaside town. It didn't seem right. We didn't have that breed of youngster surely, but apparently we did.

'There's a close-up of a newspaper, taken at the same time, so you can check the date,' I added.

'It could be any day's newspaper. Means nothing.'

'No one can get hold of tomorrow's paper. It's the same date as the accident.'

'So then they were eating at Miguel's,' said James, shredding duck meat on to a sliver of pancake, adding spring onions and hoisin sauce. The second course had arrived. I nibbled a spring onion.

'It was Derek Brook and Nina Deodar who were at Miguel's,' I said, wondering if I could find room for the Chinese idea of a pancake, so paper thin you could see through it. 'They were together. The connection is odd.'

'Maybe they're having an affair?'

Did James know anything about affairs? Would he have an affair with me? I'd go along, pretending. I wasn't proud. He could share my bed anytime and I would massage his back, sinking my fingers into his flesh, take away the pain, ease the sorrow. But that was pillow fantasy. Dream on, dunderhead.

'It looked more like business than an affair,' I said, hoping I knew the difference. 'They weren't looking at each other in that way, that special way.'

'What way?' He was looking at me keenly over his duck pancake. I felt my cheeks becoming warm.

'That way. The way people look at each other when it's something special. You know, into their eyes.' I was faltering over the words.

'I wouldn't know,' he said.

'They could be cooking up records, X-rays.'

'Maybe. Anything else?'

'They would need doctors' reports for an insurance claim. Perhaps this woman could supply them.'

'Can you falsify reports?'

'Of course. Go to A and E with a bump on your head and give a false name and address. It's then recorded on computer. It's never deleted because no one knows if or when you get better. Any insurance company would accept that as a genuine injury. Or Nina Deodar might be simply creating an entirely false record out of nothing.'

'I don't think I like the sound of this.'

James was on to his third duck pancake. I was sipping the pink wine. I'd drink pink lemonade if it was in his company. I was almost enjoying this. An array of Chinese dishes arrived on hotplates, a bowl steaming with egg fried rice. There was no way I could manage more than a beansprout.

But James was hungry. The Chinese food vanished down his lean body in minutes. I found room for a few cashew nuts and a slice of water chestnut. I wondered if he would take me for a walk along the beach. It would be cold but bracing. The pier was laced with lights all the way to the nightclub. The promenade would be deserted except for a few dog walkers and late-night clubbers. We could find an empty shelter. Sit for a while, admiring the crescent moon. The beach would be too lumpy to sit on, all those cold pebbles.

'You look tired,' said James, noticing my face.

'It's been a long day,' I said.

'Perhaps I should take you home,' he said, calling for the bill. 'You didn't eat much.'

I didn't want him to take me home but he did. No seductive walk along the promenade, arms entwined. No coupling on the pebbles under the stars. But he did put his coat over my shoulders. My body ached with longing for him, like floating on a silver-streamed tide. It was the worst kind of slap in the face. To be walked home and left on the doorstep.

'You need some sleep, kiddo,' he said as I fumbled for my keys. I couldn't care less about sleep. And I hated being called kiddo. It was so patronizing. I tried to think of a hurtful reply but nothing came. Police slang would pass over his head. Nobody used it much these days ... gumshoe, mob squad, the Sweeney ... these words were being replaced by newer insults.

'Thanks for the seaweed,' I said. 'Pity about the pebbles.'

James did not have a clue what I was talking about. He took my key with a kind of old-fashioned gallantry and opened the street door for me. He put the key back into my hand.

'When you can remember where that photo was taken, give me a ring,' he said. 'Night, Jordan.'

'You'd better have your coat back.'

I set my alarm for four a.m. I had other things planned, like wrapping up in old clothes and camping out under the deck of the pier. This had come to me suddenly during a forkful of seaweed. The workmen were putting new decking on to a section of the pier and they had erected a steel fence round the replacement area, so that tourists etc. would not fall down the hole. I planned to climb down and find myself a nook or cranny under the girders of the pier, wait for high tide and the anglers. Maybe I'd catch a rod disappearing. Bingo.

I checked the tide timetable. Four point six was not too high a tide. I did not want to be swept out into the English Channel, to be found clinging to some blinking beacon by a boatload of grinning coastguards.

I force-fed myself a bowl of lukewarm

porridge, packed a torch, radio, camera, mobile and a flask of black coffee into a rucksack, and set off for the seafront. Dawn can be beautiful. The pale grey sky was streaked with a wash of pink and gold as night gave way to the next day. An off-sea easterly wind was testing the palm trees along the front. The palms were still wearing their winter hairnets.

They never close the pier, which is really trusting, nor do they charge admission. One day they will and I'll have to buy a season. I'm a pier freak. My daily walk is a must.

There was no one about at this time of day, or was it still night? The sea air was fresh and uncontaminated by any other breathing. Even the gulls were still asleep. I'd heard their dawn chorus many times and it could awaken the dead.

The workmen had not reckoned on anyone wanting to jump down a gaping hole, and the steel fencing was only loosely fastened together. It was easy to force two segments apart and slip through the gap. I climbed down the girders and eased along, under the decking, to the area most favoured by the anglers. There was not a great deal of purchase for my rear end, and I was glad I had brought along a wedge of Dunlopillo from the shop so I could lean against an upright, with my legs astride one of the beams. It was not comfortable. It required a great deal of positive thinking through the pain.

Sleep was the other problem. My body was telling my brain, or vice versa, that I had not had enough sleep and it was time to nod off again for another couple of hours. Nodding off on a girder under a pier was not a good idea. I might easily become fish fodder.

My tiny cheap pocket radio was the salvation. I plugged it into my ears and listened to nameless DJs rabbiting on in the small hours about totally unknown people and bands and gigs, but their voices kept me awake. I nearly phoned in a couple of times as I knew the answers to their quiz questions. I could have won a holiday to Bermuda. I mean, everybody knows that the Vatican is the palace of the Popes in Rome, don't they?

The strong coffee was rationed. I was glad when the anglers began to turn up. They gave me something to focus on and listen to. They were early risers, so was the sea. It was washing round the legs of the pier, dark and foamy. I hoped four point six was as low as I thought it was. The wind off the sea was not helping and the waves were starting to run big below my perch.

Now that there was fishing going on, I had something visual to watch apart from waves. If you like watching paint dry. It seemed an endless wait before a line began to twitch. Someone said that a fishing line had a hook one end and a fool the other. It was someone famous, like Samuel Johnson. Don't blame it on me.

A line twitched and almost flew into my face. A slim, wriggling silver fish was impaled on the hook. It looked very small, used as I am to a plateful of succulent white-flaked fish at Maeve's Cafe. I hoped the angler had a heart. He did. The tiddler came flying back into the water, its mouth ripped.

This was not a good moment for me.

Workmen arrived above, stamping about, cursing the fencing, starting to bang and hammer. It kept my brain awake. I was so stiff. I had to flex my aching legs, my sore bottom, my arms, which had nowhere to go but up or out, or carry on clinging. I massaged my neck, drank more coffee, tried to concentrate on the music, desperate not to fall off this precarious perch.

The tide was rising. It was rising far higher than I had expected and faster. That damned wind had whipped up the tide. Rollers were rolling in, groaning with the weight of pebbles and sand that they were carrying. I was horribly exposed yet no one could see me. I was a dark mass huddled under the decking, clinging to a rusted iron girder. Even if I shouted no one would hear me.

Waves were starting to thrash against my legs. I was getting wet, not something that usually bothers me. I can cope with a bit of wetness. There must be more than twelve foot of water under me now. I would have welcomed a boatload of coastguards.

A huge wave splashed halfway up the girder, drenching me. The radio went dead. The thermos was wrenched from my hands and went spinning down into the swirling depths.

I clutched my mobile to my chest, protecting it from the waves and clung to the upright girder as the tide surged in. This was no four point six. I started to shout but no one could hear me. They were using a noisy drill to put the new decking in place. I was underneath, shaken by the vibration. This surveillance had gone drastically wrong and I was some kind of pig in the middle.

Monster waves were surging diagonally across the beach, foaming and churning. They could sweep me away in seconds. I found some rope in my rucksack and looped it round myself and the girder. I might drown but I would not be swept away. My watch said it was six twenty a.m.

On second thoughts, the rope might not be so clever. Drowning was an awful death. They said Dick Mann had drowned. Perhaps I ought to swim for shore while I still had a chance. Someone might see me and launch a boat.

No one had taken a fishing rod. I had not seen any activity except lines occasionally being reeled in. It was a hobby without drama or trauma unless you were reeling in a shark.

I thought I ought to let someone know where I was, in case of the worst. I ran through the phone list keyed into my mobile and wondered who to alert. A wave washed over me and, in the lurch to save the mobile against my chest, I accidentally pressed the ring pad. I heard a call ringing, pressed on my wet ear.

'Maeve's Cafe,' came Mavis's voice.

'This is Jordan,' I shouted, water dripping from my face. 'I'm under the pier. Roped to a girder. I'm going to drown.'

Bless her, she asked no questions. A sensible, fish-frying person. Her response was instant.

'Of course you're not going to drown. Hang on there, Jordan. I'll ring the coast-guards.'

Mavis did better than that. She rang her bronzed fisherman friend, who was nearer, and, through the spray of water, I saw a sturdy fishing boat put out from the shore, tossing on the waves. Then when it was over the surge, the boat turned right and chugged in a straight line towards the pier.

I thought I recognized the tall, burly figure at the tiller. It was Bruno, the latest in her line of lovers. He didn't like me. Yet he was coming to rescue my skinny bones from under the pier. Mavis must have a powerful hold.

I was knee-deep in sea now, teeth chattering, every new wave a personal battering. The workmen above were still rivetting everything in sight. The fishermen were swopping tales and burgers. No one noticed me at all.

It was a turquoise fishing boat with a broad hull and two masts, fore and aft, a spluttering engine in the stern. The boat was piled with nets. Bruno was leaning on the tiller, steering the boat between the legs of the pier. Once under the pier, he switched off the engine. He was standing proud in yellow oilskins, a knitted cap covering his curls.

'Jump!' he shouted. He was holding on to the girder with both arms, taking the pull of his boat on the waves with every muscle in his body. 'Jump now.'

My fingers were frozen, trying to undo the knot in the rope. The boat was tossing beneath me, almost in danger of crushing my legs. Bruno's eyes were glaring. He still didn't like me.

'I'm trying, I'm trying,' I gasped.

He couldn't wait much longer. That boat was his livelihood. He could not afford to have it damaged. Selling fresh fish was his living.

The rope slithered through the loop and without thinking I just leaned over the girder and dropped. I didn't care where I fell. But Bruno had turned the hull of the boat and I fell straight into a pile of wet and smelly nets, into the mess of seaweed and spider crabs and bits of torn plastic bags. I got a mouthful of wet.

'Thank you,' I said, the breath knocked out of me.

'Don't ask why I'm here,' said Bruno, putting the boat into reverse. She barely moved at first against the strong oncoming tide, but slowly she made some distance from the pier. When she was a good way out, he turned the boat, then we were running with the tide, heading for the shore. It was a glorious, exhilarating feeling.

His thick lashes were spiked with seawater. It was dripping off his tanned face. No friendly hand offered to pull me up off the nets.

'Take this,' he bellowed. 'You might as well start making yourself useful.'

He handed me a mallet. 'Smash the crabs,' he said.

Twelve

Bruno was not my idea of a friendly rescuer. No sympathetic cluck-cluck or shoulder patting. He barely said a word. His attitude was of disapproval and he made it quite clear that he had only put out to sea on the insistence of Mavis. I think she had now paid off any debt she thought she owed me.

I sat on the wet nets, shivering with cold, not making any attempt to hammer spider crabs. They were very little crabs, some no larger than a fifty-pence coin, not doing any harm. I pretended not to hear him.

It was a rough journey back, tossing on huge waves. I could not see how we were going to make the shore, let alone how I was going to be able to climb out of the fishing boat in such water. Perhaps I would have to stay with the nets until the tide turned and the sea receded, leaving the boat high but not dry.

'What the hell were you doing under the pier?' Bruno shouted eventually, curiosity overcoming his hostility.

'I was on surveillance,' I said with as much

dignity as I could muster. 'One of my cases.' I could have said one of my many cases, but that would have been an exaggeration. I had learned nothing from the last few hours except always to check the wind force as well as the tide timetable. I would probably be laid off the anglers' missing rods case as the disappearances seemed to have stopped. No more had been reported as missing.

Dick Mann's life had also stopped. I wondered if it was a coincidence or not. But there was no reason for Dick Mann to have been involved. Witness protection or not. I wanted so much to find out why he was being protected. Yet his home had been devoid of anything personal. Except that one small item which I had purloined. And I had no idea if it would lead me anywhere.

DI James had told me nothing about their investigations into Dick Mann's death. He would never tell me what routes he was following or who were his suspects. Perhaps it was time to probe a little more. Did I have any information to barter? It always worked better if I had something to give him. Time to return to Dick Mann's cottage and carry out an in-depth search. But why? It wasn't one of my many cases...

The fishing boat had reached the shingle but the churning waves made it difficult to beach the boat. She tossed and slewed. I stood up to see if I could help.

166

'Sit down!' Bruno yelled. 'You'll tip her over!' He sounded like a dictator. I wondered if he shouted at Mavis. Perhaps he shouted in an extremis of emotion.

Bruno leaped down into the water, thigh-deep, hauling a rope over his shoulder, actually pulling the boat up on to the pebbles, using the energy of the oncoming waves to help lift a two-ton weight up the shore. It was an exhibition of physical strength of awesome proportions. It made me feel quite puny. Sometimes I couldn't lift my laundry.

The bow of the boat crunched deep into the sliding pebbles and refused to move any further. She was high up, water swirling around her bow as the tide was still coming in. I thought I was marooned.

It all happened so quickly. Bruno appeared at the side of the boat, still thigh-deep in water. He leaned over and wrapped his arms round me as if I was a sack of something disgusting. He lifted me into his arms and over the side of the boat. My face was against his wet oilskins. He staggered on the shifting shingle and carried me through the sea and on to the beach.

For a moment, one brief moment in time, suspended in disbelief, I actually enjoyed the sensation. He was strong, smelt so masculine, and I could imagine I was being rescued by a knight on a white fishing boat. I did not look at his face. It was not the face

I wanted to see, even if the arms were all right.

He dumped me on the pebbles, thump, dump, knees giving way. And the romance disappeared as the pebbles crunched into my aching flesh.

'Count yourself lucky,' he growled. 'I could have dumped you overboard with the crabs.'

'Thank you,' I said, catching my breath. 'My mother taught me good manners ... so I'll simply say thank you and ... my thanks are genuine. Mavis is a good friend and I will always help her out, even if she chooses the oddest of friends. You must have some talent I know nothing about.'

He was momentarily without a blunt retort, eyes shuttered. Then he turned his back on me and his attention was on making his boat fast with anchors and tarred boards slid under her belly. He attached a winch wire to the prow. I no longer existed. Somehow I had to make my way home. His pitch was on East Latching beach so I had a long walk along the front.

My rucksack was full of water and I tipped it out as I clambered up the slope. Everything was soaked. My wet clothes rubbed and chaffed. Time for the talc and Nivea cream. Time for a coffee that was not diluted with seawater. My mobile had gone again. No wonder these companies make huge profits.

Maeve's Cafe was on the way home. It was empty at that time of the morning. I went in, bedraggled, dripping and still shivering. Mavis took one look and pushed me into a seat, whipping off my wet anorak and hat. She went into the kitchen and returned with a towel quickly heated in a microwave and started towelling my hair and my face.

'Did Bruno pick you up?' she asked.

'Yes,' I said, teeth chattering. 'I'm very grateful.'

'But then he dumped you on the beach?'

'Well, he had to think about b-beaching his b-boat. The sea was pretty rough. I was all r-right by then.'

Mavis pursed her lips. 'I'll have a word with him. His manners are gross. I've nothing dry for you to put on. Keep towelling and I'll bring you a hot drink. Then I'll phone for a taxi to take you home. You need a hot bath straight away, my girl.'

It was a mug of hot chocolate with foam on top and sprinkled with grated chocolate. Chocolate has a hidden pick-me-up. It triggers the release of endorphins in the brain, which give a feeling of relaxation and goodwill. I let goodwill drift into my veins, the heat curling into crevices that were frozen, my tongue detecting flavours that brought my senses back to life.

'Can you provide someone to scrub my back...?' I murmured, overflowing with goodwill.

'I'm not lending you Bruno.'

'I wasn't thinking of him.'

Mavis knew who I was thinking of but said nothing. For a second her eyes twinkled. She was busy getting ready for today's onslaught of hungry tourists. How she did it all on her own was a wonder. Would she take me on as an assistant, chopping chips? It might be more rewarding.

A coachload of disabled men and women, some in wheelchairs, suddenly arrived. Mavis was rushing around, serving everyone at once. I left a pound coin on the table and disappeared. I was sufficiently warmed up now to get home under my own steam. Huddled in the next beach shelter was the homeless bundle who was Gracie, surrounded by her loaded shopping trolleys and bin liners. It was beyond me to say more than 'Hi'. I looked worse than she did.

My two bedsits were a haven. It seemed as if I had been away years. I had to recognize the rooms as mine all over again. I stripped off and lowered myself into a *Lavandula officinalis* bath. Lavender for healing. And I needed healing. They say that halfway through the woods and you are still grieving. Was I grieving for Ben? Or was I grieving equally for James whom I could never have?

Amazing the power of a deep, warm bath. More people should take them. Showers don't have that power. They are merely a temporary sprinkle. I climbed out, invigorated, towelled, talced, sprayed with deodorant, creamed with moisturizer. Clean clothes and I was ready for a day's work. But not in my shop. She was closed for redecoration. Maybe for the duration.

I drove the ladybird along the lanes to Dick Mann's cottage, hoping a heave would open the back door as it had before. But I had my pick keys with me, just in case. DI James and I had missed something. It was up to me to find it.

But I was not sure why or what. I felt I was still involved even if Dick Mann was dead. No one seemed to be bothering about his death. It was not fair. He was ... had been a person. Someone should care. Someone from this life, or his previous life.

The police had been along and secured his cottage with tape and a new padlock on the door. Suspicious lot.

I wandered around, looking at the small windows. They were doll's house windows, barely big enough for me to climb in, even if I could reach upstairs. The garage would be the place to find a ladder.

The police had padlocked the front doors of the wooden garage, but forgotten the small back door. It was half hidden by an overgrown shrub. It opened squeakily to my touch. I climbed over a lawnmower and

171

several garden brooms. There was no car, only a motorbike and a rusty bicycle. And his angling gear. I have never seen so much stuff. Do lines break easily? Does each prize catch carry its own health warning and the rod is officially retired?

I counted over forty rods. It seemed excessive for a hobby. I started to make a list of the makes. Greys, Catchmaster, Daiwa. WPP must have paid him well. Arnie would have taken his rods away when the police secured the garage.

The inside of the garage was dusty and dark. The one small window at the back was festooned with cobwebs. Even the cobwebs had cobwebs. Tools were hanging from nails hammered into the walls, drills and hammers and screwdrivers. Nails and screws were stored in old coffee jars. Folded bills and receipts were tucked behind struts of wood. I cannot resist bills and receipts. They are like a personal history book, the minutiae of life.

I collected a pile of bits of paper and put them into a supermarket carrier bag. I saw a corner of something that had been well tucked behind a strut, and pulled it out carefully. It seemed brown and fragile but it came away without tearing. It was an old photograph.

I held it to the light, peering at the dim figures. It was a photo of three young men in open-necked sports shirts, arms entwined, grinning, holding up pints of beer. I looked carefully into their faces and the front page of a dozen tabloid newspapers swam back into my memory.

I knew who he was now. I knew who he had once been. And I could guess who had strung him up. A chill of fear took me by surprise. I got out fast. No way was I going to get mixed up with that lot. But I was already involved and I hadn't known it.

First Class Junk needed a dust. I did my vigorous magnetic-brush disco dance before changing the window displays. If the tourists were starting to return to Latching, then I needed to attract them with goods that were eye-catching.

This spurt of earnest shopkeeping was in order to take my mind off Dick Mann. The shop felt safe. I did not want to be mixed up in his past life. I liked a quiet time. Nothing more violent than rough handling by a disgruntled fisherman in full view of people walking their dogs.

I did a final invoice for the anglers' syndicate. This case was finished. I could guess where the rods had gone to but not how or why. And I would never know why. Mrs Gregson's invoice could wait until I had some work to show for it. The bills and receipts were laid out on the floor of my back office. I thought I might as well have a look at them before passing them on to James. He ought to show some gratitude ... but he would probably ask how I got hold of them. Life was so complicated at times.

There was an itemized phone bill which might be worth looking into. Not many local numbers. The bills and receipts were mostly for small items used in the repair of the lawnmower, the washing machine, the motorbike and an electric saw. One receipt was more puzzling. He'd been to Guilberts department store and paid forty pounds for a bottle of Chanel No 5 ... Was there a woman in his life? I decided to keep quiet about this one.

James's answerphone clicked on. I left a brief message, resisting the temptation to listen to his voice over and over again. One day I will burst an artery in an unexpected surge of love.

A woman came into the shop and bought two glass birds. They were not worth six pounds each, so I said it was my special bargain day and she could have the two for six pounds. She was well pleased. It paid for a passable supper.

Then my doctor friend wandered in. 'Any more glass bottles?' he asked. He was an avid collector of old bottles.

'Sorry,' I said. 'But I'm keeping an eye open for you.'

'Gracie has refused the free dental,' he added as he went out. He never lingered or talked. Something left over from his busy practice days. Five minutes per patient.

'I'm not surprised,' I said. 'I don't think she has opened her mouth for years.'

This was when one counted lucky stars. Own teeth, own hair, health, roof, friends. I had a galaxy of lucky stars. Sirius, Aldebaran, Phosphor, Hesperus. Life was a luminosity.

The phone rang. I could tell from the strident ring that it was an official call. DI James, perhaps, calling to find out how I felt after my perilous rescue from under the pier. Mavis might have mentioned it to him casually over his lunch.

'Jordan?'

'Hello,' I said.

'What were you doing at Dick Mann's cottage? You were caught on the CCTV camera.' It was James, only slightly amused.

'You fixed a camera there? Why? It's not the scene of the crime. Anyway, I didn't go into the cottage, only the garage, and Dick Mann was killed in church.'

'Not necessarily so,' he said vaguely. 'We are interested in recording his visitors. Any visitors. Might give us a lead. You've been recorded.'

'Intrusion of privacy,' I said. 'Especially when I've been doing your work for you.

Have you got his latest itemized phone bill?'

There was a pause. He was checking the list of items removed from Tan Cottage. He cleared his throat. 'No, we don't have one. Do you have it?'

'Yes. It was in the garage along with numerous bills and receipts.'

'And you removed them?' He was going to bite my head half off.

'On your behalf. I know you are short of manpower.'

There's no answer to that. I heard a swift intake of breath as he searched for a suitable retort.

'A spoonful of honey will catch more flies than a gallon of vinegar,' I said helpfully. 'Benjamin Franklin.'

There was a low chuckle. 'I suppose that's out of a book in your shop. An unsold book of quotations. I'll be round for the receipts in ten minutes. And save me the book.'

'I'm glad you are grateful,' I said.

'Gratitude goes barefooted on a wet day.'

I took it on board, puzzled. It rang some sort of distant bell. 'Who said that?'

'I did.'

He put the phone down. I sank back in my chair and wondered if, at long last, DI James was developing a sense of humour. The thought was electrifying. One human gene could lead to another.

I rushed round with the air freshener, put

on fresh coffee, bought a packet of digestive biscuits from Doris.

'What's the celebration?' she asked shrewdly. 'Won the lottery?'

'Didn't even buy a ticket.'

'Why the big grin?'

'James cracked a joke. A genuine, original joke.'

'Have two packets of biscuits. It might not happen again.'

His idea of ten minutes was several hours out. Who decided how long a minute should be anyway? Who invented seconds and said that sixty of them made a minute? Why not fifty-nine or sixty-six? I was about to put up the CLOSED sign when he arrived outside in a flashy yellow and blue patrol car. He heaved himself out and put his hand on the shop door as I was closing it.

'Sorry,' he said. 'Got held up.'

'Hope you were quicker on the draw.'

'Delayed.'

'I know what you mean. Come in. There are two biscuits left. I could make some fresh coffee.'

'Thank you, Jordan. I'd like some coffee. You know what the station brew is like.'

I installed him in my office on the Victorian button-backed chair. He stretched out his legs and looked as if he was about to fall asleep, so I put the sheaf of bills and receipts in his hand. He brought himself back to reality and leafed through them as I made coffee. It was the phone bill that drew his attention.

'Some odd calls,' he said.

'Do you monitor calls as a matter of course?'

'No. We try not to have any contact at all once the new identity is established. It's better if they are untraceable.'

'Something went wrong here, then, didn't it?'

'Obviously, and I wish I knew what it was. The system is usually foolproof.'

'Perhaps he went fishing once too often,' I said. 'That's my theory anyway.'

This was a fraction too profound for James. He looked at me with narrowed eyes over the top of the coffee mug. 'What's fishing got to do with it?'

'It was his hobby. He was down on the pier in all weathers. He was quiet but everyone knew him. Maybe he fished in his other life. When the WPS gave him a new identity, they probably didn't say that he'd got to have a new hobby as well. They never said take up bowls or tiddlywinks.'

He finished his coffee and stood up, stretching. There was no way of making him sit down with a promise of home-made soup or supper. I could rustle up a decent supper with six pounds but I needed time to shred and marinate and whisk. Two biscuits were not a substitute.

As he left my office, James came face on with the 1799 chemise dress on the stand. He stopped, then walked round it, being careful not to tread on the skirt. It was as if he had never seen such a beautiful dress before.

'Where did you get this dress?' he asked.

'It's beautiful, isn't it?' I said. 'It was made in the eighteenth century. I don't know the date exactly but I found a similiar one in a fashion reference book. It's admired by everyone who comes into the shop. It's becoming my mascot.'

'And how did you come by it?'

'Why the third degree? Why do you want to know?' I didn't like the tone of his voice. He was on his mobile, talking to someone in the office, asking for a list to be read to him. He clicked off the connection and shook his head.

'Sorry, Jordan. This valuable dress was stolen from an exhibition of antique clothes that was on show at Broom Water House recently. I'll need you to come to the station and make a statement.'

'This is ridiculous. I don't have to make a statement. I haven't done anything wrong.'

'I'm afraid you do. You're ex-job. You know the score. The dress is on display in your shop so you're in possession of stolen property. Mascot or no mascot, that's a crime.'

Thirteen

This was the first time I had been charged with receiving stolen property. I could see the headlines in the local newspaper, along with a grainy photograph:

LOCAL PI DENIES SEIZED STOLEN GOODS

DI James had not exactly charged me but he wanted a statement about how I got the dress. My story sounded tame. So I found it on the shop doorstep in a carrier bag. Someone had left it there. He looked at me with derision.

'Can't you think of anything better than that? Did you see anyone leave it? Where were you beforehand? Did they know you were going to be out?'

'I can't remember anything when you throw so many questions at me all at the same time. Can you remember what you were doing every minute of the day?'

He shook his head. 'No, some days I can barely remember my name, but that's no excuse. You are a private investigator. You are trained to use your powers of observation.'

I did not know whether to hit him or kiss him.

'If I was fabricating a story, I'd make up something really complicated, wouldn't I? Men with beards and dark glasses hovering on the corner. A speeding getaway car, throwing bags out of the back window. Thugs with coshes, threatening me not to say where I got the dress. Fancy any of those? Take your pick and I'll tell you a whopper.'

Sergeant Rawlings brought me a cup of station brew. He did not look well. He was a poor colour. 'Sorry, no biscuits, Jordan. Biscuits are banned in this new building in case we encourage the mice.' He went out and closed the door.

'What's the matter with Sergeant Rawlings?' I asked. 'Is he ill?'

James raised his eyebrows. 'Sarge? I don't know. He hasn't said anything.'

'Well, he doesn't look well. Perhaps you ought to find out. Show the caring boss side of you.'

'There isn't time for TLC in a police station. We have to get on with our job. Keeping the good people of Latching safe in their beds at night. But I will ask him.'

I nodded. 'Any leads on stolen puppies?'

His face almost found a grin to wear and I

rephrased my question. Sometimes he made me feel so insecure. Innocence is a slippery path.

'Have you any underground info on stolen puppies? Small dogs, chihuahuas in particular.'

'Have you looked on the website for missing pets?'

'Didn't know there was one.'

'You'd be surprised what you can find these days. We caught a local burglar recently who had advertised stolen property on the Internet. There was a list of goods for sale.'

'Pretty stupid.'

'He thought he was being clever. We got him. He was up in court last week.'

'Can I go now? I've got work to do. Or are you going to give me an update on Dick Mann?'

'Nothing to tell you, Jordan. Anyhow, it's out of our hands now. The Met have taken over. It's more their scene.'

'He must have been someone pretty important then,' I said casually. 'Great train robber? Bullion bank snitch?'

'I've no idea. I'll get your statement written up and you can sign it before you go.' James was leaving the room with the single page of my statement. I'd had nothing to say beyond the bare fact of finding the dress in a carrier bag.

'This is costing me money.'

'Nonsense. You were just going to close your shop. Any luck with your Brook investigation?'

I shook my head. I could hardly scour the entire country for a pupil called Miranda Brook. 'I guess there's nothing I can do,' I said. 'Especially if the hospital records are being doctored.'

'Try the insurance companies. See if Derek Brook has made any other claims, or his wife. Of course, they may be using a variety of names and addresses. It's not much to be going on.'

'Are you going to take the dress away? I'm looking after it with great care. You'll only stuff it in a box, store it in a room with the wrong temperature and it could easily get damaged. If it does belong to Broom Water House and they can identify it, then, of course, they are entitled to have it back. But, in the meantime, it would make more sense to leave it in the shop.'

I had given the good Detective Inspector a problem. He knew the way stolen goods were sometimes handled and this was a valuable and delicate item. He would get into trouble if it was damaged in transit.

'I suppose I could bind you over, or issue some kind of bond. I'm not sure. The curator of the collection at Broom Water House will be along tomorrow to identify the garment. You are more or less trustworthy.'

Stay serene, I told myself. More or less trustworthy was a step forward. I produced a serene smile, fringed with sincerity and trustworthiness. It was a difficult procedure, especially when I was seething with anger.

'How kind,' I said. 'You obviously know an honest citizen when you see one. Years of experience.'

James looked at me sharply, to see if I was taking the michael. I kept looking the same look, straight at him. One day I would fall apart just hearing his name. I wanted him around forever. As the song goes, if we could not be the best of lovers, perhaps we could be the best of friends.

I would lay down my life for him. Maybe he would do the same for me. A glint of silver flashed across my eyes. It was odd. No idea why. There was a sting of regret.

'I'll bring the curator to your shop tomorrow morning at ten o'clock. Make sure you are there and the dress is there.'

'You've got me worried now,' I said, slinging on my shoulder bag. 'I may have to sleep at the shop. It would be awful if someone broke in overnight. If the dress is that valuable, the sooner the curator has it back the better.'

'Changed your mind?'

'No,' I said, with resignation. 'I'll look after it. I want it to last another two hundred years. How much is it worth?'

'Several thousand pounds, I guess. It's difficult to put a price on antique clothes until you come to sell them, and Broom Water House are not selling.'

'And to think I nearly put my usual six pound price tag on it,' I said. 'Sorry, only joking. I wasn't going to sell it. Too beautiful for common merchandise.'

'Do you want a lift anywhere?' James asked, thawing a couple of degrees.

'No, thank you. I need a walk. By the way, I left some gloves behind a hundred years ago.'

'I'll get Seargeant Rawlings to check lost property.'

A walk via Latching library. It was still open. I wanted to look up lost pets on the Internet. I might get lucky.

The rows of terminals were busy, mostly with foreign students mailing home in various languages. I had to wait in an impatient line even for a short-hold thirty-minutes-only terminal. I went straight to Google and keyed in 'pets lost'. It was heartbreaking. I couldn't bear to read about all the lost Rovers, Flopsies and Tiggers.

'Pets found' was more encouraging. I hoped the finders and losers would get together. 'Pets for sale' was even more illuminating, with lots of Chihuahuas on offer. Several were from reputable kennels that I recognized. There was one that stood out from the others because chihuahua had been spelt incorrectly, twice. Chiwahwas was a phonetic spelling, how it sounded. I took down the name, H. Ford, and the phone number. I spun through a few other websites but there was nothing of any interest.

There was a sleeping bag at the shop for emergencies, and this was definitely in that category. Doris's shop was closed, so I couldn't get any extra milk. Supper was going to be frugal unless I treated myself to a Mexican. It made sense, as Miguel's restaurant was only two doors away, but he would want me to be his guest and I could not accept another lovely meal from him.

The chemise dress was still on its lonely stand. I took a closer look at the exquisite stitching and the fine material. It was amazing that it had lasted so many years. My shop did not sell sheets so I made do with a shroud of bubblewrap. The dress needed protection not only from the polluted atmosphere but also from prying eyes.

I phoned the dealer who could not spell chihuahua and he was chatty enough. Yes, he'd got a couple of nice little puppies. He couldn't keep them because his kid was allergic to dogs. He'd let them go cheap.

This sounded promising. 'I'd certainly like to see them, Mr Ford,' I said. 'You say that one is long-haired?'

'Like a little ball of fluff, he is,' the man

chuckled. 'Proper little puffball. I can bring 'em over if you like. Where are you? Latching? That's not far. I could pop them round any time.'

Problem. I did not do PI business at my shop. I do not do business at my home. Whatever I do work-wise should not be traceable to either address.

'The puppies are actually a present for my sister, a surprise present, and I don't want her to see them,' I said smoothly.

'I quite understand, miss. You just say where and I'll be there.' Mr Ford chuckled again at his rhyming pattern. He sounded pleasant but if they were the stolen puppies, then he was a thief and might get nasty.

'How about the amusement arcade on the pier?' I said, thinking of Jack being around. My stalwart mate. 'You might win a few bob while you wait, if I'm late.' This was catching.

'OK by me. How about midday? Then I'll still have time for a drink at a pub. You'll love these puppies soon as you see them.'

'How much did you say for them?'

'Thirty pounds.'

'Is that each or for both?'

'Come off it, miss. Thirty pounds each. These are pedigree puppies.' He chuckled some more.

'Have you got their documentation?'

''Course I have. I'll bring it along, don't

you worry.'

We rang off after mutual confirmation of the time and place. Tomorrow was going to be busy. If I survived the night.

Clean jeans, clean sweater, and I was ready for words with Miguel. No black dress and kitten heels this visit. Maybe he would understand. I locked the shop carefully, back and front, making sure no one could see the dress.

'Jordan,' he said, his eyes lighting up. He was moving fast around the tables for his size. 'I adore to see you but this not good time. Come back tomorrow.'

'I've come as a customer, Miguel. Allow me to pay, please. I need a quick supper.' It was blurted out, not at all diplomatically.

'Please, Jordan, I plead with you. No supper tonight. This is bad night. I am three staff down. Bad cold, bad back, this influenza stuff. I am doing everything. Sorry, Jordan. Please go home.'

I can be a quick thinker on some occasions. This was one of them. The dress was safe for the time being. My appetite took second place as I produced my trump card.

'Where do you want me? In the kitchen, or out front?'

Not quite the right way to put it but fortunately Miguel does not have that kind of mind. His dark brown eyes, which had already brightened, lit up a few more degrees.

'Jordan, you are my angel. The kitchen is desolate. No one, only me, rushing about like a hot cat. I will tell you everything to do. I will make the cooking proper if you do arranging on plates...' His fractured English was deteriorating.

'I'll wash salad, prepare vegetables, put dishes in the machine, anything you say,' I said, following Miguel into the kitchen. 'I can cook rice.'

'You are perfection in a basket.'

I might have been perfection but I was no short-order cook. I rolled up my sleeves and put on an apron. The next three hours were more than hard work. It was like being incarcerated in hot sauce, smelling of spice and peppers and garlic and turmeric, intermittently stirred, constantly leaping from hot pot to hot pot. Steam was coming out of my ears but I became a dab hand at arranging the side salads and the relishes.

Miguel occasionally, on the run, found time to plant a warm kiss on the back of my neck. 'My angel!' he repeated, at frequent intervals. It was heady stuff.

At some point later I felt the pressure easing. Orders were slowing down, meals finishing. I was making pots of coffee and people were going home. Euphoria swept over me, along with tiredness beyond

189

description. Standing up sleeping was not out of the question.

Miguel guided me to a chair at the back of the restaurant and put a simple dish of rice and vegetable jambalaya in front of me. He poured a glass of wine.

'Finish now. Eat, drink, and I pay you,' he said.

'I don't want paying,' I said. 'I want to ask a favour.'

'Anything.'

'Will you sleep with me tonight?'

That really shook Miguel. He could not believe what he was hearing. This was not my day for saying things in the right way. A gentleness fell over his eyes. He'd been trying for months, maybe more than a year, to talk me into some sort of relationship. And he had given up, lost hope.

'Jordan, you mock me,' he said.

'No, I'm sorry. I didn't mean that kind of sleeping. I was asking you to keep me company. I have to sleep at the shop tonight and I'm a bit scared in case someone breaks in.'

The story of the 1799 chemise dress came out and he nodded understandingly. He was sipping from my glass of wine, as dead beat as I was. We were both too tired to do anything but sleep. I should really be helping with the clearing up before he went home to bed, not asking him to sleep on the floor of my shop.

'There are two selections,' he said. I loved it when he used funny words. 'I go home and get many pillows and duvets. You cannot rest on a hard floor without some comfort. Or, we take valuable antique dress to my flat in the car and rest the night in peace.'

It was a tempting option. I didn't know he had a flat. It was asking for trouble. I did not want to have to fight him off. He was always so kind in every way.

'I didn't know you had a flat,' I said.

'Right on the seafront. One of the new ones in the rebuilt Georgian terrace. On the first floor with a small iron balcony for watching the waves.'

It was a seduction of words and images. I've always wanted a balcony with a sea view. I would do almost anything for a balcony. To sit watching the sea, with a glass of wine at one's side, the newspaper, a good book, maybe some jazz playing low in the background ... my idea of heaven.

I knew the terrace he meant. It was an architectural triumph. After years of pulling down Georgian houses and putting up red-brick monstrosities, some genius had kept the frontage of a sweeping terrace but completely rebuilt behind it, providing a dozen or more luxury flats. They were very expensive. More noughts than I would ever see in a lifetime.

Miguel put his hand across the table and covered mine. 'I will fetch the pillows,' he said, nodding. 'It is more simple.'

I accepted gratefully. 'Thank you. I'll clear up in the kitchen.'

I went all out with the lemon Cif, cleaning everything in sight. The skin on my fingers wrinkled and my nose twitched. Perhaps I should have asked James to sleep guard with me. But no, he was busy elsewhere, wasn't he? Looking after the citizens of Latching, his job and his pension.

It was, I suppose, an easy sort of night. Miguel arrived with mountains of bedding. He'd changed into casual clothes. We made a nest on the floor of my office, but left the door open so that I could still see the dress on its stand. Miguel was asleep in seconds. He looked so kindly in sleep, an arm flung back, his dark face in repose, his curly hair stark against the white pillow.

It took a while for me to relax. Every bone ached and I expected each moment for someone to break a window, or for Miguel to lunge at me with intensely poetic Latin passion. But neither happened. I fell asleep and at some point in the night I moved against him and his arm came round me. He murmured something. It was very comforting.

★   ★   ★

A loud knocking woke me. I staggered to my feet, trailing duvet. DI James was at the door of the shop with the curator from Broom Water House. Their silhouettes were clear against the window. I had slept in a tracksuit, so I was fully clothed but tousled.

I unlocked the door and opened it. It was a lovely morning, fresh, clean, bright. Maybe spring was on its way. I needed daffodils and cheerfulness.

'Hello,' I said. 'Your dress is safe. No one blasted their way in last night.'

DI James stepped into the shop. 'You slept here last night?' He was taking in my unkempt appearance.

'Yes,' I said. 'I didn't want anything to happen to the dress while it was in my shop. I felt responsible for its safety.'

James introduced the elderly curator, a Mr Arthur Williams. He was overjoyed to see the dress. He kept exclaiming about its perfection. Of course, I agreed with every word. We had a lot in common.

Mr Williams had brought a huge cardboard container in which to transport the dress back to Broom Water House, and layers of tissue paper. I was sorry to see it go. It had added class to my establishment.

'You have taken good care of it, Miss Lacey,' he said. 'Thank you so much. We are absolutely delighted to have it back in such good condition. You have no idea ... We'd like to thank you with these free admission tickets. You and a friend, or your partner...' For a moment he looked confused.

'How kind,' I said, coming to his rescue. 'We'd love to come. And I'm so glad the dress is going home. I wonder what tales it could tell us.'

'Many delightful tales, indeed,' said Mr Williams with a benevolent twinkle.

It was as the curator was organizing the removal of the dress into a van that Miguel woke up and made an appearance. He had slept in short navy pants, very Latin. He looked swarthy and hairy and still sleepy.

'Benuos dias,' he said, stretching lazily. 'This is a lovely morning.'

Those few words were dynamite. I dare not look at James's face. Yet, why not? My life was mine. James didn't care. He didn't show any personal interest in me. I was merely an irritating PI, a thorn in his side.

'I trust you slept well,' said James, his eyes sweeping over Miguel's dishevelled appearance, his voice like cracked ice.

'Why not? With such an angel at my side...' said Miguel, stretching. 'Breathing blossom in my ear.'

I decided not to explain. It seemed easier. At least I was fully dressed. And I had a busy morning ahead. Twelve midday with the dog man, Mr H. Ford, on the pier.

'Now, if you don't mind, gentlemen. I have

a lot of work to do. Miguel needs a cup of my excellent coffee before going home, and you, DI James, no doubt have a lot of police calls upon your time. Nice to have met you, Mr Williams. I hope you have had your alarm systems updated.'

'Indeed, indeed,' said Mr Williams, feeling on safer ground. 'No one will be able to steal the dress again. Though why it was dumped on your doorstep is still a mystery, and how they got the dress away is also a mystery.'

'A mystery is a puzzlement that only the blessed can solve,' I said.

'Who said that?' said James, turning at the door, his face etched in a storm of sunlight.

I took in the sense of him, the sight of him, with heady abandonment.

'I did. I made it up. Do you like it?'

'It could grow on me.'

Fourteen

Miguel went home in the shambling morning light with his mountain of bedding. It was a wonder that DI James had not given him a parking ticket. I assumed, from the somnolent goodbye, that Miguel was going home for an extra twenty winks. Perhaps he never got up till midday. It wouldn't have surprised me. The pace in that kitchen had been frenetic.

It was a relief, although tinged with regret, to see the dress go. James disappeared without a further word, just a curt nod. Miguel did not look awake enough to drive, but drive he did, a long silver Mercedes, filled to the roof with pillows. Back to his rebuilt Georgian flat with a balcony overlooking the sea.

Maybe Doris had been right. It could be a life of ease beckoning me, apart from the odd emergency stint in his kitchen, which I would do gladly. Miguel might teach me to cook, take me to South America to meet his family, lavish me with roses and wine. Perhaps life was coming up buttercups and daisies, except for one thing. He was not the right man. Not at the moment, anyway.

The shop looked empty without the dress on display. I had got used to it and decided to look out for something striking to stand in its place. Maybe the theatre would lend me a gown if I gave them an advertising spot for a coming show. I was still on their voluntary list for front-of-house workers, but they had not called me of late. A little bird whispering...? Could it be they did not trust me anymore? I had been involved when their theatre manager died, rather publicly.

Something was happening to the air outside. It was warming up. The council had put some old rowing boats along the pedestrian shopping areas and filled them with spring flowers. They were splashed with the yellow of daffodils and straight little dwarf tulips with frilled red petals. Spring ... just the word lifted my melancholy. It meant that summer was on its way and soon I would be walking the beach barefooted, feeling the water on my skin, catching seaweed between my toes.

I did an eight-minute walk of the pier but no one was waiting around with a box full of puppies. The amusement arcade was always busy whatever the time of day. I went over to the security booth, where Jack was incarcerated with his bags of money. He gave me a wave and keyed in the code to open the door. He was already making the coffee.

'Hi Jack,' I said.

'Hiya babe.' I didn't mind it from him.

'I haven't time for coffee,' I said. 'I'm meeting a contact who has two puppies for sale.'

'Call me if he gives you any aggro.'

'OK, thanks.'

'Someone had to be rescued from under the pier,' he said, peering at me over the jar of instant. 'It wasn't you, was it?'

'Me?' I said, all innocence. 'What would I be doing under the pier?'

He was not taken in. 'I could have got you out. I've got a trapdoor down to the super-structure. It's in case there's a fire and I need a quick escape. You should have let me know you were there.'

'I never thought,' I said with an apologetic shrug.

He shook his head as he stirred the brown brew he called coffee. 'What's your mobile for? Give me a call. Always give me a call.'

'I will,' I said.

'Wanna come out for a drink tonight?' he called as he closed the door. He was paranoid about being robbed.

I nodded but made my escape. Puppies came first.

A man was sitting on a bench outside the arcade. He was so ordinary-looking, it was hard to describe him. Usual uniform of jeans

198

and anorak, short brown hair sticking up like a brush, anonymous face, neither trust-worthy nor shifty. He had a cardboard box at his feet. It was punctured with airholes.

'Hello,' I said. 'Are you Mr Ford?'

'That's me,' he said, grinning yellowed teeth. 'You're the young lady after two pup-pies for her sister? I've got the perfect pair.'

'That's right,' I said. 'May I see the pup-pies?'

He half-opened the lid and two puppies immediately sensed the fresh air of freedom and tried to scramble out. One was short-haired and the other was a ball of fluff.

Now I didn't know a chihuahua from a spaniel till I got a book out of the library, but these two looked genuine chihuahuas. I checked the pointed ears and big eyes.

'They're lovely, lovely,' I gabbled as I looked them both over and tried to stroke the soft heads. 'And I must take a photo of them.' I did my David Bailey impersonation, bobbing about on my knees. Mr Ford was well in the picture. The long-haired looked like a prize winner of the future. An absolute poppet, trying to lick the camera. But did it belong to Mrs Gregson? 'And you have their pedigree papers? Can I see them?'

They were photocopied papers. It was obvious from the thin darkened edge where the original had not sat on the glass properly. These had been doctored with new names and birth dates.

'Why aren't you going to show them or breed from them?' I asked, fondling the small ears. 'They're nice puppies.'

'I told you, my kid's allergic to them.'

'Didn't you know that when you started your kennel business?'

The shifty look came into focus. Mr Ford didn't know how to answer. I could see his brain cells changing gear.

'It's summat new. I've recently got together with this divorced woman and its her son, not mine. Sneezes summat awful he does.'

I didn't believe a word. 'Well, I'll certainly have both puppies,' I said, diving in at the deep end, so to speak. Supposing Mrs Gregson didn't want them? 'I'll give you forty pounds for the two.'

'No way, miss,' he said, shaking his head sadly. 'I'd be cutting my own throat. Thirty pounds each. They're worth it.'

'Fifty pounds for both puppies.'

'Done.'

He wanted cash, of course. I knew that before I even got out my cheque book. He was halfway off to the pub already. Five brown ones changed hands and I took the documentation even though I knew it was false. It was lucky that I had got some cash out of the wall. I hoped I had got the right long-haired. It was a pretty little thing.

'Thank you very much, Mr Ford. Perhaps

you'd like to give me your card so that I can recommend you.'

He patted his pockets. 'Right out of cards, miss. Henry Ford. I'm in the phone book.'

As soon as I heard the hesitancy in his voice, I knew he wasn't Mr Ford or in the phone book. We'd have a job tracing the founder of the Ford Motor Company.

I took the puppies back to my shop and let them run loose in the back yard, making sure they could not get out. They loved it, sniffing everywhere and leaving a few calling cards of their own. I didn't know what to feed them on so bought a tin of spiced meat-balls in gravy from Doris and they thought it was wonderful, scoffed the lot, panted around for seconds.

I phoned Mrs Gregson. 'Could you come over to my office,' I said. 'Please don't get too excited, but I have some puppies to show you which may be of interest.'

She arrived at the shop before I could even write up my notes. She had hurried and was out of breath. I took her through to the back. She stood in the doorway, emotionally stunned, her hands clasped to her breast. Then she scooped up the little long-haired chihuahua and held the bundle of fluff against her face.

'Angel,' she sobbed, with an intensity of love. 'My baby Angel.'

* * *

The other puppy was not hers, she said, after examining it. But we were obviously on the right track. She offered to give the short-haired a temporary home, but as there were no pedigree papers, she could not show it or sell it and the puppy legally belonged to someone else.

'Poor little thing,' she said. 'Perhaps you can find its real owner. He looks pedigree. Nice little face.'

I did not explain that I was not running a charity for lost or stolen dogs. If I could find her other puppies, then I might do something. But this new puppy was not my responsibility even though I had bought it. She was more than happy that I had spent fifty pounds of her money. I said I would give her a detailed invoice. Case finished?

'Worth every penny to have my Angel back,' she said. 'I'm going to get her micro-chipped straight away.'

After she had gone, I hosed down my yard. I was never going to make a breeder. Cats, perhaps, but not dogs.

Suddenly I had no cases, or rather only half a case. There was little hope of finding Mrs Gregson's other puppies. Mr Ford could have sold them on via the Internet.

The only other work on the horizon was the fake car crashes, Mr Brook and family, with their various whiplash injuries. I might be able to save myself my no claims bonus.

Dick Mann's death was nothing to do with me, yet I still felt obliged to find out more about the circumstances. Now that I knew who he was, or thought I knew who he was.

I phoned DI James. He answered himself, which was unusual. He was doing paperwork or crime was down. One of the two.

'Are you looking for someone who steals pedigree puppies, or handles stolen dogs?' I asked.

'Not at this moment.'

'I have a name and a photograph. The name is probably false but the photograph is genuine.'

'I'm impressed.'

'Let me know when you are impressed enough to want a copy of the photograph.'

'Will do, Jordan. I'm making a note.'

There was a pause and a rustle of papers.

'Have you any further news about Derek Brook and the car-crashing scam?' This conversation was hard going. Like getting the last of a Pepsi out of an empty bottle, drip by drip.

'As it happens, there was another one last night, out on the A27. On the roundabout before the turn-off to Latching. Similar to your crash. A blue metallic Jaguar got a bent bumper, but the other car was far worse. A write-off. Went into a wall. The occupants, a couple, name of Smith, were taken to hospital with whiplash injuries.'

'How do you know that it was a fake crash like mine?'

'Because the driver of the blue Jag gave a detailed account of what happened. He also has some very up-to-date equipment installed in his car which records exactly what the car is doing, as and when, speeds etc. The perfect automated witness.'

Bells rang. 'Jack?'

'Yes, your friend, your bit of rough, owner of the amusement arcade.'

My loyalty immediately split in two. Jack was not my bit of rough and I objected to this description of him. He was not exactly out of the top drawer, but he was a kind man even if he did not have a clue about what made coffee halfway decent.

DI James had no right to talk about him this way, and I did not like it. What was happening to me? I was at some kind of divide and it made my ribs hurt.

'Jack is not my bit of rough,' I said, in a voice as cool as pond water. 'But thank you for the information. I'll go and see him immediately. We have a crash in common. Is the dress safely back in the museum?'

'Yes,' said James. He paused, as if wondering whether to apologize. 'I've put your name forward for the reward. They forgot to mention it. They were so delighted to get the gown back.'

'What?'

'They put up a modest reward for the return of the dress. It's not a fortune, so don't go mad, but it should pay a few bills.'

He rang off before I could thank him.

I sank back in my chair. A reward, even a modest one, would save me from capsizing. Life was too complicated at times. And I wanted to buy Doris a present.

It was time for a walk, maybe even along the beach. I stumbled down the shingle and on to the wet sand. The tide was out, far out, nearly as far as France. It stretched seamlessly a long, long way. There was a nice crop of seaweed. The horizon was awash with mist and low-moving clouds like Gulliver's travelling islands. I could not see the Isle of Wight, or Beachy Head or anywhere in the distance. It had all disappeared. It would be easier to stack shelves in Safeways, or Waitrose, as it had now been renamed. I wanted a simpler life. Jordan, give up, crawl under a duvet and go to sleep.

But it was not to be. My existence was about to be shot to shreds. Tell me about it. Give me a warning. At least let me know when to duck.

The pier was on fire. I saw tendrils of black smoke, curling into the air, as if from the stacks of an ocean liner. The wisps were coming from the nightclub building at the end of the pier, above the anglers' double decking. The ship-styled premises were closed during the daytime. There might not be any staff about. It came to life around eleven p.m. when the youth of Latching converged en masse to consume vodka and dance to deafening music.

I shouted uselessly. I was half a mile away and only the gulls responded, rising in waves, flapping in protest. Thank goodness I had my reserve mobile with me. Sometimes I don't take it on walks, especially beach walks where I am prone to dropping it into the sea. Shopping list: another mobile. A second spare reserve.

'Jack, Jack!' I was still shouting.

'Jordan, babe...' he drawled. He recognized my voice. 'What's th'matter? Stuck under the pier again?'

'The pier is on fire. At the end where the nightclub is. I can see smoke coming from it.'

'OK, I've got it. You phone nine-nine-nine. I'll shut the arcade, evacuate the punters and go along to see if anyone is in the club. You never know. Someone might be sleeping off a heavy night. Bye, honey.'

He was so calm about it all. I had to hand it to him. I called 999 and was put through to Fire Services in the ten seconds that they advertised. They were very efficient. I could almost hear the sirens already.

I ran and jogged along the beach, my

breath coming in gasps, cutting my feet on sharp stones, not caring about the pain. My pier, my beloved pier was in danger. It had a long, chequered history. A disastrous storm in 1913, a fire in 1933. It had been blown up during the Second World War, then badly damaged again in a storm. And this was the second fire. There was so much new wood, new resin, all that new decking, everything was flammable.

And there was Jack's livelihood. The arcade was his whole life. He lived and breathed the clink of coins running down little gullets into his bank account.

Flames were licking round the outside of the nightclub, searing the paintwork, climbing the wooden façade, dancing along the upper walkway to the make-believe bridge. I could not see Jack anywhere. He'd gone into the nightclub.

I staggered up the shingle slope near the lido, pulling on my trainers, laces untied. The front area of the pavilion was already cordoned off. Four fire engines were parked on the promenade, hoses snaking along the pier.

'Sorry, miss. You are not allowed anywhere near the pier,' said a sturdy fireman, helmet obscuring his face.

'But my friend runs the arcade,' I began.

'I'm sure he has had the sense to leave the pier by now,' he said, waving back a group of gawping schoolboys. 'Get away, you lot.'

'He was going to the nightclub to see if anyone was there,' I gabbled on. 'He might be in danger.'

'I'm sure he'll have been escorted off by now.'

The tide was far out. There was no way I could climb the girders of the piers from the sand below. How did they know if Jack was safely out of the nightclub building?

I bit my lip. A sign of anxiety. I took a wander round the vehicles parked close up to the pier entrance, police and fire, cheek by jowl, a mass of vehicles and hoses and people. I was easily lost in the crowd.

No one noticed me cruising the fire tender cabs. I waved my notebook and said, 'Press.' It worked. I was now a reporter for some paper. You name it. The *Daily Whatsit*.

This astute reporter spotted a mauve flame-resistant jacket and yellow helmet under one of the driver's seats. It didn't fit but who cares about appearances at a time like this? I snapped the jacket fastening fast and pulled on the helmet, tucking my plait of hair out of sight.

'Let me through,' I said, shouldering through with authority. I was carrying a piece of equipment, also taken from the driver's cabin. Don't ask me what it was for. It could have been for sawing through steel.

I clomped along the pier, dodging the

hoses. The fire fighters were spraying the nightclub premises with four hoses. Flames were spluttering and throwing out sparks. The smoke was dense, billowing. My asthma protested. But they were keeping the fire back from the amusement arcade.

'Hello, I'm a reporter. Where's the owner of the arcade?' I shouted to whoever I thought was in charge.

'Who?'

'The chap who went into the nightclub to see if anyone was there. I know because he told me where he was going. Jack. I'm a reporter.'

'Don't know what you're talking about. We were not told about anyone going into the building.' The fireman looked genuinely bewildered. It was the uniform which confused him. 'Are you sure?'

'Jack, the owner, said he was going to see if anyone was asleep in the nightclub,' I insisted. 'I'm going in.'

'You stay out of this, miss. I'll go.'

Hero material. Follow hero time.

I followed the fire fighter because he was bulky and tall and knew what he was doing. I'm also tall but was totally at sea. If you can be at sea in a fire on a pier.

I tried to be macho and not cling on to his belt. But it was almost impossible to see in the swirling smoke. The southerly wind was not helping. The flames had not yet taken hold of the new decking, so we could walk on it but the heat was fierce. Inside the blackened building, glass windows were cracking and exploding. Bottles of alcohol were flying off the shelves. Flames were licking at the plastic seats, melting them.

'Bloody hell!' said the fireman. 'He's over there.'

Jack was crumpled in a corner between the bar and the disco area. He was barely breathing. The fireman dragged him out on to the decking and told me to use the oxygen apparatus I had with me. So that's what it was. I fumbled with the contraption, trying to remember my first-aid training.

We fed oxygen into Jack's lungs. He spluttered, coughed and started to breathe. We carried him away from the burning building on a makeshift stretcher made of a couple of deckchairs, his feet hanging off the end. He looked awful. He was not a handsome man in the best of circumstances, but now he looked even worse. No one took the slightest notice of me, which was how I wanted it.

Even James did not appear to recognize me. And he was there, investigating the possibility of arson probably. Yes, he was there. I backed off, helmet down.

'Cor, we would have missed him if it hadn't been for that reporter,' said the fireman.

'What reporter?' I heard James ask.

'That girl reporter. The one with reddish hair.'

'Oh, that reporter...' I could almost imagine the resigned sigh.

Fifteen

The paramedics slapped an oxygen mask on Jack. He was in good hands with the team at the head of the pier. I slipped away, helmet down to my eyebrows. It looked as if they were getting the fire under control. I didn't want to be shouted at and told to hold a hose or anything physical.

The pier was shrouded in smoke. The gulls abandoned it with wild flapping wings and assorted shrieks, rising above it like white ghosts. They keeled off towards Brighton's tower blocks and unpolluted air.

I started coughing. The smoke had got to my inflamed airways. I needed a whiff of Jack's oxygen and hung over the rail, hoping to find some clean sea breeze down below.

'Is there anything you won't do to be part of the action?' said DI James, sauntering alongside the rail. He was not looking at me, so I could not see if there was any concern in his eyes.

'I've just saved a man's life,' I said, choking on the words. 'I'm emotionally stressed out so don't h-hassle me.'

'See anything unusual there?'

'What do you mean, unusual? Are you talking arson?'

'Yes, I'm talking suspected arson. Jack is involved in the crash scam. They are not above removing a witness who might blow their lucrative trade. What did you see?'

This was not nice. They could have confused the nightclub with the amusement arcade. 'I saw smoke curling from the night-club when I was walking the beach, about half a mile away. I phoned nine-nine-nine and the amusement arcade but not in that order.'

'What an upright little citizen you are, Jordan.'

'I'm not that l-little...' I choked.

His hand came under my elbow and practically hoisted me off the rail. 'Let's get you out of here before you choke to death. And get this clobber off. Don't you know it's against the law, impersonating a fireman?'

I love it when he's masterful, but not in front of a hundred gawping spectators. I was not part of the show. If they wanted a soap, they could go home and watch the box.

'Did you know that spring is here and summer's a-coming?' I said, making ridiculously small talk as he hauled me to the front entrance of the pier. The tourists craned forward, their cameras clicking.

'Is that Wordsworth? I've no time for poetry,' he said. He stripped the fireproof jacket off me, removed the heavy helmet. My thick hair fell down, wet and tangled. 'I should charge you.'

'Oh, James,' I said, exasperated, at the end of my tether. Time went warped. 'Surely you've got better things to do? For goodness' sake, come down to earth. Concentrate on the real criminals, not a small seaside-town private investigator, trying to make an honest living and get ends to meet. How often do you have spaghetti without cheese sauce because you don't have any cheese? And you have a pension. Don't you know that I will help you, do anything that makes your job easier? I still have a lot of loyalty. I was a WPC, remember? Before they got rid of me for being too bloody honest.'

James looked completely taken aback by the tirade. His gaunt face was a picture. Confusion, guilt, concern. Yes, normal concern. I knew he had had a bad time with his ex-wife and the children. And I did not know the full story, but perhaps one day he would tell me. Like, bonfire night?

I think it was time he did.

'This fire,' I said, knowing first I had to see if Jack was all right in hospital or wherever. 'It's under control? Yes? So soon you will be off your shift and we can meet? Say yes, James, or forever hold your tongue.'

It was an ultimatum with a bit of Shakespeare thrown in for ballast.

'How can I resist such a poignant invitation?' he said, his control shifting. He was thinking on several levels. Half of him wanted to meet me, the other half was ducking the issue.

'Right then,' I said briskly. 'Eight p.m.? You pick me up, please, at my flat. If you phone, saying that something has cropped up, I won't know if you are telling the truth, or ducking out.'

DI James was looking at me as if he had never seen date rage before. How many years had we known each other? His face was plains of disbelief. 'You're a hard woman, Jordan Lacey. Eight p.m.'

I had a lot to do. It was race around the clock time and I did not feel too well. Asthma is an odd ailment. It can catch you at unexpected times. Most days I ignore it, stupid breathing. That was the best thing to do with asthma. But the smoke had been lethal. It could have been me being carried out on a deckchair.

I tried to inhale normally. You know, in and out, without hurrying. But my airways were in spasm.

Help.

My inhaler was back at the flat. I don't carry it on walks. The hospital would have some Salbutamol. But if I went to A and E, the hospital procedure would take hours, all those questions and doctors prodding and form filling. I hurried to the hospital, taking shortcuts along twittens, calming my breathing, and went in through the front entrance to the reception desk. Slight hiccup. I did not know Jack's surname.

'You know the fire on the pier...' I began. 'They've brought Jack in. He was rescued from the fire ... I wondered if he's all right, if he's recovering. Could you please find out?'

'You mean Jack from the amusement arcade? He's doing fine, wanting to go home already. Would you like to see him? Perhaps you could talk a little sense into him.'

'Is he ... is he injured at all?'

'I believe it's smoke inhalation. But they always keep them in overnight in such cases. Do you want to go up? He's in Churchill Ward on the first floor.'

'Thank you.'

I took the lift, not wanting to arrive out of breath and panting. Churchill Ward was at the end of the top corridor. As a staunch Labour voter, he would be fretting at the choice of ward. I knew it well and the smell of disinfectant and dying flowers. It was an eight-bed ward and one bed had blue curtains drawn round it. I could tell from the

215

indignant voice coming from behind the curtains who was in that bed.

'I'm not staying here, I'm telling you. I'm as right as rain and I've got my business to attend to. Those firemen could be wrecking everything with their hoses and their water. Some of those games machines are worth thousands. So I'll have my clothes back now, if you don't mind, miss.'

'Now be sensible, please. You are not in a fit state to go home. It would be very foolish to discharge yourself,' came a brisk, nursey voice. 'I'll get you a nice cup of tea.'

'If you weren't a lady, I'd tell you what you can do with your nice cup of tea.'

I found the curtain opening and went in. 'But I'd like a cup of tea, nurse,' I said. 'If you've time to bring two cups. I'll keep Jack company for a while.'

Jack had the oxygen mask under his chin instead of over his mouth. He was propped up in bed wearing one of those awful hospital gowns that tie at the back. No wonder he wanted his own clothes back. All dignity disappears with those hospital gowns.

He looked at me, aghast, as if I'd found him stark naked. He probably went to bed in his underclothes and only washed them when they were too stiff to move in. He pulled the candlewick coverlet up to his chin.

'Jordan, babe,' he said huskily.

The huskiness was the clue. He had inhaled smoke and the treatment was under his chin.

'Put that mask back on, Jack,' I said, slipping on to a chair near the bed. 'Don't be daft. You need a few puffs of oxygen.'

'What are you doing here?' he asked.

'I've come to see how you are, you idiot. I think you're now classed a hero. You went into the nightclub to rescue someone, didn't you?'

'I'd seen a girl ... a woman, I mean, but I'd thought nothing of it. Their cleaners come and go at all times. Or perhaps she worked behind the bar...'

He started coughing and I had to insist, actually force him to put the mask back on over his mouth and nose. He was clearly distressed by my presence during what he regarded as a humiliating experience, a chip in his masculinity. So I retreated, giving him his privacy.

'I'll go and see where that tea is,' I said. 'That nurse must have gone to pick the leaves in India.'

I wandered about along the echoing corridor and found the nurses' station. She was talking to another nurse, the two cups of tea cooling on a tray. I hate lukewarm tea.

'Shall I take the tea?' I offered brightly. 'I can see you're busy.'

'Thanks. I've just been called down to A

and E. Another car accident. Latching seems to have an epidemic of cars crashing into each other. This is the third this week.'

'Is it serious?' I asked.

'I hope not,' she said.

I took the tray from her and went back to Jack's cubicle. The curtains were still drawn. I did not open them, thinking Jack would prefer anonymity. He had cultivated his macho arcade image for years. Being in bed, wearing only an open-backed gown, was severely denting that image.

'The tea's cold,' I said.

'I don't drink tea,' he said, removing the mask. 'I only drink coffee. My coffee.'

'If you promise to put that mask back on, I will try and find some coffee for you. Is that a promise?'

'You're a star,' he said, closing his eyes.

I found a coffee machine on the floor below. It dispensed the kind of coffee Jack would like. It was so hot I could hardly hold the beaker. I wrapped a handkerchief round the beaker in case I was heading for the burns unit. Jack appeared grateful. I'd even remembered to lace it with double sugar.

'Brill, girl,' he said, the old light coming back into his eyes. 'You know how to treat a man.'

That was the sad thing ... I did not know how to treat him, because he was not right for me. Jack was a friend, a very good friend, and would never be anything more. He lived in hope that a meteor would enter the earth's atmosphere, knock me senseless and into his arms. Some hope.

We talked fire, then small puppies for sale, then the world at large. Jack was more at ease now, drinking coffee, putting on the mask, forgetting his backless state. He was enjoying my undivided company. I had almost talked him into staying overnight.

'I'll go lock up for you,' I said. 'I can do that.'

'There's a security code,' he said reluctantly.

'I know that,' I said. 'It's Fort Knox, Latching, on the pier. You can trust me with the code for tonight surely, then change it tomorrow if you want to. Trust me. No sweat. Jack, be sensible for once. You need to stay overnight so that they can check you out. What use will it be if you rush out and then collapse halfway to the pier?'

'You'll do it properly?' he asked. 'Like I would. All the codes and everything? Leave the money in the kiosk.'

'Don't you trust me, Jack? Would I promise something that I wouldn't do? Give me a break. I'm not an idiot.'

'I know that,' he said, whipping off the mask and grabbing my hand with the same movement. It caught me by surprise. I could hardly snatch my hand away. After all, the man was a patient in a hospital bed.

His hand was rough, calloused, and his nails uncut. Bitten on some fingers. Imagine those hands on my soft skin. It was enough to send one to the nearest convent and start banging on the doors.

'So tell me the code and give me your keys,' I said, letting my hand rest in his, unfeeling. I was a martyr, an angel. St Peter, are you watching? Writing it down in your ledger?

'The keys are in me jeans. They're in that locker. Then you'll have to come close while I whisper the code. I don't want nobody hearing it.'

Everybody, the entire Churchill ward, was dozing in bed or half comatose. They wouldn't have cared if he was giving me the winning lottery numbers.

'OK. Before I go, give me a whiff of your oxygen. Thanks.'

I took a taxi back to my bedsits. I was that desperate. It was nearing eight p.m. and I had a date. A date with my soulmate, heart to heart time, but now I had an errand to do and James would have to come with me.

I stood under the shower for two minutes to rid my body of the smoke smell, hospital smell, dried briskly for another minute, dressed in one minute. Clean jeans and underwear, black shirt, black fleece sweater, newest trainers and a silky scarf. I looked like a candidate for a Mafia recruitment parade. The last remaining minute I spent on my face and hair. Mascara and grey eye-shadow. My hair bunched up with a velvet scrunchie. Do I hold the record for fast changes?

'You look very nice,' said James at the door. 'Your hair is wet.'

'It was a quick make-over,' I said. 'I'll tell you on the way to the pier.'

'We have a date on the pier?' He looked bemused.

'I promised Jack I would lock up for him. He's given me his keys and his code. Major trust in return for staying overnight in hospital.'

'Then lock up the arcade we must,' said James, leading me to his car. 'Major trust is one of the most important aspects of life. Drinking copious red wine can wait.'

It is during these brief, sweet moments that I love him to distraction. There are not many of them and they have to be savoured. Sometimes he knows exactly the right thing to say.

The drive to the pier was minimal, but I was glad not to be walking. The firemen were clearing up, the blaze now out, charred timbers still steaming and the stench of fire everywhere. It looked as if the fire had been contained to one corner of the nightclub.

The crowds had dispersed. All the fun over.

'You realize that you would not even be allowed on the pier without my authority,' said James, opening the passenger door for me. 'The pier is off-limits until it's been checked for safety.'

'If you say so,' I said demurely.

'Let's go lock up.'

The decking had been checked and declared sound, so it was safe to walk to the amusement arcade. The premises were not damaged but they smelled of smoke and the floor was wet.

Jack had said nothing about counting or removing the money in his cubicle, so I made sure the door was fast and left the bags of change hidden behind the bullet-proof glass. We locked the back entrance doors, keyed in the security code and then left by the front entrance, keying in a different code. It was a smooth operation.

'If you ever decide to leave the force, I could offer you a job,' I said facetiously. 'The pay is not good but the perks are brilliant.'

'I may take you up on that, Jordan. You see, I am being offered a transfer to Yorkshire and I may not like it there.' He was looking straight ahead, concentrating on the jam of traffic leaving Latching. He always drove well. It was one of the things that I liked about him. No road rage, no fuss, always competent, professional driving.

I did not remember much of the leafy journey to the Gun at Findon. Yorkshire? That was somewhere up north with wild and wet moors. I would never see him again. It was hundreds of miles away. The news was shattering. I did not know how to talk normally.

'That's great for you,' I began, babbling. 'Promotion, of course?' He nodded. 'Congratulations. A few more steps to chief superintendent. You are going to take it, aren't you?'

'There's nothing to keep me down here,' he said.

Knife in the ribs.

The rest of the evening was a blur. I was nothing to keep him down here. I don't remember what I said or how many glasses of wine I drank. It was a good wine, fruity and rich. James was not drinking. He looked at me curiously.

'What did you want to talk to me about?' he asked.

'I think it's too late now and anyway I've forgotten,' I said. 'You're leaving. We probably won't meet again.'

'It's never too late,' he said.

'I wanted to know about your wife,' I went on, not caring anymore whether it sounded callous or blunt. 'I want to know what happened, what has made you so bitter, so against women. It must have been something awful.'

His face went grey. I was sorry that I had spoken.

'It was something I want to forget,' he said slowly. 'Awful is not the right word.'

'Then let's forget it,' I said, gulping down more wine. 'It's none of my business. Another juice? It's my round.' I pulled out a fiver, knowing I would never forget this moment. It was even a clean note.

'She took my children and gassed them in the car,' he said, looking at a wall across the room. 'And then she gassed herself. The exhaust method, you know. Pipe through the window. It wasn't necessary. I would have let them go to her, willingly, to let them live, but she was possessed by some demon. She did not want me to have them or see them. My children, my two young sons. They were in their pyjamas. She carried them out to the car. I would have done anything to save them, given her anything. But she did not even give me the choice. She took them with her, without telling anyone. And she took away all that I have ever really loved.'

His face was without expression, stony, a grey sphere.

I was stunned, shocked. It explained every-thing. I did not know what to say, went cold. I could not even touch him. He was in a world of misery that I could not enter. James ... James.

'I know that sometimes I have been less than kind to you,' he went on, turning his glass. 'Sometimes it must have seemed cruel, a pointless cruelty. I'm sorry, Jordan. You are always so bright and bubbly and it was more than I could stand. You had no right to be so happy and content with your life. I wanted to make you suffer in some way. Sorry.'

'I didn't know,' I said, my voice subdued. 'If you had told me earlier, I would have understood.'

'How could I tell anyone? I wanted to take it out on someone.'

'Well, thanks buster,' I said, trying to normalize the level of conversation. 'It worked. You did upset me, often. And I've always wanted to know why. But it's OK now. I don't mind anymore. You can have a go at me anytime you like.' I made an offer. 'I'll try to be less bubbly.'

A shadow of a smile touched his mouth, that curved mouth. 'Don't you dare, Jordan. You stay the same sweet, zany person. Many times you've saved me from the depths of hell.'

'Me?'

'By doing or trying out something so idiotic that I have had to laugh. It works every time. Even rescuing you from disasters is therapeutic. Carry on bubbling.'

'Bumbling?'

'Both. Can you still say bumbling? I don't

know if I should buy you another wine. I think you've had enough. I doubt if you can stand. You're swaying sitting down.'

'That's not fair...' I began, but James stopped me with a hand on my arm. His eyes said don't move.

'Don't look now, but a couple have just come in. They are both wearing neck braces. The woman is leaning heavily on a walking stick.'

'Is there a young girl with them? A daughter perhaps?' I tried to swivel my eyes without craning my neck.

'No, no daughter. But there's another man with them who sells dubious second-hand cars and faked guarantees. He's well known for it in Sussex. We've had tabs on him for months.'

'Is it the famous car-crashing couple, Mr and Mrs Derek Brook? Victims of yet another appalling roundabout accident?' I asked, wishing I could see.

'Can you identify any of them without too much obvious staring?' said James.

'Of course, I don't stare obviously,' I said. I took a mirror out of my bag and touched up my straggling hair, looking at the reflection behind me. I saw Derek Brook and his female partner or wife, then I froze. The shock was from seeing an old terror emerge in reflection.

I controlled the panic. I was with James.

Nothing could happen. It was the person with them, the dubious car dealer. He was the man from the Sow's Head. The man with a knife. The thug who swore to cut me up.

Sixteen

'I know that man,' I said, without taking my eyes away from the mirror. A shiver went through me, slicing nerve ends.

'Derek Brook?'

'Yes him, but particularly the other one. The man you said has a dodgy second-hand car business. He also has a very nasty temper, as I know only too well.'

'Is he the one who attacked you with a knife and cut your hand? You were supposed to be meeting someone about a puppy at the Sow's Head when he appeared?' James had a knack of being able to watch without turning his head. The pub only saw a man enjoying a drink with a woman friend. But I could sense the alertness, not missing a trick.

I nodded, putting away the mirror, apparently satisfied with my appearance.

'Are you sure?'

'I'd know that face anywhere.'

'You couldn't describe him very well right

after the incident. Yet now you say that you'd know that face anywhere.'

'It's the whole of him,' I insisted. 'Not only his face. The feeling of malevolence. The whole evil thing.'

'I'd better make a note of that,' said James with heavy sarcasm. 'The whole evil thing...'

'You must know what I mean, James. You've seen enough criminals, big and small-time crooks.'

'And some are little old ladies that you would trust with your last penny, who can use their knitting needles like sabres.'

'That's him, anyway,' I said, gulping down more wine. A voice in my head told me that I had had enough to drink, but I didn't seem to care any more. Yorkshire ... how on earth was I going to get to see James? It was difficult enough when he only lived a couple of miles away. I couldn't see myself driving up to Yorkshire on his days off. The depth of my affection was about two inches when it came to negotiating motorway signs.

'Do you want to charge him?'

'What with? Waving a knife at me? No, I want to forget it and him. Don't do anything, please, James. Let him go.'

'I can't believe you're saying this, Jordan. You can't be serious. That man was going to attack you. He might attack someone else.'

'But I got away and he didn't get a chance. So you can hardly charge him with intent.'

'I could and I would. He had a knife.'

'Perhaps he was going to sharpen a pencil.'

'They're moving. They're leaving. Jordan, I'm going to call for assistance. We can't do this on our own. They could split off. Can you get yourself home? I'll call a taxi.'

'I'm coming with you,' I said, as sober as a High Court judge suddenly. I drank the rest of his glass of orange juice. 'I'm good on surveillance. Pretend we are a couple, an item. Put your arm round me and I'll gaze up into your eyes with adoration. Make like we are heading for the car park and some serious snogging.'

'Snogging? I'm surprised at you, Jordan. Where did you learn such language?'

James put his arm round me as if he had been doing it all his life. It felt so right. I could smell his scent. Not just aftershave and deodorant, but the smell of his body. I tucked myself against his arm as if I was tailored to fit. We walked out of the pub, eyes only for each other. I could dream.

'Keep walking,' said James.

'Will they recognize your car as a police vehicle?'

'No. It's my own car. No police marking.'

'Shall we get in then? You'll have to pretend to kiss me.'

Any moment I was going to wake up. This must be a dream. Smoke inhalation might have induced hallucinations. If so, I liked this one. James might not kiss me with intent but I was going to kiss him. I was good at my job.

I had barely noticed the make of his car, only that it was fairly new and a dark navy, some silver touches somewhere. A line, like a streak of moonlight. It was tidy inside, not a sign of litter, no crumpled crisp packets or beer cans. Quite different to the casual dis-order inside Marchmont Tower.

He had to sit beside me in the car because he was still the driver. It was dark and leathery. Neither of us knew what to do next. All my good intentions evaporated. There was no way I could kiss him now. He was remote, but then he turned and smiled at me, that funny smile.

'Not so easy, is it, Jordan?'

'I'm no good at this.'

He leaned over in the darkness. 'I think you are very good at this,' he said.

Then he kissed me. And it was all sweet-ness and warmth. I floated away into some starlit sky where angels sang and cherubs played harps. Or was it a soft blues jazz player taking a melody up into another octave, higher than the one before, finding notes that radiated emotion and joy.

Could a kiss really mean so much? One single, light kiss on the mouth? But it was James and his mouth was firm and sensitive, something I had dreamed about for years.

The touch of skin on skin was feather-light, warm and soft, but there was a sincerity that was unmistakable. The cover was blown. This was for real. My arms crept around his neck.

For a moment my cheek rested against his cheek and I could breath him in. I felt the brush of an eyelash. It was like a whisper that can barely be heard. Any moment now I was going to kiss him again.

But then he moved and the moment was gone. We were back into the woods. We were sliding down to earth, not in harness but two separate people. I felt tears welling in my eyes. I'm such a softie.

'Don't cry, Jordan,' he said, touching my cheek.

'Sorry,' I said. 'I don't get kissed very often.'

'I don't believe that,' he said. 'You have a string of admirers from Latching pier to South America.'

'They can admire but not touch,' I said, quite unable to explain these unusual relationships. 'They are my friends.'

'Loving friends, I think perhaps.'

Loving friendship ... that's what I wanted from James. I wanted him to be a loving friend. The phrase was near perfect. It summed up all I ever wanted from this man.

'We are supposed to be following a dodgy car salesman,' I said, arriving back to earth

231

with a bump.

'The two men are coming out of the pub, but without the woman. Careful, Jordan. Don't let them see you.' He pulled me close to him, holding my face against his shoulder, but there was no affection now. It was purely professional. We were a team on surveillance, acting a part. I could go along with that.

'Are they going separate ways?'

'No. They are getting into the same car.' He was watching them over my shoulder. My nose was buried in his neck. I hoped he would not get mascara on his shirt. It was hard to wash out.

The other car, a red Suzuki, began to ease out of the pub car park. We waited, not wanting to be observed. James made a quick call on his mobile, repeating his request for back-up. The Suzuki turned right and James immediately shot his car into gear and we were away. To where, I did not know. I didn't care. He could have driven me to the moon, craters and all.

I put on a pair of tinted glasses. James looked at me without comment. It was a token cover.

The other car began to head towards Brighton using the back roads route. A rabbit's eyes were caught in the glare of the headlights. The little creature froze, half hidden in the grass verge, ambushed by the sudden spate of traffic.

'Brighton isn't your patch,' I said.

'Let me take care of that.'

'I'm not sure why we are following them.'

'The fake crashes, remember? We may find where the cars used in the crashes are kept. They may lead us to a garage or repair workshop, wall to wall with old bangers that can be crashed without compunction. They get these cars from somewhere. They're not stolen vehicles. The paperwork is bona fide. They may even get patched up after a crash and used again. It's the insurance claims that are suspect.'

I was barely listening. 'Will you get promotion if you move to Yorkshire?' I asked.

'Yes. It's a step up.'

'You'll need a stick.'

'What?'

'To help you up the next step.'

'Don't talk such nonsense. Watch where they are going and tell me. This is the outskirts of Portslade. We could easily lose them in these backstreets.'

'I don't know this area at all,' I said, peering along the rows of terraced Edwardian houses. They were solid and well built, although with run-down gardens, many cemented over for parking. The Suzuki had slowed. James stopped and let another car overtake. He did not want to be too close. He kept the engine running, pretending he was consulting a street map.

The Suzuki was turning into a yard next to a double-fronted grey-stone Victorian villa with tall windows and an impressively pillared porch, but close to a line of shabby lock-up garages that had been built in its garden. There was hardly an inch of grass left. A few straggling shrubs struggled for survival in the remaining patches of earth. Some moron had gravelled over the entire garden.

James put the car into reverse and eased back a few houses into the shadowy darkness between street lights. I released the seat belt and waited for instructions. Something was going on. I could sense it. There was an uneasy gloom, undeclared and unnamed, that seeped out of the barrenness of the house.

'What do you want me to do?' I asked.

'Nothing. Sit tight. We'll wait till back-up arrives.'

'But they might get away. We ought to have a look round and see what's going on. The curtains aren't drawn. I could have a look. We might catch them red-handed at something.'

'Catch them at what? Dividing the spoils between them? Don't be daft, Jordan. Even if the lock-up garages are full of old cars, we can't prove anything until one of them is in another crash.'

'At least we could take the registration numbers and run them through police

234

computers.'

'They probably change the plates.'

I was starting to fidget. Something was happening in that house and I wanted to know what it was. Waiting outside was not going to produce any evidence. I wanted to know if there was a daughter, another wife, people hobbling about with injuries.

I knew why I was fidgeting. It was all that wine. My body was protesting at the heaviness of the liquid and wanted to relinquish the burden. Oh dear, this was hardly the time to tell James that I needed to find a loo. But although my control is excellent, I could not last forever.

'James...' I began.

'There was a pub on the corner further back. Be quick and don't look at the house.'

I was out in a flash, slinging my bag over my shoulder. The night air was cold and I didn't have a coat. The street was empty and I hurried towards the lights of the pub. A sign swung eerily over the door, depicting another Rose and Crown. I pushed open the door with relief.

A few people were leaning on the bar, talking and drinking in a smoky haze, their voices low and muffled. It was not busy. The fire in the grate was smouldering coals, not enough to warm the place. I nodded at the landlord as he wiped the counter with a cloth. I bought a bottle of sparkling water and a packet of cheese and bacon crisps. He charged the earth. Perhaps that was why the pub was half empty.

'Meeting someone,' I said, heading for the loos.

The toilets were shabby and running out of paper. The hot-air dryer didn't work. But I would have been thankful for a hole in the ground. As I washed my hands and shook the water off, I moved towards the doorway to the bar. A man was buying a bottle of whisky over the counter. I recognized him instantly and cringed back as if adjusting my clothes, brushing specks of nothing off my shoulders.

He paid the landlord and went out, the bottle tucked under his arm.

My instincts were to stay close. I knew something was going to happen. Perhaps he and Brook were organizing another fake car crash right now. Maybe the woman was painting an ivory foundation on to her cheeks and hollowing under her eyes with a faint smudge of bluey-grey shadow.

I untwisted the scarf from round my neck and tied it over my hair, tucking most of it out of sight. I slipped outside and crossed over the road, as if home was in a different direction. James's car was still parked ahead but he was not in the driving seat. That was strange. I tried a bouncy new walk, a hurry-home-to-Eastenders sort of walk, swinging the water and the crisps.

I passed the Brook house and went on further up the road. The man with the whisky had gone inside, a burst of light lit up the front door as it opened, and then darkness again. A light went on in a downstairs room and someone drew the curtains. I wanted to know what was going on. There was no sign of DI James. Where was he?

This was time for action, despite the worry. Without stopping to think what I was going to say, I went back to the villa and walked up the front path. I rang the bell. It sounded shrill and cheap. The door opened.

The man stood there, still in his outdoor coat. I tried not to look at his face, but concentrated on the second button lower on his shirt.

'Hello,' I said cheerfully. 'Have you been at the pub? The landlord told me he'd given you the wrong change.'

'What change?' the man growled.

'He didn't give you enough,' I prattled on. 'He was distracted by something and didn't give you enough change. So, as I was passing, he asked me to drop by with it.'

I rattled a handful of change. 'I only live up the road, so it was no problem for me. This is a lovely house, isn't it? I've always admired it from the outside. Is it very old? Looks old.'

'It's Victorian,' he said. 'All the houses in this road are Victorian.'

'Well, I'm no expert.'

'Want a quick look round?' he offered. 'The rooms downstairs ... my brother and his wife won't mind. It's their house.'

'Oh, I'm terribly sorry, I didn't know.'

'Come on in.' He opened the door further. 'I've got a minute.' I could not bear the thought of seeing this man again, but I'd started it so I had to go on. He stepped back as I went in.

'Just a very quick look then,' I said merrily.

I admired the high ceilings and the dentil cornices and original wood doors and marble fireplaces. It was well furnished. Insurance money? I looked around without really looking, anxious to get out now. This was not a good idea. A small controlled panic was starting inside me. A girl was bent over her homework at a gate-legged table. She looked about fourteen.

'My niece,' he said. 'Always studying.'

'She's got the right idea,' I said. And I knew without a doubt that she had not been in the car in that roundabout crash. She was a tall gawky fourteen-year-old with lots of floppy fair hair and not easy to miss.

'Hello,' I said. 'What's your name?'

'Miranda.'

'That's pretty. And what school do you go to?'

'It's a convent actually.'

'There's an original Victorian sundial out

in the back garden,' the man interrupted. 'I could show it to you.'

'Oh don't worry about that,' I said. There was no sign of Mr or a Mrs Brook. I was starting to get anxious. I was alone in this house with a fourteen-year-old girl and a maniac with a knife tendency. I needed to get out. 'It's too dark to go outside. Thank you very much. I'd better be going. My husband will be wondering where I am,' I added for good measure. I wanted to say he was a six-foot-two, black-belt judo-fighting fireman, but thought that might be overdoing it.

'Won't take a sec. I've got a torch.'

'Just a quick look then...'

I followed him out into the back garden. It was unkempt and untidy, with a few straggling overhead branches and perimeter shrubs. I couldn't see any sundial or garden.

It happened so quickly, I didn't have a chance to fight or yell. My arms were pulled behind me and my head pushed down. Another pair of hands yanked up my knees so I was off my feet and crushed between two men like a sandwich. I heard the clang of a boot lid opening and I was being bundled inside, head first.

I started yelling and shouting. A hand clapped over my mouth.

The lid clanged shut. I struggled around and began banging on the inside with my clenched fists.

'Let me out!' I yelled. 'Let me out. What's this all about? You're making a terrible mistake.'

'You made the mistake, sister.' The man was jeering now. 'You see, I gave the landlord the right money for the whisky, so there weren't no change. Got it?'

They were talking but I couldn't hear what they were saying. I stopped drumming for a moment and tried to listen.

'Is that the one?'

'Yes, that's the one. She's been making enquiries, I'm sure. At the hospital and everything, Nina said, asking questions. Too bloody nosy for my liking.'

'Far too nosy. Let's take her for a little ride, somewhere nice and quiet. See how she likes it.'

The car jolted forward and I was thrown against the lid. It hurt.

Seventeen

It was a nightmare journey of panic and fear. I was thrown from side to side in the small space, joggled against rope and boxes and tools, all the usual junk carried in boots. I'd given up yelling and banging, conserving the oxygen. I tried prising open the boot from the inside but it was a waste of time and energy. I could hardly breathe. The shuttered air was petrol-fumed and stale.

There was no way I could tell where we were going. I tried memorizing turns and traffic lights but got confused. We had left Brighton and the main roads and were speeding along lanes, some very bumpy. Once I thought I heard water, river water, not the sea. We might be nearing Arundel.

And where was James? I tried using my mobile but could not get a signal. They would take it from me if they knew I had one. I could hardly hide it in my bra or jeans. The bottle of water and crisps were miraculously still with me. There was an old crumpled Safeways carrier bag under the rope and I put all three in the bag, the phone

241

underneath. I groped about and added a pair of pliers, some wire and a handful of rusty nails. They might come in useful but I could hardly make a bomb out of them.

Cramp was knotting my twisted legs. I rubbed the hardened muscles, my head down, brow damp with perspiration, sweat trickling down between my breasts. I could barely move for the excruciating pain. I didn't care where we were going as long as I got out soon before my legs were paralysed.

It seemed like a good thirty minutes of agony. It could have been fifteen. I'd lost all sense of time.

The car turned into a short driveway and slowed down. I heard the mechanism of a garage door opening automatically and the car inching inside. I braced myself for what might be ahead. Bluff was on my side.

The boot opened and the air was almost sweet. I could smell river again. It must be the Arun. They heaved me out and I folded down on to the ground, quite helpless, unable to stand. My legs were not working. They lifted me up in the half light, dragging me indoors and then down some wooden stairs, my feet clomping on every step. It smelt damp. I held on to the plastic carrier bag as if my life depended on it, as it did. They were in too much of a hurry to notice my luggage.

'Get her down here.'

'Is she conscious?'

'Hardly. Her eyes are closed.'

I closed my eyes.

'She needs air.'

'Don't worry. There's enough air.'

'We don't want her dying on us.'

'She won't die. She's a tough cookie.'

They threw me on to a damp stone floor, my head hitting some boxes. I sprawled in whatever pose I landed, the bag hidden under me. Crushed crisps. My face was against something hard. This was hardly the Holiday Inn.

'What are we going to do with her?'

'Dunno. Let me think about it. We don't want her interfering no more. No more snooping around, asking awkward questions.'

I heard their footsteps retreating up the steps and a door slamming and being bolted. Darkness descended on me. There was no light, not a glimmer. I squeezed my eyes and tried to find some light from somewhere. It was imperative that I could see what I was doing and where I was.

The cramp gradually retreated as I was able to stretch my legs. The relief was an oasis of calm. My breathing eased too. It was a moment of tranquility before the next nightmare began.

I began to explore the area, feeling around. It was a wood and stone cellar, about five foot square, somewhere near a river. Maybe one of those old warehouses along the riverbank that had been converted into desirable flats. I felt along every wall and crevice, looking for a means of escape. I could just stand up. There was a very small trapdoor in the sloping roof, hardly big enough to push a cat through. I could not see the purpose of such a small trapdoor. I had a go at it with the pliers, hacking at the wood round the hinge, and managed to open it. The night air was beautiful, a dancing sense of space. There was even a star, winking at me. I drank in deep gulps before moving on.

Yes, the river was flowing quite near, dark water and gentle. I imagined I saw the ghostly shapes of swans, homeward bound to some sanctuary.

There was no way I could get out of the trapdoor. It was far too small. I could barely force my head out. I slid back to the floor and had a drink of water and ate four crisps. It was WWII ration time. The cheese and bacon flavour was more-ish but I knew how to discipline myself. They had to last.

DI James. I still had the mobile phone. I climbed on to a crate and held the phone out of the trapdoor up into the night air. I got a signal. The relief was overwhelming. The tears arrived but I wiped them away.

'James?' I said after keying his number.

'Where the hell are you?' he snapped.

'I don't exactly know. Sorry. I'm in a cellar, somewhere near a river. Locked in.'

'Are you all right?'

'Not exactly.'

'Why didn't you come back to the car?'

'I did, but you weren't there. I couldn't see you.'

There was a grim silence. I heard him clear his throat. My heart steeled itself against further recriminations but none came.

'I was checking the cars in the lock-ups at the back. There are some interesting number plates. Several have been involved in accidents.'

'Good, well done. Time not wasted then,' I said hurriedly. 'But what about me? I'm being held prisoner.'

'Stick with it, girl...'

This was a different voice. Apparently a former colleague incarcerated in a cellar somewhere in West Sussex was somewhere on his list of priorities.

'Are you in any danger?' he went on. 'Can you wait?'

'How do I know if I am?' I hissed. 'Those two evil men brought me here, angry that I am being too nosey, want to put a decisive end to my enquiries. So what do you think? Are they going to slap my wrists and send me home without any supper?'

'Can you get out?'

'Not unless I lose at least a stone in the

next ten minutes. There's a trapdoor above but it's only phone-size.'

'Can you barricade yourself into the cellar so that no one can drag you out? It'll take us some time to track down your signal.'

'There's some wood and boxes lying about and I have some nails I took from the boot of the car.'

'Are you sure you are in danger? I don't really have the resources for this.'

I nearly blew a gasket. 'I'm a rate-paying citizen. I was kidnapped, thrown into the boot of a car, bundled in with excessive force and am now locked in a cellar against my will. If that doesn't warrant some of your resources ... but, of course, if they had gone through a couple of speed cameras, parked on a double yellow line, half the force would be down on their heels by now.'

'I don't make the rules,' said James grimly.

'But you interpret them.'

'To a degree.'

'Isn't that why you are being promoted?'

It was below the belt. James was always fair, had come to my rescue many times. Long, long ago. But I was crippled by disappointment and was working myself up into a terrible temper. This sort of passion is dangerous. I knew I would regret it but there was no control left to me in this cellar-based abyss.

'I could send out a patrol car with a

tracking device. They can follow a mobile phone signal these days, as long as your battery lasts.'

'Yes, I do want you to send out a patrol car. Yes, I do want you to find me before I am hacked up and dumped in the river. Yes, I demand my rights.'

'I'll contact Arundel. They might be nearer. Meanwhile, do what you can to barricade yourself in. And put something out of the trapdoor that can be spotted easily.'

'OK, like I always carry around a Union Jack.'

'Ring off now but leave the phone switched on. You've got to conserve your battery.'

This was where the wire came in useful. I twisted it round my mobile and put it outside on the cellar roof, attached firmly to the catch which I had broken with the pliers. I levered open some of the boxes. It was impossible to tell in the faint patch of moonlight what was inside, but I did find a bundle of books.

Now it goes against my literary grain to tear up books. All that hard work. The sweat and tears of the author burning his particular midnight lubrication. But my need was the greater.

I found the whitest non-print pages and tore them out and stuck them on a wire spike like receipts in an old-fashioned office. It had a Christmas tree look. Then I put the arrangement outside the trapdoor and some-how fixed it upright, or almost upright. It leaned over like a paper Tower of Pisa. I hoped it would last a few hours before the wind blew it away. My reward for ingenuity was four more crisps and a gulp of water.

I was clambering down when I heard the bolt being shot back. I fell into a huddled heap on the floor, hoping they would not notice the open trapdoor above.

'Water, water,' I moaned faintly.

The two men were standing at the top of the steps. One was Derek Brook and the other my attacker from the Sow's Head.

'What are we going to do with her?'

'Get rid of her. She knows too much.'

'How do we know what she knows? She might have been asking questions for a different reason.' This was Derek Brook. He sounded reluctant to get rid of me. 'It's only guesswork on our part.'

'Look, mate. We got a nice little craft going. You and the missus and the girlie daughter. We've made a quarter of a million this year already, bought two houses. Who knows what we'll make next year? Then you can retire to that villa in Spain that you own. And I'll be off to Las Vegas.'

'But you said nothing about killing anyone, Les.'

Ah, a name at last.

'Who said I was going to kill her? How

about a few little minor alterations to her head so that she can't remember anything? They got nice homes for people like that these days, and if you feel generous now and again, you could send them a donation.' Les chuckled but there was no mirth in it.

'Water, water...' I said again feebly.

'I don't like this at all,' said Derek Brook, retreating. 'This is going too far.' I heard his footsteps going somewhere and then the sound of a tap gushing upstairs. He came back with a glass of water and knelt beside me.

'Drink this,' he said.

I drank. 'Thank you,' I murmured with a degree of shaking. 'Why am I here? Please t-tell me, mister. I've d-done nothing wrong. I don't even know you. You've got the wrong person. I've never seen you before.'

'You've been following us,' said Derek. 'In a car.'

'Me?' I coughed and spluttered. 'I been at Tesco's all day, the big one on the main road. I work there, shift work. I'm in supplies, stack shelves. You can check on it. I ain't been in no car.' My voice rose a few octaves, very Eliza Doolittle. This was Oscar role-playing.

'She's lying,' said Les, at the top of the steps.

'We could check it out.'

'This is the girl, I tell yer. I've seen her

before somewhere. I'm not stupid. She's trying to fool us.'

'Believe me, guvnor, you got the wrong girl,' I sobbed. 'Lemme go home and I'll say nuffing about this.'

'I think we ought to be careful. We might have the wrong girl,' said Derek Brook, sitting back on his heels. 'I don't like it.'

'Didn't she come to the house with this cock and bull story about change from the pub?'

'Perhaps she mixed you up with someone else. Easily done, in the dark. She's not very bright. Maybe there was some other chap buying whisky.'

'Sometimes I wonder who is the brains of this outfit,' said Les, clearly irritated. 'Leave her. We're late already. The traffic is piling up. We'll deal with her when we come back.'

They shut the door and bolted it again. Les obviously didn't recognize me from the Sow's Head episode, which was a blessing. I'd been wearing the big hair-do and slinky dress. I felt light with relief. *We're late already.* They were due somewhere else. I had time to barricade myself in.

I heard a car drive off and silence descended. They had gone. Was it to fake another crash, a multiple crash?

I pulled down my mobile and keyed in James's number. It clicked to answerphone. 'They have gone out to fake another crash,'

I said clearly. 'They said they were due somewhere, as if it was planned.'

'Roger,' said James, breaking in. 'We'll follow up.'

At least I had done something useful.

My attempts to barricade myself were pathetic. The nails were bent and wouldn't go into the wood. I hauled boxes up the steps and put them against the door but they wouldn't stop a mouse. A diagonal plank propped against the door might delay them for a minute. That minor alteration to my brain did not sound at all pleasant. My brain was my own business.

In another box I found an old battery radio. It wasn't working. But then I found an alarm clock and the battery out of that fitted the radio and lo and behold, we had a station with a tinny, clamorous noise. It was foreign-sounding, blaring out music and foreign voices gabbling in a dozen tongues. I stuck it outside the trapdoor on the roof, wedging it with a bit of wood so that it did not slide down.

I rewarded myself with some more crisps, drank a little water, wondered what else I could do. I was starting to shake for real. It was very damp in the cellar. Water was seeping through the floor bricks. Was the river tidal? There was nothing to wrap round me for warmth.

Perhaps this was the end of Jordan Lacey.

Years loomed ahead in a home for the mentally retarded. My shop would gather dust until the lease ran out and then the stock would be sold or given away. My friends would wonder where I had gone. Doris and Mavis would be bewildered and baffled by my sudden disappearance. I hoped my ladybird would go to a good home. Thank goodness I didn't have a cat.

I was sitting in the dark, helpless, angry and weepy. It was some minutes before I was aware that people were clambering about outside and banging on things. Someone banged on the cellar roof.

'Is anybody there?' a voice called out. It sounded miles away.

'Of course I'm here, I'm here,' I yelled, coming to life. I stood up, clumsily, almost falling over as I got to my feet. 'I'm in here, down here, in the cellar.'

I stuck my hand out of the trapdoor and waved it about frantically. Suddenly a big hand caught mine and held it firmly. 'Don't worry, miss. We'll get you out of there.'

I heard them breaking down doors and then battering the cellar door. My barricade held up pretty well. It took several minutes before it gave in.

I couldn't move. I was quivering like a half-set jelly. DI James was kicking debris out of the way as he came down the steps, flooded in light from upstairs. He looked pale and dishevelled.

'I didn't say barricade yourself in like it was Fort Knox,' he said, lifting me up. I leaned against him for one moment. Did he never know how his nearness affected me? He was reaching into the trapdoor and pulling down my mobile, the radio and the shredded book.

'Didn't know you listened to Radio Luxembourg,' he said. 'Any good?'

'Passes the time,' I said, my teeth chattering.

'And look at this book,' he said with sharp disgust. 'That's scandalous, Jordan. Ripping up a book. You're turning into a vandal.'

Somehow my breathing steadied itself. I was safe. I was with him but it had not registered.

My hands were trembling as I opened out the crumpled packet. 'Would you like a crisp?' I asked politely.

Eighteen

My jeans were damp and the clinging cuffs wet and I wanted to take them off. Not a good idea. All that undignified wriggling in a car. A WPC wrapped a blanket round me, to contain what was left of my body warmth. I was about to thank her but she got into a different patrol car.

'Have they caught them?' I asked, my teeth chattering. 'Have they got them yet?'

'We will,' said James. 'Every vehicle is out and that's the Arundel police as well. If they make any kind of move, they'll be spotted. I checked those plates. Some of them had been used before. Very careless.'

'I can't get warm,' I said, shivering.

'Not surprising. That was a pretty damp cellar they put you into. I should imagine it floods with a high tide.'

'They were going to alter my brain.'

'Pretty difficult.'

I think he was being sarcastic.

'It's been a wet few weeks,' I said, still shivering, remembering the rescue from my watery perch under the pier. 'It's all this fishing and piers. This is the last time I take on any water-based cases.'

'Have you still got a fishing-rod case?'

'No, the thefts seem to have stopped.' I didn't mention Dick Mann's amazing stock of fishing equipment. It wasn't relevant now. 'Have you any news about Dick Mann?'

'The post-mortem report reckons that it was a suicide attempt that went wrong. No case for us. The enquiry has been closed.'

'A suicide that went wrong? Odd way to put it, but it worked, didn't it? He achieved the desired effect. He died, didn't he?'

'They said he meant to hang himself but somehow slipped and the noose went round his foot and he hung upside down until he drowned of fluid in his lungs.'

'Why didn't he pull himself up?' Jordan asked. 'A sort of vertical sit-up?'

'These was an abrasion on his forehead. As the rope swung, maybe violently, he hit his head on a beam and knocked himself un-conscious.'

'But why should he want to kill himself? He seemed to have a fairly contented life with his fishing and his drinking mates, even if his job at the hospital had packed up.'

'Maybe he thought someone was on to his previous identity and that made him ner-vous.'

A degree of warmth was seeping into my bones. James had put the heater on and the inside of the car was beginning to feel comfortable and pleasant. 'What had he got to be nervous about?'

James did not answer. He was not going to tell me. There was a lumbering forty-four-foot container truck in front that needed careful overtaking. 'You tell me.'

'Maybe he knew something no one else knew?'

'Maybe.'

'Perhaps it wasn't suicide. Perhaps it's murder and someone made it look like suicide.'

'You have a suspicious mind. I'm glad you don't work for me. You'd be chasing red herrings every day.'

'At least I'd get paid for having a suspicious mind. No one pays me for brain time in my present capacity.'

'Call it paperwork,' he suggested kindly.

'Was he?'

'Was he what?'

'Was Dick Mann a bell-ringer?'

'Yes, apparently, that part is genuine,' said James. 'He was learning. Anyone can learn. It could have been an accident in the bell chamber itself. If he was up there amongst the bells when they were down, that is facing mouth downwards. If someone downstairs, either mistakenly or deliberately, began to ring one of the bells, the person upstairs could be seriously injured.'

I was confused. Upstairs, downstairs. 'So that might have happened?'

'Maybe. The other bell-ringers were very shocked. They played a special grandsire in his memory.'

'How kind. He'd have liked that,' I said drily.

'Where am I taking you?'

'Home, please.'

'I will take you home only if you promise to come to the station in the morning and make a statement this time.'

'I promise.'

'Do these thugs know where you live?'

'Derek Brook would know my address from the insurance claim. Oh hell, that complicates things, doesn't it? No, it doesn't. He hasn't connected me with the woman in the ladybird crash yet. This particular incident was tied up with following them and making enquiries at the hospital with the woman who later had a meal with him at the Mexican.'

DI James swung the wheel, taking a left turn. 'I don't understand that. They might have connected you with the crash by now. I guess you aren't going home. It's Marchmont Tower again, Jordan. You might as well move in with me and pay me rent.'

I wish.

I dozed off at this point. Out like a flickering nightlight, fear vanishing. It was the warmth and an easy sort of giving up. Maybe I was trying too hard, too hard at everything. Someone once said, wear life as a loose garment. I'd belted a notch too tight. Time to let go and start to float with the wind.

Marchmont Tower loomed ahead in the dark. The patrol car had left us miles back. The folly was beginning to look like home, although I still yearned for the simplicity of my two bedsits. I was a person who needed to live alone. I liked the uncomplicated freedom.

DI James parked round the back. I could already feel what was going to happen. This man would dump me indoors and then go back to work. I gathered the blanket around me as if I was the Indian woman, Pocahontas. As he unlocked the door and switched off the security system, I swept in.

'I'll have a hot bath if you don't mind,' I said with resolution. 'I'll eat something hot if I can find anything. And then I will sleep in Ben's bed. Thank you, James, but you don't need to worry about me any more.'

'Good,' said James, his mobile glued to his ear. 'There's been a car crash reported outside Arundel. I must go. It may be our friends, spreading their wings to new territory. Sleep well, sweetheart.'

He bent and kissed my cheek and then he was gone. The room was empty. It was the first time he had kissed me voluntarily. It took me a few moments to recover.

I shed my clothes on to the bathroom floor, had a hot bath, water up to the armpits. No foam, no bubbles, just soap, nothing feminine around. I made a chicken and noodles cuppa soup in a mug, which was all there was in the cupboard, and then trailed in the bath towel upstairs to Ben's bedroom.

Nothing had changed in the room. No one had removed his belongings. It was as if he was still alive. I wept a few tears into his pillow and then fell asleep, parcelled-out. Dear Ben. He hadn't been the right man either.

A shaft of light lit the morning to my eyes. It came between the blinds. It took a few moments to realize where I was. This was when I longed desperately to be in my own place. My own bed, my own bath, my own towel ... my body was never going to be right for James. The pain of what had happened to his children could never be eased. No ordinary woman could ever make it feel right. It was a losing battle. And Jordan Lacey had lost before even the first shot was fired.

The air was laden with a pale sea mist rolling up the valley to the tower. I could hardly see out of the door. My jeans had dried stiff. This was instant replay. Hadn't I done all this before?

No instructions to stay put this time. I could go whenever I wanted to and I wanted to leave right now. I tidied the duvet, the pillows, cleaned the bath, folded the towel, washed up the mug. You could hardly see I had been there.

I knew my way round the countryside now. I walked briskly down the hill and into Findon, waited at a bus stop and eventually a single-decker Stagecoach came along. The fare into Latching was more than I had on me. I searched my pockets in a panic. A nice woman offered to pay the difference and declined to give me her name for repayment.

'Do the same for someone else one day,' she said. 'Keep the good-turn ball rolling.'

I could feel myself itching to do a good turn already. It was extremely catching.

'Thank you,' I said. 'I have to get home.'

'I could sense the desperation,' she said with a smile, standing up to get off at the next stop.

Latching looked the same, such a small but thriving seaside town, all that wild sea and remote beach, the elegant Georgian architecture, the same municipal eyesores. Nothing had changed while I'd been away. It felt like years, yet had only been hours. Perhaps it was me that had changed.

There was a message on my answerphone. I didn't recognize the name ... Annie. Annie who? When had I, in the last century, met an

Annie? She sounded disturbed. She wanted to see me but wouldn't say what it was about, only that it was urgent. She said she would be waiting at the Nico cafe at eleven a.m. Cafe Nico was an 'in' coffee place.

'Please, please be there, Miss Lacey. I must see you.'

So much for a quiet morning, laying low and recharging. A surge of adrenaline rushed through my veins. Things were moving. This had to be something. I flipped through my notes and files. No Annie anywhere. Who was she? I might be walking into a trap. If I was, then at least I would have clean undies.

My clothes were filthy. I threw them into a bowl of hot suds and swirled them around. Shopping list: washing machine, spin dryer, even a new washing-up bowl would do. I'd settle for anything.

I put on clean indigo jeans, black T-shirt and dark-blue fleece. Boots. My trainers were ruined. Shopping list: oh, to heck with shopping lists.

For insurance, I went into Doris's shop to tell her where I was going. At the same time, I picked up some groceries, fruit and veg. My cupboard was bare.

'What's all this about?' said Doris suspiciously. 'You don't usually give me your itinerary. Is this a new leaf turning? Are we bonding? Or are you scared of something? This is not like you, Jordan. And where have you been lately? I haven't seen you for ages.'

'It was in case. I've been around.'

'In case of what?'

'In case I don't come back.'

Doris counted out my change. 'Can I have first refusal for your car? I could learn to drive.'

Annie was already seated inside Nico's, perched on one of the brown leather sofas. She looked ill at ease, biting her nails. I knew who she was now. She was the plump Annie Rudge, Arnie's wife, the woman with a brood of noisy children and several dogs, hens. Dick Mann's next-door neighbour.

She looked up with a quick nervous smile. I think she was pleased to see me.

'Hello,' I said cheerfully. 'Would you like some coffee?'

'Yes please, Miss Lacey. Milk, two sugars.'

I went to the counter and ordered coffee for Annie and a hot chocolate for myself, cream extra. I required building up. Carrying the brimming cups back to the table was a tricky business. We moved to another sofa for privacy.

'That's lovely,' she said, trying to tear open the sugar sachets with shaking fingers. She spilled the granules over the table. 'I'm so glad you've come.'

'It's nice to see you again,' I said. 'Who's looking after the children?'

'Arnie's at home. He's got a streaming cold. All that fishing off the pier. Caught a chill. He's taken some sick leave.'

'Best not to spread the germs,' I agreed. 'And how are all your children?'

'Growing fast. Noisy. Demanding. And far too many of them,' she said, with a shrug. 'Don't tell me about family planning. Arnie's never heard of it.'

Surely everyone these days knew how to limit the size of their families? Maybe Annie and Arnie wanted lots of children. I liked children. Not much possibility of me having any of my own. This was not something I wanted to dwell on.

We talked children and dogs for a few minutes. Annie was calming down now, with the coffee and the comfort of Nico's sofa. She was enjoying some peace and quiet, time to herself. I guessed she did not get much of either. She put down her coffee.

'I expect you're wondering why I asked to see you,' she said. Any minute she was going to start biting her nails again.

I nodded. 'I was wondering.'

'It's about Dick Mann.'

'Your neighbour.'

'Yes. He was a very nice man. Quiet and reserved, of course, a bit lonely. But I liked him.'

I was beginning to see a glimmer of light, but she wouldn't look at me. 'And did Dick

Mann like you?'

'Oh yes. He often came in for a cup of tea and a slice of fruit cake. You see, he was lonely and my house is noisy and chaotic. Not something he'd like all the time, you understand, but it made a change. Kids and dogs everywhere.'

'Very understandable. You were kind to him.'

'No problem. It was easy to be kind. Arnie and Dick were fishing mates after all. It was normal for him to pop in now and again. The kids liked seeing him. And so did I.'

'Of course, it was so ordinary, so natural. A nice, noisy family next door and he was lonely,' I said.

I was trying to make it easy for her. She smiled at me. Annie was not a great beauty but her face was genuinely kind, even if her long blonde hair was wild and untamed. Or maybe that was a look that attracted these days. Perhaps it appealed to Dick Mann.

'So you were seeing quite a lot of him...' I went on.

'Oh yes, quite a lot.'

'And he liked you.'

This was when the shutters came down. She looked closely at her coffee as if reading the grains. She smoothed the knee of her size twenty navy polyster trouser suit. I had to get her back on track.

'But you wanted to see me about some-

264

thing,' I said.

'It was nothing to do with me, you under-stand,' Annie said, searching for the right words. 'It was Dick. I'd done nothing to encourage him but he seemed to take every-thing so personal. It were queer really. Him being so quiet for months and then suddenly getting all het up and demanding.'

'It's the quiet ones,' I said. 'They're quite unpredictable.'

'That's it,' she said with sudden vigour. 'I didn't know he was going to come barging in with declarations of needing me and us being an item and pleading with me to leave Arnie. Leave Arnie and all my kids? They were my kids. He must have been loco. And I told him so. He didn't like it, of course, went off with a face like bloody thunder. I was quite upset, I can tell you.'

'Naturally,' I said. 'I can imagine. What a thing to suggest. What happened next?'

'He came back in minutes and said we were meant for each other and that he didn't know what he would do if I didn't go away with him. And he meant it. It was sort of threatening. That's blackmail, isn't it?'

I nodded. 'Sort of. Emotional blackmail.'

'Well, I wasn't having any of that and any-way my youngest was coming down with a cold. I told Dick to be sensible and go home and cool off. It was none of my business. I'd got enough on my hands. I couldn't cope

265

with all that stuff.'

Annie was really upset now, sniffing and gulping. I gave her a tissue and went for more coffee. I got her a chocolate muffin as well. Muffins were known to work wonders.

'And that's not all,' she went on, breaking up the muffin till the plate was full of brown crumbs. 'Then there was some man came knocking at my door real loud, asking for Dick, looking for Dick, quite soon after he'd left. I told him I didn't know anything. I didn't like the look of him. He wasn't very nice. I'm sure he wasn't one of Dick's friends, although he insisted he was.'

'Can you describe this man?'

'I dunno if I can. He was sort of thin and nasty-looking. I didn't like him. Sort of shifty.'

'Do you remember any details about him? Anything odd.'

'Not really. Nothing much. He smoked a lot and he had a couple of comic books. He was reading them while I cleaned up one of my youngsters. He'd pulled down a packet of flour on top of hisself.'

'The man?'

'No, Toby, one of my kids. Proper mess it was.'

'Why did this man want to see Dick Mann?'

'I don't know, Miss Lacey. He said it was

urgent. But he wasn't the kind of friend Dick would have. He looked sort of devious. I bolted the door after he'd gone. I wasn't taking no chances.'

'Very wise,' I said. 'You can't be too careful these days. What happened after that?'

'Well, it was Dick again. He phoned me up. He said he was going to kill himself if I didn't go away with him. I was really fed up by now and told him so. The next thing I hear, he'd hung himself in the church tower. It wasn't my fault, was it, Miss Lacey? Please tell me it's not my fault.' Annie was genuinely upset.

'No, not your fault, Annie, I can assure you. His death was a horrible accident. There are sometimes bell-ringing accidents. Those great bells, each weighing several hundredweight. He probably slipped. That's what really happened. All his threats were only trying to make you change your mind, so please don't worry about it. I think I should give you this, Annie. I know Dick Mann got it for you as a present. It shows how much he cared for you, doesn't it?'

I gave her the gold brooch with the initial 'A'. A flash of light caught on a fragment of glass embedded in the crossbar of the letter 'A'. I hadn't noticed it before.

'Did he? Why, it's lovely.' Annie smiled at me and took the brooch, turning it over with a sort of wonder. 'How kind of him. I've never had a brooch with my initial. He was a nice man. I shall always wear it.'

It might help to make her feel better.

Nineteen

Arnie was down on the pier, fishing. I did not enquire who was taking care of the kids. Perhaps he had cleared off as soon as Annie got home. There was a dampness in the air and he was done up to the gills with his waterproofs.

'Hello, Arnie,' I said. 'I thought you were off sick?'

'I decided a bit of fresh air would get rid of the germs. Got catarrh something rotten. Clogs you up.'

'You're probably right,' I said. 'I'm still interested in Dick Mann's death. His garage is overflowing with fishing rods, all sorts and sizes. Have you any ideas about them?'

'Yeah, sure. I know all about them rods. Some of them are mine. He let me store them there. We ain't got no space at home with all the kids.'

'And what about the others? There seems an awful lot of rods for one angler.'

'So what? None of my business.'

'But you wanted me to find out who was taking the rods.'

I did not remind him that no one had paid me yet. Perhaps the invoice I'd sent him had not made any sense. Memo: present another copy.

'Yeah, well, it doesn't matter much now, does it?' He cast his line far out to sea. It sank immediately into the grey-green depths. The sea was surging, turbulent with fish, not knowing they were destined for a plate.

'So you knew all along that it was Dick Mann who was taking the rods off the pier?'

Arnie was chewing gum. He was surprised at my statement and for a moment forgot he had a mouthful and swallowed the gum. He nodded awkwardly, coughing, trying to dislodge the gum from the back of his throat. I hoped I wasn't going to have to do mouth to mouth resuscitation. There was a horrible, gagging sound and the blob of gum flew into the air and over the rail.

'Yes, I knew Dick was taking them,' said Arnie when he had recovered. He opened a packet and started chewing mints. 'But I couldn't say anything, could I? He was my mate. So that's why I got you on the case. I thought perhaps you would say something to him, or at least frighten him off. It didn't make sense. I didn't know he was going to kill himself, did I?'

'Have you any idea why he did it?'

'I guess he was upset about summink. Perhaps it was the rods. Perhaps he knew he'd been found out.'

'A rather drastic reaction, don't you think?'

'Yeah, I suppose so. A bit over the top.'

'I wonder if you could tell me what you were doing the evening that Dick Mann was found dead?'

I had no right to ask him. I was not a police officer any more. But he might not know the difference. It seemed important now to find out if Arnie had been around at the time. He was a big man. He could have been mad with jealousy at Dick's interest in his buxom wife.

'Me?' He looked surprised. 'I went home after work and had me dinner. Shepherd's pie and chips. Annie does a good shepherd's pie. Proper gravy and lamb and carrots.'

'Did you go out at all?'

'I went down to the pub after me dinner like I always do. Nothing unusual in that.'

'Which pub?'

'My usual.'

This was like getting blood out of concrete. 'And there are people in the pub who will be able to corroborate that? You know, confirm that you were there.'

'Of course, because I was there, wasn't I? I always go there. It's my usual pub. I need a pint or two most nights. Lubricate the gullet.

Doesn't every man?'

'That's something I've no real knowledge about. But I do need to know where you were. You see, Dick Mann's death may not be as simple as we first thought. Has Annie told you anything? Anything at all unusual?'

'No, why should she? Has she got anything to tell me? What are you getting at?'

He was reeling in his line in a demented fashion. I'd said something which upset him. The bait flapped on the hook. There was nothing but a spill of seaweed.

'Look, I've had enough here. There ain't no fish running. I'm off home. My cold's getting worse.'

Arnie sniffed and spluttered, blew his nose, was ruffled. He was scowling, not as amiable as usual, packing up his rod with short, abrupt movements. This was a different side of the big fella. He didn't like my line of questioning. Perhaps he had not been at the pub, like he always was, after his dinner. I hoped Annie was not going to be caught up in this aftermath.

'So you don't know anything more about Dick Mann's death?'

'No, I don't. Why should I? I wasn't there in that church tower. I don't know nothing what happened to Dick. Nor do you, Miss Nosey-Parker Lacey. You're guessing about all this stuff. My Annie weren't going off with him nor nothing. She lives with me and the kids, always has, like always will.'

Arnie was steaming, nostrils blowing like an old bull. His eyes were swivelling, not looking at me.

'I didn't say anything about Annie going off with Dick Mann. What made you say that? Did you think she was going to go off with him?' I shouldn't have asked but I couldn't stop myself.

But Arnie Rudge was striding along the pier, feet turned out like a copper, rods over his shoulder in a zipped-up bag. He did not look back. There was no point in going after the man. I wouldn't get any more out of him, but he sure was rattled.

'No, I didn't. I didn't think anything!' he shouted back. 'Leave me alone.'

Ah.

I knew where I was going. It was going to take a long time, but my teeth were into the bait and I was not going to let go. It was a hunch but something told me that there might be, just might be some truth somewhere, waiting to be found. This is what I should have done a while ago before I got distracted.

James was eating at Maeve's Cafe even though she was near to closing. Mavis was feeding him up with a huge plate of cod and chips. He had decorated it with half a pint of tomato sauce.

'It's as well that they've decided tomato sauce is good for you,' I said, sitting down at his table. I helped myself to a chip.

'Who decided?'

'Some Public Health Authority.'

'Never heard of it.'

I took another chip. James frowned at me.

'You know the photograph that I found of Dick Mann and his pals, circa 1990?' Had I told him about it? Somewhere along the line I must have told him.

'If you say so...' He was concentrating on the fish now. The flakes were creamy-white and succulent. He didn't offer me any.

'Well, I know you won't tell me who Dick Mann once was, before he became Dick Mann, that is, but I think I know his previous identity,' I said slowly.

'So?'

'I think I also know what happened in the bell tower of St Luke the Divine that evening.'

'More guesses?'

'Calculated guesses.'

He went over to the counter and took a clean fork and paper napkin. He pushed them towards me. 'I can see you're starving. Help yourself. Mavis always gives too much.'

'Thanks,' I said, savouring the prospect. 'James, I think I've worked it out. But I'm

273

not sure if I'm right. I need your expertise. You don't have to tell me anything. But I need a nod now and then.'

'I might manage a nod. Shoot.'

'It took a long time,' I said, spearing a large chip. 'Running through microfilm of a decade of newspapers is time-consuming, and I've just spent several hours in the library, going cross-eyed.'

He nodded, eyes like lasers. 'Thought there was something different about you.'

'I found front-page stories about the Gaskon Street safety box raid. Ring a bell, does it? Heck, I shouldn't say ring a bell ... not a good choice of words, but you know what I mean. National headlines for weeks. There were three thieves, working this pretty neat scam in the vaults of a jeweller's, but two of them got shopped by the third. And that third thief, who happened to be a security guard at the jeweller's, mysteriously disappeared while the other two got jail sentences. Odd isn't it?' I took advantage of a pause to fork up some fish. Mavis knew how to cook fish.

'If you say so.'

'Do you think this third man might have possibly been uprooted and replanted in Latching? In a small cottage out in the wilds, down a country lane? Somewhere obscure?'

James said nothing. Not even a nod.

'And the loot has never been found, has it?

So I guess those other two thieves are still incredibly annoyed and will be looking for it soon. Am I right?'

'Want any more tomato sauce?'

'No, thank you. I prefer runny tomatoes to be in a soup. And the older of those two robbers has recently been released from prison on parole. I checked that too. Robber Number Two is out. I should imagine his first concern would be to find the geezer who shopped him, and maybe the jewellery that was stolen and never found. It's stashed away somewhere.'

James stood up and fetched two coffees from the counter. Mavis was looking curiously at me. She was probably wondering why I had been talking non-stop. I don't usually say so much.

'You know I can't say anything, Jordan. So don't ask me. Would you like some coffee? You must be getting dry.'

'Thanks. Do you want this last chip?'

'No, you can have it.'

I stirred my coffee. I don't know why, as I don't put sugar in it. One of those childhood habits.

'So do you want to hear that the robber who has been released from prison is swanning around here now, in Latching?'

'You can tell me if you like.' His expression never changed. It was one of cool appraisal. I would never be able to cope with his distance.

'He's been spotted, twice. His name is Johnson. And he has a passion for comics, especially old comics.'

'Beano Johnson,' said James, with a nod. 'I've seen him. He's been in my shop.'

A glimmer of interest crossed his face. 'Did he buy anything?'

'Vintage comics.'

But I didn't tell him the other interesting facts that I had uncovered from the newspapers. Only a few safety boxes had been opened and one had belonged to Lady Annabel Shrewsbury. Among her jewellery stolen had been a small gold brooch with the initial 'A' and set in the centre of the 'A' was a flawless diamond. Not a fragment of glass as I had supposed but a genuine diamond.

Some of the boxes had contained money and other bits of jewellery. But the last box had belonged to a South African gem dealer. In it was his last delivery of uncut diamonds, blue, white and pink diamonds ... a haul of immense value. Where were they now? They had never been found.

No wonder Dick Mann went to ground.

'Do you want to speak to this Beano Johnson?' I went on. 'You might have some questions you want to ask.'

'I think I probably do,' said James laconically. 'What do you suggest?'

'We could set a trap. He's mad about

collecting old comics and I have goods that he wants. Some old annuals. Now, I know they are valuable and I'm not letting them go for peanuts. But I could put them in the window with some enticing price offer. He'll come in and you could nab him.'

'And where will I be? Hiding under your counter?'

'No, but you could be my assistant, serving in the shop. I could pretend I've had an accident or something, put my serving arm in a sling, and you could be helping me out in the shop. Everything above board.'

My dream come true. James and me running a little shop. I couldn't help starting to laugh. James couldn't understand why I was laughing. We were worlds apart.

'You need to know why you want to question Beano Johnson,' I prodded helpfully. 'It is possible that he had something to do with Dick Mann's death, isn't it?'

'It's more than possible,' said James, thawing at the last minute. He was scenting a breakthrough. 'Forensics have found traces of skin and blood under Dick Mann's fingernails. And they don't belong to him.'

'That's it then. Beano followed Dick to the bell tower and tried to get out of him where the haul is hidden. Maybe he ties him up to force the information out of him, threatens him and then Dick Mann slips with his foot caught in the noose and it's too late. He's down there, dangling. Beano isn't strong enough to pull him up. Or he taunts Dick Mann for the whereabouts of the loot. I don't know. You tell me.'

'It is possible. OK, we'll go for it. Do I need training for this shop assistant business?'

'Oh yes. Training. Definitely.'

'How long for?'

I thought of the delicious possibilities. 'It could take quite a long time,' I said, thinking weeks.

'Twenty minutes,' he said, getting up to pay the bill.

Next day I cleared the front window and arranged the precious annuals in a picturesque group. I added a few other extremely ancient, dog-eared paperbacks. My notice was to the point:

COLLECTORS' ITEMS
NO REASONABLE OFFER REFUSED

There was an ancient pillowcase out back, on its last legs but too pretty to throw away. I tore it up and fashioned a sling. James fixed it round my neck with admirable efficiency.

'I took a first-aid course,' he said, noticing my amusement.

Doris came in bearing a packet of jam doughnuts. She stopped when she saw the sling.

'My God, Jordan. What have you done now?'

'Nothing,' I said. 'Don't look so horrified. It's work, not real. It's a set-up.'

'I never know when to believe you.' She inspected the knot and looked at me closely for bruising. 'It looks for real,' she said.

'Well, that shows how lifelike it appears. If it fools you, then it'll fool anyone.'

'I've brought these doughnuts,' she said. 'I want to barter them for the Penguin copy of *Jane Eyre* in the window. The notice says no reasonable offer refused.'

'Done,' said James.

'Don't be silly, Doris,' I said. 'You can have *Jane Eyre*. I wouldn't charge you.'

'But I could really murder a doughnut,' James muttered.

'It might be a first edition,' said Doris, leaving the doughnuts on the counter. 'Then I'll be laughing.'

James took off his jacket and, with total commitment, began wrapping the book in a second-hand white paper bag.

'No charge,' he said, handing Doris the packet. 'In all seriousness, Doris, may I suggest that you don't come back in here, or anywhere near this shop, today.'

Doris looked at him sharply. 'I don't like what I'm hearing and I don't like what you are saying. First sign of trouble and I'll call

279

the police.'

'Thank you, Doris,' I said, ushering her out of the shop. 'Don't worry. It's nothing dangerous really.'

'Next time I see you, you'll probably have both arms in a sling.'

The annuals would have sold twice over. I had to turn down several good offers, but at least James made a note of interested names and phone numbers for me.

'You aren't very businesslike,' he said.

'This shop is a cover, not a business,' I said.

'So how are you getting on with your other cases?' he asked.

'I found one of the puppies, the long-haired female, but not the other two puppies. Mrs Gregson was overjoyed. But I didn't find out who stole them.'

'Why not?'

'My remit was to get the puppies back. That's all.'

'And...?'

'The stolen fishing rods case has come to a natural end. They stopped disappearing about the time that Dick Mann died. Apparently the anglers knew that it was Dick Mann taking them, but they wanted me to find out and warn him off. They didn't want to do it themselves because he was a drinking mate.'

'Heaven help the angling fraternity. So you are currently unemployed?'

'Underemployed,' I said. 'I still have a shop to run. Would you like to make some coffee please, James?'

'Yes, Miss Lacey. Anything you say, miss.'

There was a kind of milky stillness to the atmosphere in the shop. James was here and I was here and we were working together, if you can call turning away genuine customers working. James sold a pop-eyed glass frog and looked immensely pleased with himself as he put the money in the cash box.

'This shopkeeping is a piece of cake, Jordan. Nothing to it.'

Then the door opened and Beano Johnson walked in. James was not out front. He had gone into the back store to find some replacement items for the side window. He had become quite enthusiastic about shop-keeping.

'Hello,' I said politely.

'So, I see you've decided to sell those annuals after all,' said Beano. His days of freedom had put some colour back into his face but he still looked shifty. I wondered why Dick Mann had ever taken up with such a creep. 'Come to your senses, have you?'

'Yes, I'm open to offers,' I said, raising my voice, hoping James would hear out back. 'I remember you buying the old comics. You were very keen then.'

'Always liked old comics and old annuals. They take me back to my youth. Fifty pounds the lot.' Beano Johnson was inching towards me. If he could rob the safety boxes of a top London jeweller's, then ripping off a junk shop in Latching would be nothing.

'That's a pretty good offer,' I said hurriedly. 'But not quite good enough. Annuals, after all, fetch a very high price these days and they are in immaculate condition. Condition counts, you know...' I rabbited on, wondering where on earth James had got to. I was on my own in the shop.

'I think perhaps I'll have them and you'll accept my fifty pounds,' said Beano, producing some filthy notes. 'I'll just help myself to them out of the window. I could break the window, by accident, of course, smash it to smithereens, if that will help you make up your mind. And then I'll be on my way.'

I started to chill out, gripping the counter. Beano Johnson was a nasty piece of work.

'I don't think you are going anywhere,' said James, standing in the doorway. He had nipped out the back and come round to the front of the shop. He was holding out his badge. I was so glad to see him.

'Beano Johnson, I'm arresting you for the murder of Dick Mann. You do not have to say anything. But it may harm your defence if you do not mention, when questioned, something which you later rely on in court. Anything you do say may be given in evidence.'

Beano looked at James and then at me. His eyes were narrowed. I tasted the ash of fear.

Twenty

Two flashy-coloured patrol cars were round in minutes and uniformed officers were leaping out to surround the shop. It was very Eastenders. A crowd gathered like flies to sticky paper. Beano Johnson wasn't going anywhere. He looked stunned by the speed at which the situation had changed.

'Leave me alone. What's going on? I don't know any Dick Mann,' he kept saying, over and over again. He was handcuffed by now. 'Who is this geezer?'

'Move along please,' said an officer to the crowds. 'There's nothing to see.'

'I know my rights,' Beano spluttered.

'I bet you do,' said James.

They bundled Johnson into a car, head down, and then it was all over bar the clapping and the patrol cars drove away. James had gone, leaving only his essence. People waited on the street, wondering if something else was going to happen. They were hoping, maybe, to see me carried out on a stretcher.

Doris came round with an opened packet of tea bags. She bustled in and made a mug of tea. It was hot and strong. She did not know about my preference for weak tea and honey. She handed it to me, checking for bruises, broken limbs.

'You're all right then,' she said briskly.

'Yup. Ready for another day.'

'You want a proper holiday, that's what you want. Nothing but trouble this year.'

'Can you recommend some pleasant town by the seaside, preferably with Georgian architecture? Four-mile beach, plenty of walks, pier, not far from the South Downs?'

'Come off it, Jordan. You live there already.'

'Then why do I need to take a holiday?'

I took the sling off and rubbed my arm. It felt odd to have two arms again. Useful, though. I put up the CLOSED sign and shut the door. James had left a list of telephone numbers and I guessed I ought to sell the annuals to one of those people. It was only fair. No point in keeping the annuals. They had served their purpose long after publication.

'Why don't you take the rest of the day off at least?' Doris suggested. 'It's a lovely day. The sun's out for once. Spring is on its way. Go check on the sea.'

It was indeed a lovely day. I hadn't noticed.

Perfect for walking the beach.

'Maybe I will. Thanks for the tea, Doris.'

'It was your milk.'

Half the dogs in Latching were already on the stretch of sand, chasing seagulls, prancing through the waves, catching balls and sticks, shaking wet drops all over their owners. The new passion for big kite flying was in full glory, some controlled by people walking the sand, others out to sea dragging their owners on surfboards. I watched how the kite-surfers, clad in wetsuits, lay on their backs in the water and pulled themselves up on to their boards as soon as there was enough drag. A real skill.

I pulled off my trainers and rolled up my jeans. It took courage. Somewhere I have a pair of denim shorts cut down from old jeans. Time to dig them out. It was glorious to think of summer coming.

The sea touched my toes, cold as ice. It trickled through my toes, shocking my skin, washed over my feet, a lace of bubbles fringing the foam. I missed barefoot walking in the winter. It was always wellies. This was marvellous, my face to the sky, breathing the clean air, swinging my trainers. Only one life thread was missing from the web. Don't ask me who.

This is where dogs and children should be with acres of sand and miles of sea, somewhere to race around and let off steam.

These were the lucky ones. A dad was pushing a big double-wheeled buggy through the waves, the toddler inside shrieking with excitement. I hoped the child was well fastened with a harness.

'You're mad!' I called out.

'He loves it,' said the dad.

Fortresses of the less durable kind were already being built. Small streams of water were being dammed. Brothers were being hurriedly buried, sisters splashed, toddlers dabbling podgy fingers and tasting strange stuff called seaweed. A youth was lying in the water, while his giggling girlfriend improved his assets with piles of wet sand. He was tough.

And I was walking with a purpose. My thinking time. It was tricky avoiding the sharp rocks and stones which the tide moved to different areas every day. There was little more for me to do for Mrs Gregson unless I got lucky. The anglers should be reminded to pay my invoice. Any minute now my insurance company would get a hefty claim for a written-off Vauxhall. I wondered how much the Brooks were claiming for their various injuries and traumatized, but non-existent, daughter in the back seat.

'It's not my case,' I told a seagull feasting on a dead fish head. The head looked revolting, glassy-eyed, but the seagull obviously thought it was a gourmet take-away and took no notice. 'It's up to the police to sort that one out.'

But Jack's car, also crashed into by Derek Brook, had all this highly sophisticated recording equipment. They might not find it so easy to stake a claim against him. He was armed with damning information that proved otherwise. And what about Nina Deodar? Whatever she was doing must be criminal. I hoped James hadn't forgotten my little gem of observation at Miguel's restaurant.

Then the chemise dress ... I was going to get a reward for its safe return. Brilliant. I spent a happy ten minutes planning how to spend it, whatever the sum. A lick of paint for the shop – essential, barely-white with saffron trim. Valet service for the ladybird and new seat cushions. New trainers for me. Decent haircut at Hair Affair, those split ends. Glittery eye make-up. Hang on, it might be thousands ... world cruise, New York, Australia.

'Ouch.' I stubbed my toe on a sharp rock and bit back the pain. Perhaps it was time for me to wear plastic footwear on the beach. I was always hurting myself. Plastic sandals were ageing, I thought, and I didn't feel that old. But only one more birthday and I would be facing the big three zero. Nearly half my alloted span and where had it gone?

The sounds of the beach cut into my

drowsing thoughts. Barking dogs, children crying, voices calling, waves slapping, seagulls screeching, a police helicopter droning overhead. I waved airwards in case the officers knew me.

By this time I was deciding that I should be taking the whole day off. The world could continue without me. There was a Don Lusher Big Band concert tonight at the pier pavilion and that would be a treat of mega proportions. It was a long time since I had heard the world famous trombone player, and he, like me, was ageing. But his music never aged. It was fresh and timeless.

I had time for a late supper at Maeve's Cafe. A day off included no cooking, no shopping, no fasting. I had a freshly caught Dover sole with new potatoes and peas.

'Did Bruno catch this?' I asked.

'Yes,' said Mavis. 'He still doesn't like you.'

'I'm worried,' I said putting a pat of butter on the Dover sole. It melted elegantly.

'He doesn't like you even more now,' she went on.

'That's not fair,' I said. 'Why doesn't he like me even more now?' I got round the grammar somehow.

'You know when he rescued you from under the pier? Well, his boat bashed into one of the pier girders and now there's a crack in the hull. It's going to cost thousands to repair. And that boat is his livelihood. He can't exist without it. So, natural, ain't it, he don't like you even more.'

I saw my reward for the period dress disappear into a boat. I would have to offer him a major contribution to the repairs. To hell with the glittery eyeshadow.

'Don't worry, Mavis. Tell Bruno that I can help out. I've something coming to me, an unexpected reward. However much it is, and I don't know how much yet, I'll see that Bruno gets enough to pay for the repairs. You will tell him, won't you, Mavis? Now, this fish is wonderful. I'm going to enjoy every mouthful.'

Mavis grinned at me. Her hair was a vibrant cherry-red this week, cascading like Cher, but clipped back for hygiene in the kitchen. 'I knew you'd come up with something, Jordan. I'll phone Bruno right away. He'll be relieved. Perhaps he'll like you a bit more now.'

It was beginning to blow a bit as I walked from the cafe to the pier. The afternoon warmth had soon faded. Crowds were converging on the Pavilion but it was too early to go in. I strolled the pier and was unexpectedly faced with nine black creepy crawlers ahead on the deck.

They were huge, too big for spiders. First I thought they were locusts, but they were grey-backed crabs, marooned on the decking, metres above the sea.

They were so lost, being ignored. It was horrible to watch the poor creatures, crawling about. Alien country. No one helping them.

Now, I have never handled a crab before and have no idea of the best way. Those claws looked lethal. Their backsides appeared less vicious. Timidly I grasped one by the back, ran to the railing and dropped it into the sea below. I hoped it could stand heights.

Eight more to go. I began with the smallest, hoping the fall would not kill them. The last crab was a monster daddy crab, the size of a bread plate. Its claws were waving in the air. I wished a shovel would materialize.

I grabbed it from the back and began my run. It fought sluggishly, sinking a claw into my fourth finger. Ouch. I dropped it over the rail and watched it sink into the waves. My good deed for the day. St Peter, please note, no blood.

Don Lusher and his Big Band were drawing an enthusiastic jazz-mad crowd of fans from the deepest corners of Sussex. I got one of the last seats, right at the back, but I didn't mind. No one would be upset if I jogged about a little to the rhythm of the music.

I'd changed into top jazz gear. Black with a touch of pink. Black jeans, black shirt, pink scarf tying back my hair. Pink doesn't go

with my colour hair but sometimes the outrageous works. This was an outrageous
night. I even wore earrings, which shows
how serious I was about my day off and this
special night out.

Don Lusher is every jazz woman's dream.
Slim, dapper, immaculate dinner jacket,
silvery hair, sparkling eyes behind his metal-
rimmed glasses. And he could play like an
angel. His trombone was melodic, mellow,
mellifluous. He played the old favourites. It
was drifting on clouds, trading on dreams,
rainy days that were warm and forgiving.

His energy was amazing. I could not
believe he was eighty or anywhere close. But
that's what he told the audience he was.
Now he was announcing a change in the
programme.

'One of my lead trumpets has had to back
out because of a family problem. But
instead, I am proud to present one of this
country's top trumpet players. And the piece
he's going to play is "Memories of You".
Please give a big welcome ... at very short
notice, he's only just arrived from Gatwick,
having flown in straight from the United
States. Ladies and Gentlemen! Here he is!'

I knew who it was before Don Lusher had
finished his announcement. My spine was
already tingling, hardly believing my luck. I
could sense his presence. My trumpet player
walked on, his tie already at half-mast, but

291

the black suit was pure Savile Row, brown hair flopping over his heart-throb eyes. He put the trumpet to his mouth and blasted his way back into my life with a sound that could split an atom.

I barely remembered the rest of the concert. My eyes were only on him. It had been so long since I had seen him. Months and months. I would never have James because he did not want me; this man I could never have because he was already married.

The audience did not want to let him go either. They knew they were listening to a genius, dynamics that were too subtle to remember. Those pure, soaring notes, dipping down into roots of melancholy, astonishing interpretations of classics. They shouted for more and more. Don Lusher gave in with a grin and they played number after extra number, but at some point they had to stop. Their energy had spiralled and the musicians were exhausted. They trooped off the stage, waving to the audience. The red curtains closed and the last echoes of their music lingered in the glass dome of the roof.

I did not move. He might look for me. He might have forgotten me. He might have to rush home. He might be jet-lagged.

But he came out of the side door from beside the stage, carrying his trumpet case, a coat over his arm, and he walked straight towards me. He seemed to know instinctively where I was in the theatre.

'I knew you would be here, sweetheart,' he said, kissing my cheek. 'I knew you would wait. I've missed you.'

'I've missed you,' I said.

'Tell me what you have been doing in sleepy old Latching.' His eyes were smiling behind his glasses. He had a new pair, a neater shape and without rims.

'Do you really want to know?' I asked. 'What you've been doing in the States sounds much more exciting.'

'Films, television, the same old stuff,' he said, dismissing his career. 'I want to know about you.'

'Well, I got marooned under the pier and had to be rescued by a boat,' I began. 'I was deliberately crashed into on a roundabout and am being taken for a ride with false injury claims. I was threatened by a man with a knife in a pub but escaped. Later I was kidnapped by the same man, bundled into the boot of a car and locked in a wet cellar that occasionally gets flooded.'

He took my arm and we walked out of the theatre, out into the breeze-chill of an early spring night. He put his coat round my shoulders.

'So nothing much has changed,' he said, grinning.

* * *

We had coffees at a nearby late-night cafe. It was almost empty and the staff wanted to close but we talked without stopping, and ordered more coffee. Then reluctantly he had to go. He had to go back to his wife. I tried to print his face on to my mind. He was looking older, a little worn, a slight sagging of the skin. He was tired but he still walked me home. He had always walked me home, whatever the churchyard hour.

We walked passed Christchurch, the old church with flintstone walls. A white mist was rising from the fallen tombstones and I shivered. I was crushed between the past and the future.

'I hope it won't be so long, next time,' I said, trying not to sound pushy or nagging. I gave him back his coat and he shrugged into it, taking my warmth with him. My key was in the lock.

'Every time I play "Memories of You", it will be only for you,' he said, not giving me a proper answer. 'Never forget that.'

Then he kissed my cheek like a touch of thistledown and was gone. Again.

It was another day and the dream was still with me. But the trumpeter had gone, back to his fame and travels over the world, back to the jazz-playing that heralds the credits of many major films. Back to his family and a life that only had moments in mine.

There were some loose ends to tie up. Derek Brook and his evil associate, Les, were still around, searching for me. They had not been caught in Arundel. Would they get to me before James got to them?

Hold on Jordan, I told myself. You're supposed to be a detective. Go out and do some detecting. Resolution: find dodgy car dealer Les, whose car boot needed cleaning and disinfecting. Why wasn't I following the Brook family? Surveillance is my ace skill. I knew where they lived now.

My ladybird was too conspicuous and they would remember her spots from the crash. I took a train to Portslade with my bike in the guard's van, and cycled to the Rose and Crown. My cover for the day was traffic warden supreme. Supreme because no one got a ticket. I had borrowed a spare uniform from a friend who doesn't ask questions, and spent a long, tedious morning patrolling the same street, putting DRIVE CAREFULLY stickers under windscreen wipers. I had lifted these stickers at some road-safety exhibition and they were coming in useful. I also made notes in my notebook, such as 'this car is parked badly' and 'needs a wash'. I waited hours before anything happened, at one point leaning languidly on the wall opposite the Victorian villa and yawning.

Then everything happened at once. Derek Brook and his wife came out of the house and got into a different car, a grimy old green Renault. No neck braces, no sticks, no slings, no limps. They were both carrying tennis rackets and bags. Next came Miranda in skinny pants and crop top with a coltish hop, skip and a jump, hair bouncing, normal teenager.

Lastly came Les, looking as dodgy and chirpy as always. He was carrying a wodge of newspapers under his arm. He opened the driver's door without looking around. He did not notice me. I had merged with a tree. And it had started to rain, a fine misty drizzle swept in from the sea.

'Let's try this banger out,' he was saying, quite loudly. 'See how it goes for a start. Got it for a song, an absolute gift. Could be useful. I'll try it out for a few miles, then you can take over.'

There was no time to take photographs. The Renault was already backing out on to the street. It was time to move. My bike was chained to a street lamp a hundred yards back. It took minutes to unfasten the padlock. The Renault was going slowly along the road with noisy gear changes. Les was having trouble getting the hang of his latest vehicle.

The car was picking up speed cautiously, taking corners in an unsteady way. I didn't like what I was seeing. Their slowness gave me a chance to get nearer. Perhaps the steering was faulty. I am not the world's expert on cars but it looked to me as if the suspension mountings were adrift, maybe the result of incomplete repairs after a previous crash. I'd picked up the jargon from Bert, the whizz mechanic.

Something wobbly was going on. I hoped they'd call off this trial run. I remembered the tennis bags and gear. They wanted to get to some indoor courts. I had no idea where we were in these streets, but peddled furiously to keep up, the fine rain blurring my sight.

Les had a reputation for dealing in dodgy cars and this was without doubt one of them. It did not look good. The steering was unpredictable. The wheels on the right side were not properly aligned and the car was vaguely feeling its way down the middle of the road, the driver not paying much attention. He was talking.

I caught sight of Miranda's face in the back of the car. She did not look happy. Les was getting more confident, putting his foot down. The car was taking a dangerously erratic course, wheels scraping the kerb. Houses and parked cars were passed. There were no trees, a few bare hedges. Les must decide soon that the car was too dicey to drive any further. Surely he had some sense? I might get my photographs after all. Come on, stop, stop...

They were in the middle of a small industrial estate of warehouses and small factories, junkyards hidden behind brick and concrete walls. It was a bleak place, no obvious activity, the rain distorting the edges of the buildings.

I saw it coming before they did. Einstein said that time slows down before you are about to have an accident. Time slowed down for them. I saw it all in slow motion.

A large, high-sided lorry was reversing out of a yard. The Renault was in the wrong place, the wrong side of the road. Les spun the steering wheel violently but the car did not respond as intended. The wheels went outwards instead and took the car straight into the side of the lorry.

The crash was horrendous, the sound deafening. The Renault reared up like an animal, rolled over on to its roof with a sickening crunch, then over again, slewing sideways across the road and jamming straight into a lamp post and traffic sign.

I forgot everything that they had tried to do to me. I could only cycle as fast as I could, stagger off my bike, throw it down and then run towards the steaming car. The bonnet was crushed back into the front seats. The driver was stumbling out of the lorry cab, staggering, running over to the scene.

'I never saw them ... I never saw them at all,' he was crying. 'They came right at me.'

'I know, I know. I saw it happen.'

'I couldn't do anything. I couldn't stop.'

'I know. I know...'

My training as a WPC came instantly to my aid. I'd attended many accidents and there was no time to waste. First I made a 999 call. There was a ten-second response. I checked the name of the street with the lorry driver, gave it to the responding officer and asked for help.

'We need an ambulance and rescue equipment,' I said urgently. 'The car is badly smashed up and there are four people trapped inside.'

I could see Miranda. She was trying to open a door, tugging frantically at the handle, her face white and panic-stricken, banging on the splintered window, soundless with fear. She was mouthing words that I could not hear.

'Help me, help me,' stretched the shape of her lips.

Twenty-One

Derek Brook and Les were both staring into space, eyes fixed and glazed. I think they were dead, crushed by an engine catapulted into the centre of the car by the force of the crash. The woman was pinned under metal wreckage. She was moaning and bleeding. It was a job for the fire fighters to cut her free. It looked like very nasty multiple fractures. She was bleeding from numerous cuts but was still conscious.

'Miranda? Miranda...' she was saying. I leaned into the open door.

'Miranda is fine. We've got her out. She's with me,' I said, but I don't know if she heard anything. 'Your daughter is all right.'

Miranda was weeping by the side of the road, wrapped in a blanket, her injuries minor, cuts and bruises. I sat with her and talked, tried to keep her mind off what was going on as the paramedics attended to her mother, putting in lines, giving her oxygen. Miranda was shocked, shivering, trying to talk.

'Why d-don't they get my d-dad out?' she wept.

'Your mother needs help first.'

'They gotta get my dad out. He's hurt.'

'They will ... they will,' was all I could think of saying. Totally inadequate. 'Do you have any relations, anyone I can call? You need looking after.'

'My Aunt Daphne,' said Miranda. 'She lives in Latching.'

'Perhaps I should phone her.'

The noise of the cutting equipment was horrendous, then the paramedics were swiftly lifting Miranda's mother on to a stretcher to carry her on board the ambulance. They came over to Miranda.

'You come along too, missie. You need checking out, just in case. Anyway, your mother would like it. She's asking for you.'

Miranda climbed aboard the ambulance without a backward glance at me. She was staring at her mother and all the life-saving equipment galleried around her.

'What's your aunt's name?' I called out.

'Gregson. Mrs Daphne Gregson. She breeds dogs.'

Little dogs. Some little therapeutic animals might be what Miranda would be needing after this accident. This one was real, tragic, fate taking a hand. No false claims after this accident.

The driver of the lorry was sitting on the pavement, his head in his hands, white-faced. A police officer was talking to him. I did not recognize him. He was new and even to me they are getting younger every day.

'Did you see what happened, miss?' The officer turned to me.

'Yes, I did. I was right behind.'

'Are you willing to give a statement?'

I nodded. 'Yes. Not willing, but I will.' I was becoming a professional witness. Not exactly a good career move. I shed some of the traffic-warden image, putting on my own anorak, then went to the Brighton police station and gave my statement. It took ages. The WPC couldn't spell. Later I cycled to the train station and put my bicycle in the guard's van, sat on the tip-up seat provided and returned to Latching on a tedious train which stopped at every station along the route.

James phoned as I knew he would. His voice was an enigma. I was not sure if he was annoyed or relieved.

'You saw this accident then?'

'Yes, I was right behind. Well, not right behind, because I was on my bicycle, but near enough to see what happened. There was something wrong with the car but I'm not sure what. It wasn't steering properly. The lorry driver never saw them.'

'We've got experts who can check the steering, even from what's left in the wreckage.'

'Great. Fine. So what are you phoning

me for?'

'To see if you are OK.'

'I'm OK.'

'They won't be making any more claims. Both the men are dead. Instantaneous, by the look of it.'

'No more claims. It's all finished then.'

He put the phone down. For a moment I absorbed his words, burdens lifting, then I rang back immediately.

I cleared my throat before speaking. 'James, can you spare five minutes to come with me and look at Dick Mann's shed? I have a theory I'd like to share.'

I thought the share line might hook him.

'Five minutes? Is that all? I'll give you ten and I'll even give you a lift there. I hope this is not going to be a waste of time, Jordan. My shift is nearly finished. Your theories are pretty hare-brained.'

'This is special,' I said, hoping it was. 'There's a link, something I feel.'

'I'll pick you up outside your flat in five minutes.'

This was all happening rather fast. I only had time for a quick wash before putting on my own clothes. Uniform jeans and checked shirt, extra sweater slung over my shoulders. James arrived outside while I was still tying my trainers. My hair was crumpled from wearing the cap but he did not seem to notice. I climbed into his car.

'So what's with the shed?' he asked.

'I have a theory.'

'So you said.'

'Dick Mann was in the Witness Protection Programme because he gave evidence which lead to arrests in the Gaskon Street security box raid? Right? And the loot has never been found. It follows that perhaps Dick Mann knew where the loot was because he had put it there.'

'I'm amazed at the way your brain works.'

'Now, rods were disappearing off the pier. The other anglers knew that Dick Mann was taking them but didn't want to confront him. They wanted me to do that. He even pretended his own rod was stolen. Weird logic but then they were paying. Or rather, I hope they will soon be paying me. But before I could talk to him again, he disappeared off the pier, only to be found dead in the bell tower.'

'I'm still with you.' He was driving steadily through the lanes to Tan Cottage.

If only.

'So Dick Mann was stealing rods for a reason. And he had a good reason. Rod bags are fairly big. They can take two rods, I've checked. Supposing he went on to the pier with one rod in his bag, but left with two. It would be simple for someone as experienced as him to dismantle a second rod and pop it into his bag when no one was looking. The anglers are a sociable lot, eating, drinking, chatting around. They are not watching each other.'

'Very sociable.'

'The question is why did he want the extra rods?'

'I am completely mystified,' said James. He could be really sarcastic without saying a word.

'The extra rods that Dick Mann has been acquiring are in his shed. But at one point, he stopped. Why?'

'Yes, indeed. Why?'

'Because he found the rod he wanted.'

'Lead the way.'

I could feel that James was interested but he was thinking along mundane lines. Jordan off on a limb, as usual. I gripped my hands. I hoped I was right. There was very little to go on. It was a fishy hunch.

'So we are going to look at these rods?'

'Yes. We are going to dismantle rods.'

'My idea of a perfect evening.'

James had a key for the shed at Tan Cottage. Nothing had changed but the yellow scene of crime tape had been removed. At what point did they decide it was no longer a crime scene? I followed him into the shed. The air was stale. I propped open the doors and switched on the lights. The weak bulb lit up the rods and the cobwebs. The spiders had spun their magic again.

'What are we looking for?' said James.

'A rod that is different.'

'OK,' said James taking off his jacket and hanging it on a nail. He rolled up his sleeves. There were thirty or forty rods. 'You start this end and I'll start the other.'

James did not need telling how to examine a rod. I watched him at first and then got the hang of it. Most of the rods were split into two pieces or three. They were made of carbon fibre and uniformly hollow. The pieces fitted together with fold-down eyes. It was a long and tedious examination. There were so many different makes and styles. I should be dreaming of rods at this rate. I hoped that wasn't Freudian.

Then I found the Beachmaster. It was a thirteen-foot rod that broke down into three pieces. It was grey and blue in a swirly pattern with a sturdy black handle. The third and largest segment did not feel as light and hollow as it should. I shook the lowest part, the widest segment leading directly from the handle.

'James,' I said. 'This rod is different.'

He was over in seconds. 'Show me.'

'It doesn't feel as hollow as the others.'

It was nothing to go on. Just a feeling. I looked down the shaft but there was nothing to see, all blackness. No light at the other end, because it led to a handle. I had nothing with which to probe the hollow. James was searching on the workbench for some kind of instrument. He found a piece of bent wire.

'There's something there,' he said, poking about.

Slowly he drew out some foam packing. Perhaps rods were always packed with foam. How would I know?

He shook the rod and a plug of foam reluctantly fell out. Then, without any warning, a slim packet of bubblewrap followed. It was small, barely larger than a matchbox. The bubblewrap had been folded inwards and sealed with sellotape. We both looked at it.

'Shall I open it?' I asked, not wanting to be thrown into a cell for unofficially opening evidence.

'Please.'

We could hardly see in the light and moved together under the hanging bulb. And I was afraid of what I might find. Bubbles popped as I mishandled the package. I opened out the folds so carefully, and there in the palm of my hand lay a small scattering of uncut stones, a dozen or more, white, pink and blue. Beautiful, catching shafts of light. I felt measured, precise and very chilled.

'Here they are,' I said quite unnecessarily. 'The loot from the security box.' I peered at the tiny stones. 'They don't look very pink or very blue to me. But they are diamonds.'

They glinted in the light, sparks of radiance catching the dust motes, frozen crystals. It was only a handful but I could see that they were beautiful gems. No wonder Dick had wanted to find them. No wonder Beano Johnson was keen to get his hands on the loot.

'The experts will look at the collection. They can be identified from the diamond trader's report,' said James. He was folding up the bubblewrap and putting the package casually into his inside jacket pocket. 'Thanks, Jordan. You've been a real help. Your theory was spot-on. Clever girl. I'll drop you home now.'

I was so tired I did not really care that I was being dumped off home. I wanted to sleep, let James climb the paperwork mountain.

'I wonder how Dick Mann lost the rod in which he had hidden the diamonds,' I said. 'It seems pretty careless, doesn't it? He must have known which rod had the loot. Then he would not have had to steal all the others.'

'Perhaps someone took it home by mistake. Or he lent it to a mate or he forgot where he had put the diamonds in a panic. He must have been in quite a state. These were new friends, not old friends, remember. Maybe he had two rods of the same make.'

'So he brought the loot down with him to

Sussex after he had been rehoused?' I had to ask before James put up the barricades.

'So it seems. Don't know how he did it. But it is very small. It would have fitted into a packet of paracetamols or a packet of cigarettes. They don't bring many personal belongings.'

'Where was he from originally? Surely not London? Sussex is too close to London.'

'No, he was from the Tyne area. Brought down to London for this particular job. Recruited along the grapevine. Planted as a security guard.' Crime was a continual education.

'We'll never know. We can't ask him.'

'We shall never know.'

We did not talk much on the way home. He dropped me at my bedsits, thanked me again, slid his arm across to open the door.

'You look awful, Jordan,' he said. 'Get some sleep.'

'Thank you. I'll write myself a note.'

The phone woke me. I was stretched out on the bed, nothing on except the duvet. It was almost a spring day outside. The herald of summer was blowing a few notes through a light breeze and the branches of the church tree were dipping in chorus.

'Hello,' I said sleepily.

'Did I wake you?'

'You told me to get some sleep.'

'Jordan. We should go out this evening and celebrate.'

Excuse me? Did he say celebrate? Did he say we? Had something happened that I knew nothing about? Maybe I had been awarded the Nobel Prize ... my fame may have spread from Latching. The world is not always blind to kindness, sensitivity and truly noble feelings.

'Great.'

'You don't sound very enthusiastic.'

'I'm being wary, James. You'll buy me a glass of claret and then arrest me for some misdemeanour that I know nothing about.'

I could hear a low chuckle. 'You don't trust me, do you?'

'Why should I? You've thrown the law at me so many times, I am bruised mentally and physically. If you say we should go out and celebrate, then fine, but I want to know what it's all about first.'

I sat up in bed, covering my skin with a T-shirt in case anyone could see. How did I know? There could be a camera planted behind the Monet print on the opposite wall.

'Those diamonds. Yes, they are the ones stolen in the security box raid. They have all been identified and authenticated. None missing. The company are overjoyed to have them returned.'

'Good,' I yawned. 'I'm glad they are overjoyed.'

'So that's why we should go out and celebrate. How about that new place along the A27? The old barn that has been recently converted to Tudor. It's supposed to look like a medieval hall with a gallery and suits of armour.'

'But is the wine medieval?'

'I suggest we go and try it. You're the wine expert.'

James was running out of patience. It was something that he was asking me out. But he was not one to persist. If I sounded reluctant he would put the phone down. And that would be that. Another lonely evening walking the front, watching the tide turn.

'You're on,' I said quickly, with a degree of pumped-up enthusiasm. 'I will put on a damsel in medieval distress type outfit and you can pick me up at half past seven.'

'Don't overdo it,' said James. 'It's only a pub.'

Twenty-Two

The day went in a daze of activity. Don't ask me what I did. Then it was shower, shampoo, deodorant, clean jeans, classy blue linen shirt with flowered yoke embroidery, very line dancing, nearest to medieval in my wardrobe and one of my favourites. Feet in open-toed sandals, toenails painted red, wanting this new summer to arrive. Waterproof mascara.

I had not eaten. Who wants to eat when you can't think? I was doing a Mother Hubbard. My cupboard was bare. Perhaps James will buy me a bag of crisps.

James was waiting outside for me. He too had changed but into his off-duty uniform. Black-belted jeans, black shirt open at the neck, rolled-up sleeves, usual gangster gear. His neck was brown and muscular. I looked away.

'You look better,' he said.

'That's a first.'

James actually seemed relaxed and happy. His shift had ended on a high note. Finding those diamonds had been an amazing plus.

He was riding on the acclaim from head office. His career was moving. For once he was at peace with the world.

'So am I going to meet my long-awaited knight on a white charger?' I asked with a tinge of sarcasm.

'Of course,' said James. 'I've made all the arrangements. He'll be there.'

'And why are we celebrating?'

'Be patient. I'll tell you soon enough.'

'I hope it's worth waiting for.'

'It is. Believe me.' He smiled so I had to believe him.

This converted pub was way out on the fringe of West Sussex. I lost track of where we went, winding lanes, overhung trees, old farmhouses, but when James drove into the car park, I could see the shape and slope of the barn's close-thatched roof. Music was coming from the open doors.

'They're playing music,' I said, car door half open, astonished.

'You like jazz, don't you? It's their jazz evening. I heard you liked jazz. So we've come here, very special. Just for you, Jordan.'

I went in on a dream. Not my famous trumpeter class of jazz, but blues and beat enough to stir my effervescent blood. Not the quirky beauty and blazing tone of classic jazz, but a fifteen-piece local band playing their hearts out in rehearsal, all the old favourites, Glenn Miller, Count Basie, Stan

Kenton. It was a heaven of sorts. The soprano sax was good.

We moved to a corner of the downstairs bar. It was packed to suffocation. The band was playing on the other side of an ivy-decked baronial fireplace. Oak stairs led to an open gallery also packed with people. The staircase was standing room only.

The new owners had called it the Medieval Hall and there were sixteenth-century recipes etched on the walls, ancient scrolls and coats of arms stencilled on the plaster-work. But dominating the room was a knight in shining armour. It was a full-size suit of armour with the helmet visor down. He sat on a canopy over the bar, feet sticking out, his scissor-sharp pointed steel shoes daring anyone to misbehave.

'Do you like it?'

'I love it,' I said.

'Red wine?' James asked, when we'd found seats on the other side of the room, ready to launch himself on to the crowded three-deep bar.

'No, thank you. It's too hot in here for red wine. White – medium, sweet or dry, I don't care what kind, please, with some ice. Red would be too heavy.'

I should have been warned by my change of taste. It was like an impending sense of pain. No one changes their taste in wine without reason.

The music was fun. They did not play each piece for long, no reprises, not many solos, keen on quantity rather than quality. It was one standard after another and they were good, full of enthusiasm and ancient in-jokes. The jokes were truly dreadful but people still laughed. No wonder the bar was crowded.

James returned, several numbers later, with a brimming glass of white wine and his usual shandy.

'That's a very large glass,' I said dubiously.

'I told them we were celebrating.'

'It's at least half a pint.'

'Don't exaggerate. Three-fifty mills.'

I didn't want to hear that he was being posted to Yorkshire next week or even earlier. I didn't want to hear that this was the last time I would see him. That this was goodbye.

'So,' I said with forced gaiety, swallowing the first icy sip. It was delicious even after years of red. The perfect grape. 'What are we celebrating?'

James was clearly enjoying this, his eyes smiling. He took his time.

'Let's go back a few hours,' he said. 'It was your hunch that took us to Dick Mann's shed, wasn't it? Your hunch that made us search through the hollow base ends of the rods. You linked Dick Mann with the missing diamonds and you, Jordan Lacey, found them in my presence. The insurance company are sending a courier down for them tomorrow. In the meantime they are locked in the safe at the station.'

The chilled Chardonnay was excellent. It cleared my brain. 'I'm glad it has all worked out well,' I said, savouring the pure taste. 'You must be pleased.'

'I am but I haven't come to the best bit,' said James. His dark-blue eyes were full of light and hidden laughter. Something I rarely see. 'I won't tell you what the diamonds are worth now, but years ago the insurance company offered a reward. Ten per cent of their value for their return intact. The reward still stands, Jordan. And guess who is going to get the reward?'

I went quite weak. They were playing 'Moonlight in Vermont', a Sinatra standard, and my brain wouldn't function against the plaintive music which I loved. 'The Police Benevolent Fund? Widows and Orphans?' I suggested lamely.

'No, you, Jordan Lacey. Idiot girl detective in person. You're getting the reward. Private investigator supreme. Every single penny.'

His words barely sank in. Another reward? A reward for returning the chemise dress had been prize enough, but now another, even bigger reward? This was the lottery twice over, rolled into one, Christmas every day. But I did not want money, I only wanted him.

'I don't believe it,' I said, dry-mouthed. I took a big gulp of wine. 'More money?'

'You'd better believe it when you meet their representative tomorrow. He's coming down to Latching to present their cheque to you personally.'

A smile started on my face and wouldn't stop spreading. 'You really mean it? I'm getting another reward for following a hunch?'

He nodded. He didn't seem to mind that it was me and not him. There was nothing stingy about my James. He was generous in heart and spirit.

'What are you going to do with it?' he grinned.

'What am I going to do with it?' I repeated like the idiot he'd called me. I repeated the same shopping list. 'The shop needs repainting. The ladybird needs new front seats. I need new trainers and, oh yes, there's a fishing boat to repair. A present for Doris is a must, something special. I'd really like a computer, internet and databases, email, be a high-tech PI. There's so much I could spend it on...'

I smiled at James and he smiled back.

An idea struck me. An idea that had been dormant for a while. 'And I could have a party on the beach. A really big party, asking everyone I know. All my clients from previous cases. There'd be hundreds and hundreds of people on my guest list. The wine would be top quality and all the party food from M & S. I'd serve the wine in proper glass glasses.'

'Not on the beach, Jordan. Broken glass is dangerous.'

'Then I'd get pretty plastic ones, not those awful plastic beakers. And a barbecue, the best meat for the carnivores but lots of fish. Salmon fillets and sushi.'

'Waitrose does sushi trays for parties. A dozen different ways with raw tuna.'

'Perfect. Sushi trays, salads, rolls. Fireworks! Oh yes, James, we must have fireworks. Shooting stars and twinkling lights. I adore fireworks.' I was getting carried away. 'I can get a few trusty men to set them up for me. I love that one that looks like golden rain, a cascade of golden sparks like a huge umbrella shooting towards you. What's it called?'

'Golden Rain. You've got to get permission for fireworks.'

'I'll apply for permission.'

I remembered the last time I had planned a beach party and why it had to be cancelled. Ben had died in a car chase, a senseless waste of life.

'Is Sergeant Rawlings well enough to come? I heard he was off sick.'

'He's getting better. I'm sure he'd make an effort to come to your party. Everyone will come.'

'Will you be at my party?' I asked. I had been dreading his answer, too scared to ask. He had said nothing about when he would be leaving. 'Or will you have gone to Yorkshire?'

'No, I'll come to your party wherever I am,' said James. 'Nothing will stop me. I'd like to relax on the beach with a glass of cold beer, watching fireworks, listening to your ridiculous chatter.'

'I don't chatter,' I said.

'Yes you do,' he said. 'But I like it.'

He smiled at me and it was the sweetest smile I'd seen for years. Was DI James mellowing? Had I broken through the barrier at last?

'Would you like another glass of wine, Jordan?' he asked, getting up. 'Your glass is empty.'

'Yes, please. The same. White with ice.'

It was the last thing we ever said to each other.

He moved over to join the crowd at the bar. The band was playing 'Georgia' with persuasive, languorous outbreaths.

I saw it moving, an uncanny glint of silver. I'd seen that glint before. It had been in my mind for months. No one else saw it. They were either listening to the music or chatting among themselves, taking no notice. Georgia ... Georgia...

The knight in his shining suit of armour was swaying on his precarious perch above the bar canopy. His pinnings, his weight, were not stable. He was about to topple, pointed feet of metal, sharp as razors, poised to slice through someone's neck.

Right below stood James, for once relaxed, a glass of beer in one hand, my wine in the other, about to return to me, but stopping for a moment to enjoy and listen to the soul-searing, plaintive sound of Georgia, Georgia.

'James, James!' I shouted but no one heard me through the soaring notes of the solo flugel horn.

'Look out! James!' I cried again. I stumbled to my feet, knocking over a chair, shouldering people, treading on toes, not caring.

'Look out!' My voice was anguished.

I threw myself across the room to push James out of the way as the suit of armour came crashing down on to the drinkers, steel-pointed shoes slicing through clothes and flesh. I saw that flash of silver as I had many times before, crimson blood spurting, some of it seemed to be mine.

James's face was suddenly aghast, then both shocked and grave. I made room for pain.